ECHOES OF EXILE

The Prince's Pursuit

By Blake Noack

First published in 2025 by the author
Western Australia, Australia
Self-published

ISBN: 978-1-7640723-0-4

Cover design by the author

A catalogue record for this book is available from the National Library of Australia.

Helge
Aerathil
Dornhold
Mynic Mines
Arndell
Sahraka
Tryn
Kareth
Thuldrek
Serpentia
Tharnveil
Ragnol

𝔓rologue

The rain hammered relentlessly against the cabin's thatched roof, the wind's mournful howls adding to the din of the storm outside.

"Ahh, that hit the spot," the large burly man said to his small friend, his hands resting on his bulging stomach as he leaned back into his wooden chair. With each creak, the chair protested under his weight, struggling to hold him.

Suddenly, the old wooden door burst open with a smash, hitting the wall and denting the logs that formed the cabin's structure. Freezing air rushed in, followed by large raindrops, as a robed figure with a crooked pointed hat and long flowing robes rushed inside. The unexpected entrance caused the two inhabitants to snap to attention, their movements quick and alert.

In the commotion, one of the large man's chair legs gave way, snapping cleanly in half. With a loud groan, he tumbled backward out of the chair, the clang of his plate armour hitting the stone floor echoing through the room. The robed figure slammed the door shut, panting as he leaned against it, muttering to himself.

"What the hell is going on?" the large man grunted as he clambered to his feet, regaining his composure. He ran a hand over the back of his bald head, feeling for a lump.

The robed figure began to shake the water off his robes and long black beard like a wet dog, before rushing over to a small alchemy workbench, positioned at the rear wall of the small wooden cabin. Still mumbling to himself, he used the flickering candlelight that shone down onto the work area, allowing him to sort through the various scrolls and maps that lay unorganised and sprawled over the bench.

"Malkhia, what is it?" a small half-elf with flowing blonde locks of hair covering half her face said as she stood up and moved next to the heavy-set man, concern etched on her face while adjusting her emerald green hooded cloak, which had somehow managed to tangle itself in the dark handwoven leather chest strap of her quiver hanging on the chair, making it twist off her back.

"They are coming, I told you they would. They were right behind me. I thought I lost them; we need to find it and get out of this place," Malkhia said hurriedly, scattering papers and maps around the alchemy workbench.

"Find what and who is coming? I think the magic's finally gotten to him and he has lost his damn mind," the large man said, glancing down to the small rogue.

"Stop it, Horethian, this looks serious," the rogue said, brushing her fringe from her eyes before thumping at the man's chest, her hand met by a painful thud against his iron plate.

"The map to the Forgotten Lands, I know it is here, and I knew we should not have listened to you, Horethian, and taken out that scouting party. They knew what was in that dungeon same as us," Malkhia replied.

"Slow down a minute, that snobby prince's scouting party? And that silly old parchment with random lines and drawings we almost sold to the provisioner?" the rogue questioned.

"Yes, the prince wants it. It's not silly, Atlas — the Forgotten Lands are real and they're coming. We need to find it and get out of here quickly," Malkhia insisted.

"I don't see what the big deal is around these Forgotten Lands," Horethian said, peering out the front window, squinting through the downpour. He spotted a trail of torches off in the distance. "Shit, he's not joking. Quickly, gear up, Atlas — we have company, and a lot of it," he said, turning away from the window.

"I told you!" Malkhia snapped.

Atlas rushed to the other side of the house, grabbing an exceptionally hand-crafted yew bow off a hook and slinging it over her shoulder. Meanwhile, Horethian opened a wooden locked box, tossing a bundle of arrows over to Atlas.

"Ah ha! Here it is! We must leave!" Malkhia exclaimed urgently, his voice tinged with a mix of adrenaline and anxiety. As he spoke, he grabbed small leather pouches, potions, and a handful of scrolls, stuffing them inside his dark royal blue robes.

Horethian peered out the window once more, noticing the trail of torches flickering much closer than before. "Hurry, Malk, get us out of here," he said, wrapping his iron-clad fingers around the hilt of a blued metal sword resting against the wall.

Malkhia continued to search the table, grabbing a rolled-up note held with a blue ribbon and a broken red wax seal, stuffing it into his pack. He picked up his staff and started to chant the incantation as his free hand flowed through the air, forming different shapes with his fingers.

"Trea Ango Mov." A small fizzling sound followed the words as a puff of dark black smoke shot out.

"I don't think this is the time to fail casts, Malk," Atlas said.

"Trea Ango Mov," he chanted once again. This time, a small blue lightning bolt shot down to the ground and swirled at his feet. Malkhia stepped back to watch the portal grow to above head height, a whirlpool of white starting to swirl inside as the room glowed bright blue.

"Quick, everyone through," Malkhia said, stepping through the portal with Horethian and Atlas close behind. The three vanished, and the portal along with them.

1

The resonant thud of leather shoes on well-worn cobblestones reverberated through the air as a middle-aged man, draped in an elegant red tunic adorned with intricate gold filigree and a small snake emblem intricately embroidered on the chest, briskly traversed the main pathway of the bustling city.

His hurried strides carried him toward a stone bridge, its arch spanning the deep moat that encircled the castle grounds. Along the bridge's edge stood meticulously carved grey stone pillars, each bearing the likeness of a serpent.

Before he could reach the bridge, a dishevelled figure in ragged attire carelessly intersected his path, resulting in both men stumbling and crashing to the ground.

"How dare you!" the impeccably dressed man exclaimed, as he brought himself to his feet, brushing the dirt off his clothes and adjusting his crooked cap.

"How dare I! You almost busted ma lute! That thing is finely made, I have you know." the other man retorted, rushing over to pick up his instrument.

As the man leaned over to pick up the lute, a chestnut brown dog rushed towards him, stopping at his feet before affectionately licking his hand. Suddenly, the dog turned towards the noble and began to bare its teeth, growling viciously.

"Recall your mutt or I will have you both executed before the sun has a chance to set," the well-dressed man threatened.

"Ahh, Jolly won't hurt you unless he needs to. Over 'ere, boy!" the man added with a sharp whistle at the end, while he was still hunched over inspecting the instrument for damage. With a wave of his arm, he gestured as if to brush off the noble's concern.

"The two of you are lucky I have somewhere to be," the noble said.

"Pfft, you're lucky me lute ain't broke," he replied.

"C'mon, boy, let's keep moving," the man said to his dog as he leaned down to scruff the fur on its head.

The dog let out a small bark, its tail wagging happily, before turning away from the noble. With a loyal demeanour, it walked alongside the man.

"Serpentia is turning to filth," the noble said with a hint of disdain as he broke back into a run across the bridge, heading towards the castle's entrance.

The noble's pace faltered as he reached the castle's entrance, coming to a sudden halt as two imposing figures clad in heavy armour stepped forward. Their polished helmets glinted in the sunlight as they crossed their long wooden-handled halberds, forming an intimidating barrier that blocked the path to the large double doors of the castle.

The middle-aged man clasped both knees, his chest heaving as he panted loudly, trying to catch his breath after his brisk run.

"Now... is not... the... time for this," he finally managed to say between breaths.

"I must see the prince at once, so stand aside," he demanded arrogantly, his words punctuated by laboured breaths, the weariness evident in his voice as he struggled to assert his authority.

"The prince said not to be disturbed!" the smaller of the two guards retorted sternly, his voice carrying an undertone of warning as he reinforced their orders.

"Let me through at once or your superiors will be informed of this. I am not in the mood," the man said, his impatience evident.

The guards exchanged glances before eventually lowering their weapons, stepping aside to open the entryway.

"As you wish, my lord," one of the guards eventually acknowledged, yielding to the man's authority.

"That's what I thought," the man said as he straightened up the white feather in his ruby-red Tudor and adjusted his tunic.

"Bloody entitled nobles," one of the guards mumbled quietly as the man walked past.

The man almost came to a stop after hearing the insult but chose to ignore it, realizing they had already wasted too much of his time.

"There is no such thing as respect these days," he thought to himself as he continued down the lush, carpeted entryway, adorned with hanging portraits of past and present royalty.

"You there! I must speak with the prince at once. Where is he?" the man demanded of one of the handmaidens, who was attempting to walk past the large main stairway in the foyer towards the kitchen, her arms precariously overflowing with gleaming silver plates and delicate crystal goblets.

"In his bedchambers, my lord, but he said not to be dis—" she began to reply, but her words were abruptly cut off by a dismissive wave of the man's hand.

The man quickened his pace, striding down the candlelit, long winding corridors of the castle. Eventually, he came to a halt at a large, imposing dark wooden door, reinforced by sturdy iron strips. With a deep breath, he straightened his outfit once more before reaching out to grasp the handle and slowly pushing the door open.

"Beg thy pardon, Prince Blackscale, but I have urgent news," he said as he opened the door fully.

The prince turned to the door in shock.

The man shielded his eyes as he saw the naked body of a chambermaid, lying on her stomach with her head positioned at waist height to the prince. The rumpled red silk sheets clung to her form, tangled in disarray around her. A large red woollen quilt, adorned with intricate patterns, was bunched up at the foot of the bed, adding to the scene of intimacy. The bed itself, a grand wooden four-poster, loomed imposingly in the opulent chamber, its carved details hinting at its regal heritage.

"Have you never heard of knocking, Belfor?" the prince said, his voice tinged with irritation as he pushed the woman away from him. He hastily pulled the woollen quilt firmly to cover his small and frail frame before reaching for a robe hanging on an intricately carved bedpost.

"Deepest apologies, my Liege, but I have urgent news of the map," Belfor said, still shielding his eyes.

"The map? The actual map?" the prince said, his surprise evident in his tone.

"Yes, my liege."

"Leave at once, girl," the prince ordered the woman, who quickly grabbed a white dress from the floor to cover her body, preserving what little dignity she could salvage as she hurriedly exited the room.

"Out with it then!" the prince demanded as he walked over to a small table, picking up a flagon and pouring deep red liquid into a goblet.

"There are rumours it is deep in the Dungeon of Echoes, my liege," Belfor said as he walked closer to the prince.

"You come barging into my room after I said not to be disturbed, to talk rumours!" the prince said, giving Belfor a stern look while taking a drink.

"We have these rumours on good authority. Yet there is one issue, my lord," Belfor replied.

"Just spit it out already," the prince said, with a hint of anger coming through in his tone.

"We sent a small group of scouts into the dungeon, and only one returned. He informed us that another hunting party had ventured into the dungeon and slaughtered our scouts, save for one. He only just managed to recall out in time to bring us the news," Belfor explained.

"Interesting. I wonder if they knew what is in there," the prince said, placing a hand to his chin, lost in thought.

"I must see this scout at once," the prince demanded.

"He is currently in the infirmary, sir; he has been unconscious for quite some time, and his condition is stable but critical," Belfor replied, his voice tinged with concern.

"Find out what he knows immediately and send out all the scouts to find this hunting party," the prince commanded, his steps echoing across the luxurious room as he paced back and forth.

"This map is rightfully mine, and I want it!" he declared with unwavering determination.

"But sir," Belfor interjected, hesitatingly.

"Now, Belfor!" the prince snapped, gesturing towards
the door with a swift wave of his hand.

"As you wish, my prince," Belfor replied, swiftly
turning on his heels and striding towards the door. With
a fluid motion, he exited, closing the door behind him.
As he left, he couldn't help but mutter curses towards
the prince under his breath, his discontent palpable even
as he disappeared from the room.

The prince walked over to the open window, gazing
out over the vast city below.

A sea of deep grey stone-walled buildings filled the
landscape, clustered closely together. In the distance,
the town centre unfolded, featuring a grand fountain.
At its centre, a marble statue of a petite naked female
poured water from a large pot. Surrounding the
fountain were meticulously trimmed hedges, arranged
in a circular pattern that enhanced the elegance of the
town centre.

"Finally, the map to the Forgotten Lands has been
found. It will soon be mine, as it should be," the prince
murmured to himself, a smirk crossing his face, before
he gulped down his wine.

2

"Hear ye, hear ye, the Festival of Night Nye!" the town crier bellowed, his voice echoing through the bustling streets as he shuffled back and forth at the corner of the town bank.

"You'd think he'd get sick of saying the same blasted thing, wouldn't ya, Jolly?" the man mused to himself as he strolled past the bank, still inspecting his lute.

"Let's see here," he muttered, turning a couple of tuning pegs at the top neck.

The man's fingers began to pick at the strings, producing a low tune. He adjusted the pegs once more and plucked again.

"Ahh, back in business, Jolly," he said with a satisfied grin as he started to play a slow, peaceful melody.

He began to whistle along with the song as he and Jolly walked side by side, cutting through the busy crowd that was gathering in the town centre for the festival.

The large open square was filled with villagers from all areas of the town, vendor carts lining the outside like a ring enclosing the crowd.

"Get your ingots, freshly smelted ingots!" the blacksmith beckoned, his voice ringing out over the clamour of the marketplace.

"Fletched arrows, buy in bulk while they're still here!" yelled the bowyer, his voice competing to be heard above the other calls.

"Oooh, look 'ere, Jolly, a butcher. Let's say we get some fresh meat an' head on back to the docks. I'm sick of fish, so I'm sure you are too. Who am I kiddin', you'd eat the same meal every day," he said with a chuckle, looking down at his canine companion.

"Five succulent harpy steaks, my good man," he said, his voice carrying a hint of anticipation as he locked eyes with the butcher.

"Twenty-five gold pieces," the butcher replied briskly, his hands busy with the cuts of meat.

"Twenty-five!? Only want a coupla steaks, not the whole animal!" the man exclaimed.

"Price is firm. Pay up or move on," the butcher retorted, already turning to attend to another customer.

As disappointment began to settle, the man's gaze swept across the market square and landed upon a young lady draped in a long black hooded robe. Slowly, she extended her hand toward the small coin purse nestled within the butcher's cart, her movements stealthy and deliberate.

"Alright, alright. I'll take 'em. 'Ere's ya gold," the man grumbled, dropping the coins onto the cart, causing them to scatter across the ground.

"Ughh," the butcher exclaimed as he bent down to pick up the gold.

The clattering of the coins served as a convenient distraction, affording the young lady the opportunity to snatch the purse and swiftly vanish into the bustling crowd.

With a frustrated sigh, the butcher straightened up and grabbed the steaks. He hastily wrapped them in parchment, the task becoming increasingly messy with each fold, before roughly tossing them into the man's hand.

The man muttered, his tone tinged with resignation, as he stowed the steaks into the bag hanging at his hip.

In the midst of securing the steaks, his fingers brushed against a small hanging rope from his belt. Curiosity piqued, he examined it closely, only to discover a clean cut. A sinking feeling washed over him as he realized his small gold pouch was missing.

"That wench!" the man cursed under his breath, his frustration palpable.

"Righto, Jolly, we need to find her or we ain't leaving here in a hurry," he commanded his faithful companion.

Jolly let out a small sharp bark and darted off through the bustling crowd.

"Oi, wait up!" the man yelled, shouldering his way through the throng of people in an attempt to catch up.

The dog navigated through the town with effortless agility, while the man struggled to keep pace. Following Jolly's lead, they tracked the elusive trail to the north entrance of town, where it disappeared down a dimly lit pathway flanked by dense trees.

As they progressed, Jolly's pace began to slow, and the hairs on his back bristled in alert. The man finally caught up, his breath ragged, and he noticed the sudden change in his partner's demeanour.

"What is it, boy?" the man whispered, his hand tightening around the hilt of his small dagger as he slung the lute over his shoulder.

"She's led us to the graveyard, hasn't she?" he murmured to his partner, piecing together the clues.

The pair advanced cautiously down the pathway, their senses on high alert as they scanned their surroundings. Eventually, they reached a looming wrought iron gate, its imposing presence marking the entrance to the graveyard.

"She go in 'ere?" the man queried in a hushed tone, leaning down to speak to Jolly.

The dog responded with a soft bark followed by a menacing growl, confirming their suspicions.

With a slight creak, the man began to swing open the gate, just enough to slip through without drawing attention.

Directly ahead, an old decrepit tomb emerged from the shadows, its weathered façade obscured by creeping vines and layers of cobwebs. The door stood slightly ajar, hinting at recent activity.

Approaching cautiously, the man edged closer to the door, his ears straining to catch any sound. Amidst the eerie silence, he detected the faint tinkling of coins hitting stone, signalling another presence within.

The man placed one hand on the door and cast a brief nod to Jolly. Without hesitation, he shoved the door open and leapt into the tomb, with Jolly following close behind.

Inside, the startled woman recoiled, pressing herself against the rear wall as she watched the man brandish his dagger, while Jolly positioned himself defensively, teeth bared and a low growl rumbling from his throat.

"Now gimme mi pouch and it'll be over," the man demanded, his voice edged with urgency.

As tension hung thick in the air, the sound of crunching bones reverberated from outside the tomb. The man spun around to behold a skeletal figure emerging from a pile of bones just beyond the half-open door.

Realising the imminent danger, he shifted his focus back to the woman, his expression softening slightly.

"Money later, lives first," he declared firmly, meeting the woman's gaze, who responded with a silent nod of agreement.

As the fully formed creature advanced, the man and woman retreated into the corner, seeking refuge behind the solid barrier of a large stone sarcophagus. With Jolly at their side, they braced themselves for the confrontation.

With a fierce growl, Jolly launched himself over the sarcophagus, his jaws snapping at the skeletal figure with primal ferocity. His teeth found purchase on an outstretched arm, ripping it from the body with a sickening thud as it crashed to the ground.

Despite the injury, the skeleton remained undeterred, its hollow gaze fixed on its intended prey. Ignoring Jolly's attack, it continued its relentless advance towards the cornered duo.

In a desperate bid to defend themselves, the man thrusted forward with his dagger, causing the skeleton to stagger momentarily. Seizing the opportunity, the woman hurled a glass bottle filled with a mysterious green liquid over the man's shoulder, the projectile finding its mark with a satisfying crash.

As the bottle shattered against the skeletal form, green smoke billowed forth, enveloping the creature in a choking haze. Undeterred, the man pressed his advantage, slashing and thrusting with his dagger, each blow shattering bone fragments that scattered in all directions.

The green liquid now covered the entire skeleton as smoke started to fill the tiny room.

Soon, the green liquid coated the entirety of the skeleton, its corrosive effects eating away at the ancient bones. With a final, shuddering convulsion, the skeleton collapsed in on itself, reduced to nothing more than a pile of cracked, green-tinged bones scattered across the stone floor.

"Poison, eh?" the man remarked, turning towards the woman with a grin. "Not bad."

"Not bad yourself," she responded with a hint of admiration. "Those were some quick moves with the dagger."

"Prefer to use ma lute, to be fair. I'm Theo, by the way," he introduced himself, extending his hand towards her.

The woman gracefully removed her hood, revealing a moon-white, delicate face framed by long, flowing brunette hair cascading down the centre of her lower back.

"Leyla," she replied, accepting Theo's hand with a firm grip and shaking it.

A small bark resonated through the stone room, prompting Theo's attention.

"Oh right, this is Jolly," Theo explained, gesturing towards the dog at their feet.

"Pleased to meet you, Jolly," Leyla said warmly, kneeling down to pat the dog. Jolly's tail wagged happily as he panted, his tongue hanging halfway out.

"So, about this gold misunderstanding," Leyla began, straightening up.

"Misunderstanding? You mean theft," Theo retorted, his tone laced with a hint of amusement.

"Well, yeah, that. Sorry, I just haven't eaten in a few days, is all," Leyla replied, her expression innocent and pleading.

"Ah, if only I were to fall for that. But no harm done. I'll take back what's mine," Theo responded, his demeanour surprisingly forgiving.

"If you're hungry, though, I've got some nice, fat harpy steaks. We were on our way back to my boat at the docks before... well, you know," he added, extending an olive branch of sorts.

Theo scraped his hands over the gold coins atop the sarcophagus, gathering them into a neat pile before loading them back into his pouch.

"There ya go, the rest isn't mine," he stated, his tone firm but fair.

"Sorry once again, Theo. If the offer is legitimate, I may just take you up on it. I don't have much keeping me here," Leyla responded, a note of gratitude in her voice.

"Whaddya reckon, Jolly?" Theo asked, glancing down at the dog.

Jolly barked loudly twice and wagged his tail in agreement.

"I'd say that's a yes. Let's get outta 'ere before any more of these bones decide to come alive again," Theo said, pushing the tomb door fully open, eager to leave the eerie confines of the graveyard behind.

Leyla swiftly gathered the remaining gold, stuffing it into a pouch hidden within her robe.

"Yeah, good idea," she agreed, turning to Theo.

The pair began to make their way back down the darkened pathway toward the town entrance. As they approached the entrance, Theo glanced back to see Leyla trailing a few meters behind.

"You alright?" he inquired, concern evident in his voice.

"Yeah, just need to conceal myself," she replied, lifting her hood back over her head and tucking her hair away.

"A face like yours, though, shouldn't be hidden away by a hood," Theo remarked with a smirk.

"Oh, trust me, we'll get through town a lot smoother if I'm not noticed," Leyla retorted with a wry smile.

With a shrug of his shoulders, Theo turned around and continued into town. Leyla quickened her pace to join him at Jolly's side.

The trio wound their way through the bustling market district, navigating past the glowing mage shops where strange noises and fumes permeated the air. Further down the road, they passed a tannery adorned with fresh animal hides stretched out on drying racks. The tanner was crouched on a small wooden stool, meticulously scraping the fat off the back of a fresh hide.

"Good evening," Theo greeted as they walked past.

"Ehh," the tanner grunted in response, waving them on before returning to his task.

"Nice city, this one, innit?" Theo chuckled to Leyla.

Leyla nodded in agreement as the trio continued down the winding lanes and storefronts, eventually arriving at the docks.

"Ah, breathe that in—the beautiful fresh fish and sea salt," Theo said, inhaling deeply before exhaling with contentment.

"Mmm, beautiful indeed," Leyla remarks sarcastically.

Theo laughed and began to walk down the creaky wooden dock, heading toward the anchored-up boats.

Jolly dashed ahead and bounded onto a rickety-looking wooden ship, its makeshift cabin awkwardly positioned in the middle with the mast shooting out from the top. An older man, clad in a woollen green cap and sporting a long grey beard, sat in silence by the tiller arm.

"'Ere she is," Theo said proudly, gesturing towards the vessel.

"Um, yeah, it's a boat alright," Leyla replied with a hint of scepticism.

"Just a boat!? This is the pride of the ocean," Theo retorted quickly, his enthusiasm undeterred.

The pair clambered aboard, and Leyla wandered off to inspect the rest of the boat.

"Hi, I'm Leyla," she introduced herself, approaching the man at the tiller.

"Oh, he's mute and doesn't really move from that spot. Kinda weird, to be honest. I just call him Tillerman," Theo yelled out from inside the cabin, where he was rummaging around.

"What have you gotten yourself into?" Leyla mused to herself, feeling a mix of curiosity and apprehension as she continued her exploration of the boat.

As she walked around, the tantalising aroma of seasoned cooked meat began to waft through the air, adding a touch of comfort to the unfamiliar surroundings.

"That smells delicious!" Leyla called out from the bow of the ship, her attention momentarily diverted by the tantalising aroma, even as she observed the ocean swirling and bubbling in a strange manner before her.

"Well, it's ready," Theo responded from inside the cabin.

Intrigued, Leyla made her way into the cabin, finding it surprisingly nicer and more well put together than its exterior suggested. Her eyes wandered to a shelf above the enclosed fireplace, adorned with a multitude of small grey animal and monster statues.

Curiosity piqued, Leyla reached out to inspect one of the statues closely.

"Whoa, don't touch them, please," Theo cautioned, swiftly grabbing the statue from Leyla's grasp.

"What are these? I've never seen such intricate work before," Leyla inquired.

"They're my pets—my family, if you will," Theo explained, his voice tinged with fondness.

"They're beautiful," Leyla replied, admiring the craftsmanship of the statues.

"Thank you, they're from pretty much every part of the globe. It's time to eat," Theo announced, placing two plates down on a small table and a dog bowl on the floor. Scrambling through some wooden chests, he retrieved a small wooden stool.

"I knew I had another one," he said triumphantly, setting it down opposite his stool.

The pair settled into their seats, pulling their plates closer as Jolly eagerly began to devour his steak.

"There's some strange movement in the water beneath this boat. I spotted it before," Leyla observed, cutting into her meal.

"That's just Ramsay. Probably can smell the harpy meat. He loves it," Theo reassured, shovelling a huge piece of steak into his mouth.

"Who's Ramsay? And why is he in the ocean? Also, you know, these sharp utensils with a wooden handle—they can cut this steak into smaller pieces," Leyla suggested to Theo, noticing his struggle to chew the large piece of meat.

Theo let out a loud gulp as he attempted to swallow.

"Apologies, milady. I'm not used to company at mealtime. Also, Ramsay is another part of the family, just like Jolly here," he explained.

"Why the name Jolly, by the way? Kind of strange for a dog," Leyla inquired.

"Well, long story short, I had a run-in with some pirates out in the deep waters. Jolly here was chained up on their deck. I managed to 'persuade' them to give up Jolly, as well as their belongings. Ramsay played a big part in that one. So, I figured Jolly Roger, and he is quite a jolly friend, so it stuck," Theo recounted, shrugging his shoulders and forcing another piece of meat into his mouth.

"He is pretty adorable," Leyla agreed, leaning off the side of her stool to pat Jolly while he chewed.

"Well, time to meet Ramsay," Theo declared, picking up his lute and heading outside.

Leyla stood up to follow, gazing out at the sun setting over the horizon, casting a beautiful array of blue and red hues through the clouds.

Theo began to pluck the strings of his lute, creating a soothing melody that instantly washed over Leyla, filling her with a sense of calm.

The water began to churn and roil violently at the front of the ship, heralding the arrival of a large, black serpent-like creature bursting through the surface. The creature towered above the deck, doubling its height as it loomed over them, its eyes locking with Leyla's. Massive, webbed fins adorned with pointed spikes shot out from behind its head, adding to its imposing presence.

Leyla gasped, instinctively drawing a green-bladed dagger from her robes in response to the sudden threat.

"Calm down, the pair of you. We're all friends here," Theo reassured, his fingers strumming the lute with increased intensity.

A wave of calm washed over Leyla once more, and she noticed the serpent's demeanour softening slightly, its spiked fins retracting in behind its head.

Theo reached into his bag and retrieved the remaining two steaks, tossing them into the air toward the serpent. With ease, the creature caught the offerings before leaping further out of the water, revealing the vast expanse of its massive body, before gracefully diving its head back into the ocean.

As the serpent's tail flicked above the surface, creating a gentle ripple, it disappeared into the dark, almost black depths of the ocean, leaving behind a sense of awe and wonder in its wake.

"So yeah, that's Ramsay," Theo said with a smile, introducing the mysterious sea creature.

"Who even are you?" Leyla questioned, still trying to make sense of everything.

"Mm, you could say just a lover of animals and creatures with extremely good music abilities, if I do say so mi'self," Theo replied cryptically as he headed back into the cabin.

Digging through a chest once more, Theo retrieved a dusty hand-woven hammock and proceeded to set it up in the cabin. Leyla watched as he hung one end to an old, rusted hook and the other to the mast.

"This should be comfy enough for the night," he said, tossing a blanket and cushion onto the hammock.

"Better than the stone floors I've been sleeping on lately," Leyla replied as she climbed into the hammock, pulling the blanket over her body and adjusting the cushion under her head.

Theo blew out a candle and settled into his own small bed.

"Night, Jolly. Night, Leyla. Night, Ramsay. Oh, also, night, Tillerman," Theo called out before he began to drift off to sleep.

"Goodnight," Leyla replied softly as she felt herself drifting off into unconsciousness.

As the first rays of dawn broke through a crack in the cabin wall, Leyla was jolted awake by a loud thud, followed by the ship creaking and rocking violently. She was thrown from her hammock onto the wooden floor, her body aching from the impact. Frantically looking around the chaotic cabin, she noticed Theo's bed was empty, and a sense of unease washed over her.

3

alkhia was the first to emerge from the shimmering portal onto an ice-covered clifftop, the frigid winds whipping through his garments as the waves crashed relentlessly against the frozen sheet below. Atlas followed shortly behind, her steps tentative on the slippery surface, inadvertently bumping into the rear of Malkhia.

Before the pair had a chance to regain their bearings, Horethian came stumbling through the portal with a lack of grace, his bulk knocking the other two off balance and sending them sprawling onto the icy ground. They found themselves in a tangled heap, buried beneath Horethian's weight.

Loud muffles escaped from beneath him as his body covered every inch of the duo. Horethian grunted with effort as he struggled to roll over and free his companions from their predicament.

"Never managed to grasp the landing of these portals," he muttered, his voice slightly muffled by the snow clinging to his arms as he finally stood up, shaking himself free.

"It's the same as walking through a door, you big fool," Atlas retorted, her tone tinged with exasperation, as she rose to her feet and began to inspect her bow for any damage.

"Why do we bring you anywhere?" Malkhia retorted as he clambered to his feet, letting out a sigh and rummaging through his bag, checking to see if any provisions had been smashed by the crushing force of their clumsy arrival.

Horethian shrugged and bent down to retrieve his sword from the snow. "Uh, I forgot to grab my shield," he admitted sheepishly.

Atlas couldn't help but roll her eyes. "You would be the only warrior who would forget their shield," she remarked with a mix of amusement and annoyance.

Meanwhile, Malkhia was still rummaging through his seemingly bottomless bag, searching for who knows what. As Horethian and Atlas glanced around at their surroundings, Malkhia finally emerged from his bag, closing the flap with a satisfied pat.

They found themselves on a vast expanse of flat ground covered in pristine snow, with nothing but miles of icy wilderness stretching out before them. In the distance, they could make out the shadowy outline of a towering mountain.

"Ice Isle?" Atlas suggested to Malkhia.

"I couldn't think of anywhere else more secluded to come," he replied, a hint of uncertainty in his voice as he took in their surroundings.

"Well, everything seems to be in order. Let's head off to the mountains. I know there's a shrine here somewhere

where we can rest and get our bearings," Malkhia declared, taking charge of their next steps.

"Lead the way," Horethian responded, his tone indicating his readiness to follow Malkhia's lead.

The trio set off on their long trek across the icy flats, their journey punctuated by the occasional sighting of a polar bear lumbering in the distance. Eventually, they reached the side of the mountain, where a small opening caught Malkhia's attention.

"There, that must be the entrance to the shrine," he announced, pointing out the opening to his companions.

With Malkhia and Atlas leading the way, Horethian followed behind, grumbling under his breath as he turned sideways to squeeze his broad frame through the narrow gap.

"Damn tiny people," he muttered to himself, shifting and shuffling along the cramped passageway.

After a short walk, the passage opened into a small clearing, with another narrow passage opposite them. In the centre of the clearing stood a large stone Ankh, its presence casting an aura of mystery and reverence over the space.

"We can rest here for a while before we plan our next move," Malkhia suggested, setting down his black wooden staff and backpack against the mountain wall.

Atlas and Horethian followed suit, placing their belongings beside Malkhia's before sitting with their backs against the cold stone.

"You know, if we weren't being chased, this would be a nice spot," Atlas remarked, her voice tinged with a hint of wistfulness.

"Nice spot? It's cold, wet, and miserable," Horethian grumbled in response.

Suddenly, a loud howl echoed through the mountain pass, causing the group to perk up.

"Can't we have just five minutes?" Horethian complained as he jolted to his feet, grabbing his sword.

Three ice dire wolves slowly stalked their way closer from the opening opposite to where the trio had come through. One of the wolves began to let out a loud howl, answered by another from the entryway.

Atlas swivelled around to see another four wolves walking through the passage they had come through toward them, in single file before spreading out into the clearing.

"Looks like they have us surrounded," Atlas observed.

Horethian wiped his nose with his armoured forearm. "Let's do this then," he said, planting his feet firmly into the snow and readying his sword.

Atlas pulled an arrow from her quiver, knocking it and placing her fingers on the threaded bowstring.

The wolves began to close in on the group, growling and snarling.

"Cre Fir Fie," Malkhia chanted as a fireball shot in front of the wolves at the far passage, and a wall of flames arose from the frozen ground.

Atlas pulled back on the bowstring and let loose an arrow towards one of the wolves at the opposite end. The wolf responded with a quick movement, dodging the arrow completely; it stuck firmly into the ground next to the wolf.

Undeterred, Atlas quickly nocked another arrow and fired again—this time, the arrow firmly hit its mark.

The wolf let out a loud yelp before rolling over on its side, incapacitated by Atlas's well-aimed shot.

A glass potion filled with orange liquid flew over to the remaining three wolves and exploded on impact just in front of them, sending flying fragments of stone toward the wolves. The creatures howled in pain as the shrapnel cut into their flesh.

Despite the chaos, the other wolves managed to clear the flame wall as Horethian lunged with force, letting out a loud battle cry. His sword pierced the side of one wolf, slicing through muscle and tissue easily. With a swift motion, he drew it back to take a swipe at another wolf closing in. The animal easily dodged the swipe and pounced, latching onto his sword arm.

Its teeth only barely scraped the skin between the joints of his armour. Horethian brought up his fist and struck the wolf square on the snout. A loud crack resonated through the clearing as the plate iron crushed into bone and fur. The animal's grip loosened as it dropped to the ground. Horethian followed up with a downward thrust from his blade, pinning the animal to the ground, ensuring it posed no further threat.

"Vanc Mov," Malkhia chanted, unleashing an energy bolt from his staff toward the remaining wolf on that side. The bolt hit the animal with a thud, causing the smell of burnt fur to fill the air. The wolf backed away, its side blackened and bleeding, before turning tail and fleeing toward the passageway.

However, Malkhia's attention was drawn away from the fleeing wolf by a loud groan of pain. He turned to see Atlas, dagger in hand, swiping at a wolf that had a firm grip on her leg, with another about to pounce.

"En Ren Mov," Malkhia chanted, aiming his staff toward the pouncing animal. The wolf froze in place, completely paralysed by the spell. Malkhia then chanted again, "Cre Mov Vlas," and a white glowing arrow shot from his staff, hitting the wolf's snout, which was rigidly attached to Atlas's leg. The wolf shook its head, losing its grip.

Seizing the opportunity, Atlas brought her dagger down through the top of the wolf's skull, causing it to go limp and drop.

The remaining wolf turned to flee down the passageway, but Atlas let loose another arrow, stopping the fleeing animal in its tracks.

"Trea Fir," a voice echoed from behind Atlas as a fireball shot toward the paralysed wolf, leaving a gaping hole through the animal, surrounded by singed fur and cooked meat.

"I think that's all of them. How's the leg?" Malkhia inquired, as he attempted to regain his mental focus and recover mana.

"A bit sore, but I can still hold my weight," Atlas replied, testing her injured leg.

"That's why you needed some plate armour instead of that leather stuff," Horethian commented as he joined the pair, thumping his hand onto his chest for emphasis.

"I wouldn't be able to move in that," Atlas retorted, retrieving her dagger from the skull of the wolf.

"Let's skin these wolves, and I can at least tailor up some warm capes with the hides," Atlas suggested, already starting to slice the hide off the wolf that had grabbed her leg.

The group set to work, skinning and butchering the animals. Malkhia and Atlas threw the pelts into a pile before settling themselves back against the mountain wall for a moment's rest.

Meanwhile, Horethian piled up the leftovers at the opposite end of the clearing before gathering a few of the damaged pelts and bringing them to where the other two were sitting.

He began to dig at the snow, his efforts soon revealing dirt as he created a nice indent in the ground. The trio then set to work stripping the fat off all the hides, tossing it into the hole Horethian had dug earlier.

"Trea Fir," Malkhia chanted quietly, creating another fireball which shot into the hole, setting the fat and scraps alight. Atlas took out three arrows, handing them to Horethian as he skewered a large chunk of meat onto each, before placing them over the now blazing fire.

She reached back into her bag, pulling out a small sewing kit, and began to make quick work of the hides. Meanwhile, Malkhia let out a deep sigh as he stared into the dancing flames, watching the meat change from dark red to a light brown. His mind began to wander into distant memories.

He raised his hand, clasping his left shoulder and moving it further down his back, then up the side of his neck.

"You okay, Malk? Did you hurt your shoulder in the fight?" Atlas asked, concern evident in her voice, as she tossed him a cape made from the sewn hides. "This should keep you warm at least."

"Huh? Oh, thanks. I'm fine, it's nothing," Malkhia replied as he snapped back to reality and threw the cape over his back, fastening it around his neck.

"And here is yours, Horethian," Atlas said, passing another cape to him as he turned the meat.

"Where's yours?" Horethian asked as he copied Malkhia's actions, donning his cape.

"Weren't enough pelts, but I'll be fine in my 'leather stuff,' as you put it," she replied.

Horethian picked up the three skewers of cooked meat and began to hand them to the others.

"Cooked to perfection," he said as he took a huge bite and shuffled his back into the wall, getting himself comfortable.

"Where else would you rather be?" he continued as he finished the last bite.

"Not here," Malkhia said as he slid down the wall, propping his bag under his head before pulling his hat over his face, ready to drift off to sleep.

4

The sun rose over the grassy hills, casting its golden light across the freshly tilled fields like a warm embrace. A small farming village nestled in the valley between two hills, its quaint cottages dotting the landscape and backing onto a dense forest.

The village stirred with life as the townsfolk began their day. Farmers gathered their workhorses and loaded carts with tools and wheat seeds, while the wives collected baskets of linen to wash in the winding creek that flowed alongside the village and disappeared deep into the forest.

"Boy! Wake up, boy!" a man's voice rang out through the morning air, breaking the peaceful rhythm of the scene. The boy's eyes slowly cracked open, welcoming the golden sunlight. He tossed his makeshift blanket aside, revealing his scrawny frame to the chill.

He sat up in bed, the morning cold still clinging to the air as he swung his legs over the side. His father's voice pressed him into action, the urgency of the day already clear.

"I'm awake, Father!" he called, his voice thick with sleep.

"Hurry now, we need to get to the fields," his father shouted back.

"I haven't even eaten yet," the boy grumbled.

"You chose to sleep—no time now," his father replied, leaving no room for argument.

Resigned, the boy rummaged through a small chest at the foot of his bed, retrieving his worn and tattered clothes. He quickly dressed, sliding into rough leggings, pulling a shirt over his head, and stepping into old socks and scuffed leather boots that sat in the corner of the room.

"Coming, Father," he called, as he stepped through the well-crafted sandstone archway that led from his room.

The sound of a wooden chair scraping against the stone floor signalled his father's readiness. Together, they moved out of their modest Yellowstone home and into the small wooden barn adjacent to it—a later addition to the original stone structure.

"Get the cart, boy," his father ordered, as he threw a pack saddle over the back of a slate-grey horse before leading it out of the barn.

The boy hurried around the side of the house, his small frame straining against the weight of the wooden cart. With determined effort, he pulled, the wheels groaning with resistance before finally giving way and creaking forward. He steered it toward the waiting horse, where his father stood ready to secure it to the saddle.

"Grain," the man instructed gruffly.

"Yes, Father," the boy responded, darting to the back of the barn where the hessian sacks were neatly stacked. He struggled to lift one of the heavy 20-kilogram bags, but with a grunt of effort, he hoisted it onto his shoulder and carried it out to the waiting cart. Back and forth he went, making several trips until the cart was nearly full and the stack inside the barn visibly diminished.

With a sharp thud of the reins and a barked command from his father, the horse lurched forward, the laden cart groaning under the weight as it rolled into motion. The pair joined a slow procession of farmers, each with their own carts and horses, making their way toward the fields.

"Your boy looks a little worn out already there, Jeremy," one of the farmers called out with a chuckle, nodding toward the lad.

"He only just woke up. Children these days—no work ethic," the father replied, glancing down at the boy with a stern look. "But we'll sort that out, won't we, boy?"

"Yes, Father," the boy answered, his tone quiet, respectful, and edged with fatigue.

The hours slipped by as the boy worked the fields with the rest of the townsfolk, his small hands sowing seeds with the other villagers. The sun began its descent, casting long shadows across the golden earth as it sank behind the thick tree line.

"I'll sort the horse and cart. Go wash up in the stream before supper," the man instructed, his voice heavy with the day's wear.

The boy didn't hesitate—he turned and ran toward the stream, eager to rid himself of the grime and sweat that clung to his skin. Just as he reached the water's edge, he heard his father's familiar voice calling after him one last time:

"And don't be late again!"

"Don't be late again. Get the grain, boy. Sort the horse," the youngster muttered bitterly to himself as he scrubbed the grime from his slender frame.

He laid his shirt on a flat stone beside the stream, intending to wash it along with his pants. But just as he began scrubbing, a sudden surge of water from upstream swept the shirt off the rock and sent it drifting downstream.

"No! Now I'm definitely going to be late!" the boy shouted in frustration, leaping to his feet and scrambling along the riverbank, determined to reclaim the runaway garment.

The shirt floated into a narrow offshoot of the river, leading deeper into the forest. The sun was now barely visible above the hills, casting long, creeping shadows that dimmed the light to near darkness.

Then, just as suddenly as it had surged, the current subsided. The water stilled.

"Weird," the boy murmured, wading into the waist-deep stream. His bare feet slid over slick river pebbles as he crossed to the far bank. Reaching for his shirt, he

spotted it snagged on something submerged—an old wooden chest banded with tarnished brass.

He grabbed the shirt and flung it back toward the other side, where it landed with a wet slap. Then, curiosity overcoming caution, he lifted the small chest into his arms and trudged back to the bank.

"Boy!" his father's voice rang out through the trees, sharp and commanding, shattering the silence of the forest.

In the distance, the boy made out the flickering glow of a flaming torch—his father's signal, burning steadily in the dark. Despite the encroaching gloom, the boy called out, his voice carrying through the stillness of the forest.

"I'm here, Father! My shirt washed away!"

He wrapped the small chest in the wet fabric and dashed toward the light, heart pounding—not just from exertion, but from fear.

"I'm sorry, Fath—"

Before he could finish, the back of his father's hand struck his cheek, the sting cutting his words short.

"I said not to be late," his father snapped, his tone sharp and full of frustration. "Your mother's worried, and supper's cold. We can't afford to waste food."

With a firm shove to the boy's shoulder, he gestured him forward.

"Now get home and straight to bed."

"It wasn't my fault," the boy murmured, his voice wavering.

"It never is. There's always some excuse with you," his father retorted, disappointment heavy in his words. "Tomorrow, you'll stay home and help your mother with the house duties."

The glow of the torch guided them through the darkening forest, casting long shadows and lighting the winding path back to the village. As they neared their home, the father fixed a stern gaze on the boy.

"When we go in, you apologise to your mother and go straight to bed," he instructed firmly.

"Yes, Father," the boy replied, his voice quiet and resigned as they stepped into the warm glow spilling from their house.

They climbed the small steps leading to the front door. The man pushed it open with a creak of old hinges, then extinguished his torch with a sharp hiss and set it into a bent wrought iron holder on the porch.

"Sorry I'm late, Mother," the boy mumbled, keeping his head low as he walked straight to his room. He pulled the curtain draped above the archway closed, the fabric whispering softly as it slid across the worn wooden rod. He stripped off his clothes, the fabric rustling as it fell into a heap on the floor.

"I found him deep in the forest, near that crackpot's house," he overheard his father say to his mother, the voice carrying a note of irritation. "No idea what he

was doing down there," came the follow-up, punctuated by a tired sigh.

"There's a house down there?" the boy wondered, his thoughts spinning with a mix of unease and excitement. "Oh—that's right, the chest!"

His heart quickened as he darted to his bundled shirt on the floor. Fumbling with the damp fabric, he unravelled it to reveal the small wooden chest hidden beneath. Its surface shimmered faintly in the candlelight, the brass banding catching the glow with an almost magical gleam.

The candlelight revealed intricate etchings of unfamiliar runes carved across the surface of the small wooden chest.

"These are weird... and definitely not English," he murmured, his curiosity piqued as he traced the markings with his fingers.

He attempted to pry the chest open, the hinges groaning in protest as he strained against their stubborn grip. After several futile efforts, he gave up with a frustrated sigh and shoved the chest under his bed with a muffled thud.

"What was that?" came a sharp voice from the other room, edged with concern and irritation.

"Just me getting into bed. Goodnight!" he called back quickly, hoping to avoid further questioning.

The next morning, soft light filtered through the window, brushing against his face just as the front door slammed shut. His father had already left for the fields.

"House duties. Yay," he muttered sarcastically as he sat up, rubbing the sleep from his eyes.

With a weary sigh, he reached for the cold, damp clothes that had lain crumpled on the floor all night. As he pulled them on, a shiver ran down his spine.

"Ugh... cold, wet clothes," he grumbled, wincing.

He emerged from his room and entered the dining room, where his mother greeted him with a warm smile as she set down a plate of eggs in front of him.

"Here's breakfast," she said gently, her eyes shining with quiet concern.

"Your father said not to," she added in a hushed tone, pouring a glass of fresh milk and giving him a playful wink, "but this can be our little secret."

She set the jug down and leaned against the table for a moment, her voice lowering with tenderness. "You've been working hard with your father these past months— and gods know he's not the easiest man to please. So today, just... rest. Think of it as a day off. Have a bit of fun, alright?"

A smile tugged at her lips as she gathered a bundle of clothes into a basket.

"Just don't leave the house," she added with a more serious note before disappearing out the front door, her footsteps fading into the quiet morning.

"A day off? Have I died?" the boy muttered to himself with a grin as he dug into the eggs, savouring the rare comfort of a peaceful morning.

He leaned back in his chair with a satisfied sigh. "What to do, what to do…" Then his eyes lit up as the memory hit. "Oh! The chest!"

Scraping back his chair with urgency, he bolted toward his room.

Dropping to his hands and knees, he peered under the bed, heart quickening with excitement. The glint of brass caught his eye. He shuffled and slid his body beneath the bedframe, grunting slightly as he stretched his arms forward, fingertips brushing the cool wooden edge.

"Come on… almost…" he whispered, manoeuvring until his hands gripped the chest firmly. With a tug, he began to drag it toward him, dust puffing up from the floor as it scraped against the stone tiles.

Swiping his arm, he managed to knock the chest closer before grabbing it with his hand and pulling it out. With a thud, he dropped it onto his bed, where the sunlight streamed through the window, illuminating the seam of the lid. With a puff, the chest cracked open.

"What the…" the boy exclaimed, leaning in closer to get a better look. Carefully, he opened the small chest,

revealing a collection of scrolls and two small vials—
one containing a blue liquid and the other, red.

Intrigued, the boy flipped the chest upside down,
scattering its contents on top of his bed. His fingers
reached out for an old scroll bound in a blue ribbon.
Swiftly, he untied the ribbon and unrolled the scroll.

As the parchment unfurled, small words came into view,
written in a dark black ink. "Cre Igni," the boy
murmured, reading the inscription on the parchment.

A puff of smoke appeared and quickly dissipated,
leaving the boy momentarily puzzled. "Hmm, that was
weird," he muttered to himself, setting the scroll aside
and reaching for another one. Undoing the ribbon, he
unrolled it, revealing another set of words: "Cre Hea
Vlas."

As he spoke the words aloud, a cloud of smoke
materialized on his bed. When the smoke cleared, the
boy was surprised to find a fresh wheel of cheese.

"Umm, okay, Cre Hea Vlas," he repeated, and once
again, smoke appeared—this time leaving an apple next
to the cheese.

As the smoke vanished, the scroll began to self-ignite,
leaving no trace behind. Intrigued, the boy picked up
another scroll.

"Ango Mov," he read aloud, causing a loud noise to
ring out, and suddenly, he found himself outside the
house, looking back through his bedroom window, the
scroll still in his hand.

"What are you doing out here?" he heard his father's voice call from behind him. Turning around, the boy saw his father approaching the house.

"Just helping with the house duties like you said," the boy replied, quickly grabbing the scroll and rubbing it on the window. "Mother asked for the windows to be cleaned."

"Dry parchment isn't going to clean them very well. Get a pail of water from the well," the father replied before heading inside.

"Boy!" he heard from inside.

"What now," he thought to himself as he ran inside.

The boy entered through the front door to see his father standing there, holding the wheel of cheese and the apple.

"Are you stockpiling food in your room among the other junk on your bed?" the man asked in an angry tone.

"No, sir, I was clearing up the cupboards and went in there to get some parchment for the windows. I must have left them on my bed," the boy replied.

"Hmph," the man responded before placing the cheese on the table and taking a bite out of the apple. "I'll be back at supper," he said as he pushed past the boy and headed back outside.

"I'm going to get out of here one day," the boy said to himself as he walked back into his room, throwing the scroll on his bed with the others.

The boy noticed the red vial roll away as the thrown scroll dislodged it. He picked it up and examined it, popping the cork on top. Bringing the vial to his nose, he smelled the aroma, noticing something sweet in the air.

He shrugged his shoulders and began to pour the liquid into his mouth. As he did, a tingling sensation spread through his body, and he felt his energy surge to new heights. A euphoric rush enveloped him, making him feel more alive than ever before.

"Woah," he exclaimed, his voice filled with amazement as he jumped around, revelling in the newfound vitality coursing through him.

"What else do we have in this magical box?" he wondered aloud, his curiosity piqued as he picked up another scroll. With trembling hands, he unwrapped it and read out the words once more.

"Mov Agi Fie."

Suddenly, a brilliant bolt of lightning streaked across the sky, illuminating the area. It struck the house with a deafening crack, leaving a charred mark on the yellow sandstone wall. Startled, the boy's heart raced as he realized the power of the words he had spoken.

"That's enough of that," he muttered in a panic, his mind racing to contain the unexpected consequences.

Frantically, he tried to gather up the scrolls, but one slipped from his grasp and rolled away, disappearing into the narrow gap between the bed and the wall. With a sense of urgency, he hastily stuffed the remaining scrolls into the chest and shoved it under his bed, hoping to conceal the evidence of his unwitting actions.

In an instant, the front door burst open, and his parents rushed in, their faces etched with concern.

"What was that?" his father demanded, his voice sharp with alarm.

Caught off guard, the boy's pulse quickened as he searched for an explanation. "I didn't do it," he insisted, his eyes wide with innocence as he met his parents' gaze.

"Leave the boy, Jeremy," she pleaded, her voice tinged with desperation as Jeremy grabbed the boy.

Ignoring her plea, the father's grip tightened on the boy's neck as he confronted him.

"This has got to do with all that junk on your bed— where is it!?" he accused, his voice laced with frustration and anger.

The boy met his father's gaze, his eyes filled with a mixture of defiance and fear.

"Where is what?" he retorted, his voice trembling with emotion.

With a forceful tug, the father dragged the boy toward his bed, his grip unyielding as he demanded answers.

"Under the bed, I found it in the river," the boy confessed, his voice barely a whisper as he revealed the location of the mysterious chest.

In a swift motion, the father retrieved the chest from beneath the bed, his hand raised high above his head. The boy braced himself for the inevitable blow, his heart pounding with dread as he awaited his father's judgment.

With a resounding thwack, the father's hand struck the side of the boy's face, leaving behind a burning sensation and a sense of betrayal. The boy recoiled from the pain, his cheeks flushed with humiliation as he struggled to regain his composure.

"There will be no magic trinkets in my home," the father declared sternly, his words echoing with finality. *"Tomorrow, we will be heading into the city to see what we can do with your disobedience,"* he announced before storming out of the room, leaving the boy alone with his thoughts and his pain.

Tears streamed down the boy's face, mingling with the blood that dripped from his injured nose onto the wooden floor. His body trembled with pain and shock as he lay sprawled on the ground, the weight of his father's harsh blow still reverberating through him.

With a shaky breath, he mustered the strength to push himself up, his movements slow and deliberate. He could hear the muffled sounds of arguing and murmuring coming from the dining room—a grim reminder of the discord that filled his home.

Gingerly, he rose to his feet, his body aching with every movement. With cautious steps, he made his way toward the archway, his heart pounding in his chest as he peered out, careful not to be seen by his parents.

"Please, Jeremy, reconsider," his mother's voice pleaded, her tone filled with desperation and fear.

But his father's response was swift and sharp, cutting through the air like a blade. "Enough, woman!" he barked, his voice laced with anger and frustration, causing the woman to flinch in fear of his wrath.

"We will be going to the city tomorrow, and I will be coming back alone. End of story." The man's words echoed through the room, final and resolute.

With tears still glistening in his eyes, the boy turned away from the scene unfolding in the dining room. He couldn't bear to watch as his father callously tossed the chest into the fire, the flames turning a vivid green before settling back to their usual hue.

As his father stumbled backward in surprise, the boy felt a pang of guilt and sadness wash over him. He knew, deep down, that the chest had held something extraordinary—something that could perhaps have changed his fate. But now, all those possibilities were lost in the flames, consumed by his father's anger and fear.

"I'm not going to the city," he whispered to himself, his voice barely audible over the crackling of the fire. With a heavy heart, he lay down on his bed, his mind filled with thoughts.

"They will be asleep soon, and I'll be out of here," he said with determination as he swept his hands down either side of the bed, feeling the end of a silky ribbon.

"Huh," he thought, intrigued, as he delved deeper between the bed and the wall, retrieving a scroll. With cautious anticipation, he unrolled the scroll, hoping it might offer a solution.

"Please be something that can stop this," he thought to himself as he read the words aloud.

"Val Trea Atur Vanc."

Suddenly, a deafening clap of thunder reverberated through the village, causing the boy to sit up abruptly in his bed. Peering out the window, he observed the sky swirling ominously, its hue shifting to a foreboding dark purple. Forks of lightning pierced the sky as the clouds gathered, coalescing into a menacing funnel.

From the heart of the swirling storm, bolts of lightning streaked downward, igniting the neighbouring houses in a fiery blaze. Amidst the chaos, a shadowy figure began to take shape at the epicentre of the lightning strike, its form expanding to dwarf the surrounding structures.

As the fire raged on, fuelled by the relentless wind from the storm, embers swirled through the air, landing on barns and rooftops, setting off a chain reaction of destruction.

The shadowy form gradually morphed, revealing hints of a deep brown hue amidst the darkness. Two formidable horns emerged prominently from the creature's head, adding to its intimidating presence.

Suddenly, immense bat-like wings unfurled from the figure's back, dispersing the surrounding shadows and fully exposing the monstrous entity.

With a resounding stomp of its hoofed feet, the creature emitted a primal roar that cut through the village, shaking the very foundations of the homes. Panic ensued as screams pierced the air, echoing the terror of the townsfolk fleeing from the raging inferno that engulfed their once peaceful village.

As the winged Daemon spread its wings menacingly, it unleashed fiery projectiles from its gaping maw, further fuelling the devastation. The flames danced wildly, consuming everything in their path with merciless efficiency.

"What have you done!?" the man bellowed, bursting into the boy's room and confronting him, his eyes wide with fury upon seeing him clutching the ominous scroll.

"I didn't know," the boy exclaimed, his voice tinged with fear and disbelief as the wooden structure of their villa roof erupted into flames, casting an intense heat that threatened to engulf them all. A main timber beam creaked ominously, sending burning fragments cascading down to the floor before splitting in half and crashing down on Jeremy, trapping him beneath its weight.

With a surge of adrenaline, the boy leapt out of bed and rushed to his father's aid. But as he hurried, more structural beams succumbed to the inferno, raining down around them until the house's roof lay in smouldering ruins on the ground.

The boy, now unable to move, found himself pinned face down by the scorching wood. Agonizing heat seared his skin, sending waves of pain rippling through his body and numbing his senses.

"En Agi!" he heard someone yell from a distance, and suddenly his vision began to blur and shake violently.

"Malk, Malk!" a voice called out urgently, pulling him from the depths of his nightmare. Slowly, he opened his eyes to see Atlas gripping his shoulders, her voice filled with concern.

"I'm awake, I'm awake," he reassured her, rubbing his eyes and sitting up.

"You were making some weird noises there, like you were in pain," Atlas observed, her brow furrowed with worry.

"Just a dream, Atlas… Just a dream," he muttered, his hand instinctively reaching to massage his sore shoulder and neck, the remnants of the nightmare still lingering in his mind.

5

The prince's regal red cape, edged in thick, pure white fur, billowed gracefully as he strode through the opulent hallway toward the throne room. Each step he took caused the cape to lift slightly off the polished marble floor. The large golden serpent buckle of his mahogany-brown leather belt gleamed in the ambient light, its intricate design catching the eye of any who passed by.

As he passed an open doorway, inside a verdant oasis unfolded, a lush garden bursting with life. The air was fragrant with the scent of freshly cut grass and the sweet aroma of blossoming flowers. Neatly trimmed hedges formed intricate patterns around a patch of vibrant green grass, where small apple and pear trees stood sentinel.

In the midst of this natural splendour stood a figure, her ebony hair cascading like a waterfall down to her lower back. She was dressed in a flowing white gown adorned with delicate gold trimmings, her slender fingers gently pouring water into a small bronze birdbath. At the sound of approaching footsteps, she turned, her gaze catching the prince as he walked past.

"Oh, Errand boy! Is that you?" she called out, her voice melodic yet teasing.

The prince halted in his tracks, his cape swirling around him as he turned to face the woman. He adjusted the position of his belt, the golden buckle glinting in the sunlight that filtered through the garden's canopy.

"Hello, sister," he replied, his tone tinged with a hint of sarcasm.

"Refer to me by my name," the prince continued, his voice carrying a subtle air of authority.

"It's just a bit of fun, Eron," she said, her words dancing lightly in the air, "plus you sort of are and have always been Father's errand boy." A small smile crossed her pale, elegant face, softening the edges of her jest.

"You may be older, but Father left me in charge during his absence. The throne is mine. So, show some respect, Charlotte," the prince said, the bitterness in his voice betraying his underlying frustration.

Charlotte let out a small, melodic laugh, the sound like tinkling bells in the serene atmosphere of the garden. With practiced grace, she placed a hand adorned with perfectly manicured nails up to her mouth to conceal her amusement.

"Speaking of Father, any news from his crew on their whereabouts?" she inquired, her gaze flickering with curiosity.

"Nothing yet," the prince replied.

"Strange, it's been a couple of months now," she said, her brow furrowing in puzzlement.

"You will be the first to know if I hear any news," Eron assured her.

"Hmm, yeah, sure thing," she replied, a hint of sarcasm lacing her words like a delicate thread.

The prince huffed in mild annoyance as he turned away from his sister, his cape swirling behind him, and headed back into the hallway to resume his path.

Meanwhile, Charlotte finished filling the birdbath, a sense of satisfaction evident in the gentle curve of her lips. With a contented sigh, she walked over to the hedges, where rows of sunflowers were just beginning to bloom.

A petite woman, also dressed in white but lacking the ornate gold trimmings, emerged from behind the hedges where she had been hidden from view. She approached Charlotte with a concerned expression etched upon her features.

"Aren't you worried he will do something while your father is away?" she asked Charlotte, her voice tinged with apprehension.

"Eron? He couldn't even orchestrate his own loss of virginity, so I highly doubt he could organize a coup," Charlotte replied with a hint of amusement, taking in a deep breath as she buried her face in one of the more mature, deep yellow sunflowers.

"I'll let a couple of the other women know to keep an eye out, just in case, milady," Gwen says, her voice tinged with concern.

"Thank you, Gwen. The pieces were slowly moving into place, but we might need to speed things up if there was no news of Father's return coming anytime soon,"

Charlotte said, standing up and turning to face the woman.

"I will also send a couple of the young boys down to the docks again, to see if there is any new info around the king," Gwen suggested.

"Keep me informed, please. We have to proceed very carefully," Charlotte replied, her tone reflecting the gravity of the situation.

"Of course, Ma'am," Gwen acknowledged with a nod before turning towards the hallway, her mind already calculating the next steps in their intricate plan.

"Send this off as well, please," Charlotte said, reaching into her dress and producing a rolled piece of parchment with a blue ribbon and a red wax seal holding it closed.

"Usual method?" Gwen asked, her brow furrowing with curiosity.

"Yes, please," Charlotte replied before turning back around to continue tending to the garden, her attention momentarily diverted by the vibrant blooms.

Gwen nodded as she turned once more, the weight of their clandestine activities settling upon her shoulders as she began to walk back to the hallway.

Meanwhile, the prince's stride had quickened, his high-topped black leather boots thudding against the stone of the hallway with purposeful determination.

"Who does she think she is?" he mumbled to himself as he entered the throne room, his frustration simmering beneath the surface.

"She will get what is coming to her one day, especially when I have the map," he thought darkly, his mind already plotting his next move as he ascended the two small stone steps leading to a small stage where three throne-like chairs sat in silent judgment.

A large throne, crafted of shiny bronze with a serpent emblem down the backrest—made up of precious jewels—sat between two smaller bronze thrones, also bearing serpent emblems, though these were intricately carved into the bronze with spiral patterns spreading out from the emblem.

The prince strode confidently towards the largest throne, his cape billowing behind him as he fluffed it up, preparing to lower himself into the grand seat.

However, his diminutive frame left substantial gaps between the armrests and his thighs, a comical sight against the imposing backdrop of the throne room.

From the opposite entrance, Belfor, a trusted advisor, walked towards the throne. He bent down on one knee before lowering his head in a gesture of respect.

"My Lord, I have news," he announced, lifting his head to look up at the prince.

"Factual or rumours again, Belfor?" the prince replied, a hint of amusement playing across his features.

"We managed to track the hunting party, my lord," Belfor reported, still glancing up at the prince.

"The map!?" the prince demanded eagerly, shifting his weight forward in the throne, his anticipation palpable.

Belfor lowered his head back down, his gaze fixed upon the dark scarlet red carpet floor runner that spanned the length of the throne room.

"Nothing yet, my lord. Our men are still searching the cabin, but it seems it was only a temporary residence," he reported, his voice steady despite the disappointment.

"What of the hunting party?" the prince demanded, his frustration becoming increasingly apparent.

"They managed to port out before we could get there," Belfor admitted, keeping his head lowered to avoid the intensity of the prince's gaze.

"So, first you barged into my private room to interrupt me and speak rumours, now you come back with basically nothing newsworthy of my time once more?" the prince snapped, his irritation evident in his tone.

"Forgive me, my lord. We have our best trackers trying to trace the location of the portal's exit," Belfor said, briefly meeting the prince's angry gaze before lowering his head once again.

He shifted slightly on his now-aching knee, pressing into the carpet with a sense of unease.

"Find them!" the prince yelled, his face now beginning to gain a red tinge, his frustration reaching its boiling point.

"Yes, my lord," Belfor responded, rising to his feet with a slight sense of relief washing over him as he straightened his posture.

Turning on his heel, Belfor began to stride towards the room's exit, his movements betraying a hint of discomfort as he favoured his now throbbing knee, the strain manifesting as a subtle limp.

"Oh, and Belfor," the prince's voice sliced through the air, arresting Belfor's retreat midway across the room.

He whirled around to face the prince once more, grimacing inwardly at the pulsating ache in his knee.

"Do not return without my map and the heads of these thieves," the prince commanded, his expression twisted into a menacing glare that sent a shiver down Belfor's spine.

"Yes, my lord," Belfor replied, pivoting on his heel once more and striding out of the throne room.

"WINE!" the prince's voice echoed throughout the chamber as he settled back onto his imposing throne, exhaling a heavy sigh of frustration.

A young woman, her features etched with trepidation, hurried forward carrying a flagon and a sizable goblet. Pausing at the foot of the throne, she began to pour the wine with a trembling hand, her eyes downcast in courtesy as she extended the filled goblet towards the prince.

The prince grasped the goblet firmly, its weight a comforting presence in his hand, while his other hand seized the woman's wrist with a predatory grip, halting her movement abruptly.

"Such exquisite skin," he murmured, his fingers coiling around her delicate wrist, exerting a pressure that bordered on painful.

Startled, the young woman lifted her gaze to meet the prince's, her eyes wide with apprehension.

"Hmm, you're a new face in the castle," the prince observed, his grip tightening further, leaving faint imprints on her sun-kissed flesh. "Where did they unearth such a rare beauty like yourself?"

"I hail from a remote town near the desert plains, my lord," the woman replied, her voice trembling with a mixture of fear and resignation, her efforts to conceal her pain evident in the strain on her face.

"Fascinating," the prince mused, a lascivious glint in his eye as he tightened his grip once more, eliciting a stifled gasp from the woman. "Visit my chambers tonight. I intend to scrutinize every inch of you."

"As you command, my lord," the woman replied hastily, withdrawing her arm from the prince's grasp with a swift, fluid motion, her eyes betraying a mixture of fear and revulsion as she retreated.

"Fetch me the commander," the prince commanded, his tone authoritative yet casual as he reclined into his chair, bringing the goblet to his lips and draining its contents in one smooth motion.

"Leave the flagon," he added dismissively as he set the empty vessel aside.

"Yes, my lord," the woman said, placing down the flagon and quickly bowing before walking out of the room.

Moments later, a formidable figure strode into the throne room, his imposing frame clad in gleaming bronze armour, a ruby-red cape cascading from his broad shoulders and secured by thick bronze chains. The clinking of his sword hilt against his plate mail resonated through the chamber as he approached the prince.

"My lord," the man intoned, his hand resting on the hilt of his sword as he knelt before the prince.

With a casual gesture, the prince bid him to rise.

"Commander Sharl, ensure that Belfor does not falter again," the prince ordered, his voice tinged with a hint of annoyance.

"As you command, my lord. And how should we handle any potential setbacks?" Commander Sharl inquired, his gaze unwavering.

"Publicly. Failures must be met with consequences," the prince declared, replenishing his goblet with more wine.

"Understood, my lord," the commander acknowledged with a respectful bow before pivoting on his heel and striding away, his hand poised on his sword hilt to muffle any noise.

Alone once more, the prince muttered to himself, his voice a low murmur of discontent. "I fail to grasp my father's regard for Belfor's loyalty."

Meanwhile, hidden behind a stone pillar, Gwen listened intently to the exchange, her mind racing with possibilities. "Perhaps Belfor can still be of use... Lady Charlotte must be informed," she pondered, silently retreating towards the hallway that led back to the garden.

6

Leyla clambered to her feet, her body swaying in tandem with the boat's rhythmic motion as she struggled to maintain her balance.

With outstretched hands, she reached for the cabin wall, seeking stability as she shook off the disorienting sensation akin to a mild concussion.

"Theo!?" she called out, her voice echoing into the void, met only by an eerie silence.

"Jolly!?" Again, her cries yielded no response, amplifying her sense of abandonment.

"They've left me here alone," Leyla lamented inwardly, a pang of isolation settling in her chest.

Surveying the cabin, Leyla's gaze landed upon a small hatch with its wooden cover ajar, positioned at the far end of Theo's bed. Determination flickered in her eyes as she made her way towards it, a glimmer of hope stirring within her.

Kneeling down, Leyla peered into the darkness below, her heart pounding in anticipation. The cacophony of hammering reverberated through the cramped space, assaulting her senses as she called out once more.

"Theo!"

"Aye, down here, Leyla. We're taking on water. Give us a hand, will ya?" came the muffled response amid the relentless pounding.

With resolve fuelling her actions, Leyla stood tall and positioned her foot over the gaping hole, her fingers finding purchase on a small rope ladder.

With a steadying breath, she began her descent into the murky depths below.

"Good morning, and welcome to the Lower Deck," Theo announced with a theatrical flourish, his arms outstretched in a mock bow, treating Leyla as if she were royalty.

Jolly, the ever-enthusiastic companion, added to the greeting with a boisterous bark and a vigorous wag of his tail as Leyla descended the final rung of the small rope ladder.

"Quick, grab some planks! There's a bucket of nails and a hammer over there. We need to patch these holes fast," Theo instructed urgently, gesturing towards a pile of wooden planks before turning back to resume hammering a board over one of the gaping holes in the ship's hull.

Leyla wasted no time, darting over to the pile of planks and snatching up a couple, tossing them towards the second hole with a sense of urgency.

Grabbing the bucket and hammer, she set to work, following Theo's lead as she attempted to secure the makeshift patch over the breach in the ship's structure.

The rhythmic clanging of hammer against nail echoed through the cramped space as they worked together in a race against time to stave off the flooding waters.

The relentless flow of cold saltwater surged unimpeded through two jagged apertures on the port side of the ship. Theo painstakingly neared completion in patching the forward breach.

Meanwhile, Leyla grappled with the unruly board, struggling to maintain its position against the force of the rushing water. Her hands worked feverishly—one grappling for nails in the bucket while wielding the hammer, and the other holding the board flush to the ship.

Just as the pressure threatened to overwhelm her, Leyla felt the burden lift from her weary arm. Her gaze darted upwards to behold Theo's steadfast form. Despite the deluge cascading over him, his grip remained resolute as he steadied the board against the ship's hull.

"Come on now, I enjoy the sea, but I'm not quite keen on drinking it," Theo remarked with a grin, his voice carrying a hint of jest amidst the chaos, as Leyla seized the opportunity to secure the board in place with newfound determination.

With synchronized efforts, the pair swiftly tended to the remaining breaches, their actions a seamless dance of cooperation amid adversity.

As the final nail was driven home, a sense of relief washed over them as the ingress of water gradually subsided.

Theo chuckled, albeit with a hint of exasperation, as he wiped a mixture of seawater and sweat from his brow, his laughter laced with a touch of ruefulness.

"Wish Tillerman actually moved and helped; wouldn't have taken on so much water," he remarked wryly, his voice carrying a note of jest despite the gravity of the situation.

Leyla's expression shifted to one of confusion as she sought answers amidst the chaos. "What the hell has happened, Theo?" she queried, her brow furrowed in puzzlement.

"Well, I woke up, went outside to gather some fresh eggs for breakfast. But lo and behold, the dock was nowhere in sight, and we were drifting towards this blasted island. Next thing I know, we're half on the rocks and taking on water, and, well, you know the rest," Theo explained.

"How does a docked boat just start drifting into the ocean? Are you new to this?" Leyla probed further, her gaze fixated on Theo with a questioning intensity.

"Excuse me, miss," Theo retorted sharply. "I've been at sea for most of me life. We tied off to the dock just three days ago, with strong knots, mind you. Jolly here can vouch for that. And until you arrived, we hadn't encountered a single problem. So, perhaps I should be the one asking the questions."

Leyla's shoulders slumped slightly as she absorbed Theo's pointed response, her gaze drifting downward in a gesture of contrition. "Sorry, Theo. I'm just not accustomed to company or being abruptly awoken and flung across a room," she admitted, her voice marked with sincerity.

"Ehh, no harm done. Let's get a coupla buckets and get this water out, eh?" Theo suggested, his tone laced with pragmatism as he bent down to retrieve two empty buckets, handing one to Leyla with a nod.

With synchronized effort, the pair hauled bucket after bucket of water up from the depths below. With each successive haul, they fell into a rhythm, their actions becoming almost mechanical as they worked tirelessly to rid the ship of its unwanted water.

"That's the last bit," Leyla announced triumphantly, her voice carrying a note of relief as she flung a half-filled bucket over the side.

Theo released a weary sigh, his hands finding their way to his hips as he arched his back, stretching out the kinks of exertion. However, his moment of respite was short-lived as his gaze fell upon the tie-off rope lying abandoned on the deck.

"Hmm," he murmured to himself, a furrow forming between his brows as he strode towards the discarded rope, his mind already racing with thoughts and concerns.

"What is it?" Leyla inquired, concern etched across her features as she settled onto the deck beside Jolly, who lay flat on the wooden planks, panting heavily and soaked from their recent exertions.

"These ropes have been cut," Theo explained, turning to display the cleanly severed end of the rope to Leyla. "No fraying or nuffin, just a clean cut."

Leyla's brow furrowed in confusion as she rose to her feet, her curiosity piqued. Making her way to the opposite side of the ship, she inspected the second rope, only to discover it too had been cleanly sliced through.

"This one's cut too!" she called out to Theo, her voice a mixture of bewilderment and alarm.

As she continued her exploration along the cabin's side, her keen eyes caught sight of a glint of gold amidst the weathered wood—a dagger, its hilt shimmering in the dappled sunlight, pinned into the wooden surface with a piece of parchment beneath its blade.

"Um, Theo, there's a note here," Leyla announced, her voice carrying across the deck.

In a flurry of motion, Theo raced across the deck, his footsteps echoing in tandem with the pounding of his heart. Standing alongside Leyla, he listened intently as she began to read aloud from the parchment.

"Let this be a warning! If I even hear of you near my wife again, there will be no saving you. Signed, Ravich."

"Do you have something to explain, Theo?" Leyla queried, her gaze fixed on Theo with a mixture of amusement and curiosity.

Theo's nervousness was palpable as he raised an arm to rub the back of his neck, a telltale sign of his discomfort. "Well, the note explains it well enough. Lucky he didn't know about his sister, eh?" he responded with a forced chuckle, his demeanour betraying an underlying tension.

"Anyway, I'll have Ramsay pull us around to shore and away from these rocks. We'd better find out where we are," Theo suggested, attempting to steer the conversation in a different direction.

But Leyla wasn't so easily deterred. "Oh no no no, I have questions. Who is Ravich, and what about his wife and sister?" she pressed, her curiosity insatiable.

"Ravich is a goods merchant from that city, or a fence, as you would call them, but for wares from the sea. He's a rather small, rotund man with a large black moustache twisted up at the sides and a huge bald spot, which he normally tries to hide—although not that well—under a black top hat. He runs one of the main trading guilds, so I'm pretty much done in that city," Theo elaborated, his tone tinged with a hint of bitterness.

"As for the wife and sister, I won't go into details, but it's pretty self-explanatory—couple of ales and some songs, you know how it is. Damn good lookers too. No idea why his wife hangs around, must be the money," Theo concluded with a nonchalant shrug, as if dismissing the matter entirely.

"Enough of that, let's go explorin'," he suggested, attempting to steer the conversation away from the topic.

"Mm, I suppose that will do for now, but I do want to know more," Leyla conceded, her curiosity still lingering.

Theo moved across the deck and into the cabin, only to be met with a scene of disarray. The contents of the room had been dramatically displaced, with pots, pans, and utensils strewn across the floor haphazardly. The large chest, from which he had retrieved the hammock earlier, had somehow broken free from its mounting and wedged itself into one of the cupboards.

"What a mess," Leyla muttered, startling Theo as her voice sounded right beside him.

"Stop stealthily walkin' round, gonna give me a heart attack," he chided playfully, his hands busy pushing aside the scattered items in search of an old leather bag buried under the table.

With a quick whistle, Theo summoned Jolly into the cabin, who eagerly responded by bolting inside and latching his teeth onto the strap of another bag wedged between the chest and the cupboard. Leyla swiftly joined in, grabbing hold of the strap and assisting Jolly in tugging the bag free from its jammed position.

Jolly dropped the bag at Theo's feet, his tail wagging with satisfaction. Theo knelt down, giving the dog's head a quick scruff as he praised him for his help.

"I helped," Leyla quipped jokingly as she walked over to join the duo.

Theo stood up, holding the two bags, and shifted one to free up his hand before playfully ruffling Leyla's hair.

"Good girl," he teased, laughing as she swatted his hand away.

Moving to the shelf where the statuettes remained miraculously undisturbed amidst the chaos, Theo took a hand and swept them into one of the backpacks.

"Righto, just need mi lute and we can be on our way," Theo declared, his eyes scanning the room in search of the instrument.

"Here it is," Leyla announced, retrieving the lute from the end of his bed and extending it towards him.

As Theo's hand reached out to take the lute, Leyla instinctively recoiled, anticipating his playful gesture. She swivelled away, dodging his hand with practiced ease.

"Nice try," she teased, taking a few steps back to maintain her distance.

Theo erupted into laughter at her swift evasion before making his way outside the cabin. Stepping to the front of the ship, he tossed a rope out into the water, unravelling it from the anchor point to allow for some slack.

Bringing his fingers to his lips, Theo emitted an ear-piercing whistle that cut through the air, followed by the soothing strumming of his lute. The melody drifted across the water, carrying a sense of calm and tranquillity.

In response to Theo's call, the water began to churn, and Ramsay, the serpent-like creature, emerged. Only the top of his head broke the surface, but his pure black eyes fixated on Leyla, seemingly peering into her soul.

"Grab that, Ramsay, and bring 'er in," Theo instructed, his strumming picking up pace as he continued to play the melody, the notes dancing upon the air.

The creature flicked its tail, twisting its body in the water, and took the rope down to the murky depths with it. In an instant, the ship jolted forward, propelled away from the menacing rocks and towards a sandy inlet.

Shielded on both sides by towering rock formations, the inlet offered a safe haven from the open sea.

As the ship straightened its course, Leyla noticed the rope slacken once more, and the swirling waters began to churn around the vessel's sides. Suddenly, an unseen force propelled the ship from behind, guiding it gracefully towards the beach. The bow dug into the pebbly sand with a soft crunch, bringing the vessel to a sudden halt.

"Let's go exploring," Theo suggested, slinging the lute onto his back before shading his eyes with one hand, scanning the horizon.

Without hesitation, Theo, Leyla, and Jolly leapt over the side of the ship, landing on the soft sand with a muffled thud.

"It's a desert," Leyla observed, her voice tinged with awe as she strode ahead of the others to get a better look at their surroundings.

"Which way ya reckon?" Theo queried, adjusting the straps of his bags for a more comfortable fit.

Jolly responded with a loud bark, as if offering his opinion to Theo's question.

"North it is," Theo decided, retrieving a small compass from his pocket and holding it out to determine their direction. "This way," he declared, pointing in the direction indicated by the compass needle.

As they set off, Theo glanced at the compass once more, only to find the needle moving erratically.

"Maybe this way," he suggested, pointing in a different direction.

"Does that thing even work?" Leyla questioned sceptically as she approached to inspect the compass.

Theo swiftly intercepted her hand, batting it away. "No touching," he insisted, his tone firm. "It's a family heirloom." He continued to manipulate the compass in an attempt to stabilise the needle.

Suddenly, Jolly began to bark loudly, his warning cries piercing the desert silence, alerting Theo and Leyla to potential danger ahead.

"What is it, boy?" Theo managed to utter, his voice barely above a whisper, just before a dark wooden arrow with bright yellow feathers lodged into the ground at his feet.

The trio froze, every muscle tense as they watched a large group of half-dressed tribesmen enclose them in a semi-circle. Theo took note of the hand-woven fur clothing and the glint of bronze at the tips of their spears as they slowly approached.

"We must have landed near a desert village," Theo whispered to Leyla, his voice barely audible.

"They're good people, just skittish. Let me do the talking and we should be right," he continued, receiving a nod of agreement from Leyla.

As the group of desert dwellers fully encircled them, their spear tips angled menacingly towards their faces, Theo took a deep breath to steady himself.

"Just passing through, our ship crashed into the rocks," Theo explained slowly, watching as the group began to shuffle around them.

A loud horn sounded out, and the group shifted into what appeared to be a defensive stance, their spears lunging forward, nearly piercing the skin of the trio now standing back-to-back.

"Let you talk..." Leyla remarked dryly, a note of sarcasm in her voice.

"Worth a shot," Theo replied grimly, feeling the sharp point of a spear pressing against his Adam's apple.

7

"So, Malk, what's next?" Horethian asked, as he stamped out the smoking coals of their now-extinguished campfire.

"We need to get this map decoded," Malkhia replied, lifting his bag off the ground and slinging it over his shoulder.

"Any idea how?" Atlas queried from her seat against the mountain wall, her dagger expertly whittling down a straight branch as she crafted more arrows.

"I have one, but I haven't seen this person in a very long time," Malkhia responded, his tone thoughtful.

"How did you find out about this map? You got that weird letter, and the next minute we're heading into a dungeon for some treasure map," Horethian interjected, bending two of his fingers on each hand to emphasise air quotation marks.

"Never mind the letter. There are these old ruins in a small valley we need to seek out. I have a rune we could use, but it's a decent walk from where I've marked it," Malkhia explained, rummaging through a small pouch and counting reagents.

"Ugh, another portal," Horethian exclaimed, his voice heavy with frustration.

"Well, unless you have a boat handy, we need magic to travel off this island," Malkhia responded, flipping through a leather book from his bag, filled with runes to various locations across the globe.

"Ah, here it is, Solstice Wastes," Malkhia announced, pausing on a page in the book.

"Isn't that a desert?" Atlas asked, her tone tinged with concern.

"Yep, not a friendly one either. From ice and freezing cold to sand and heat, whoopee," Horethian replied sarcastically, his voice dripping with cynicism.

Atlas rose to her feet, securing the newly crafted arrows into her quiver. "Right, ready to go," she declared, slinging on her quiver and bow.

"Trea Ango Mov," Malkhia chanted, blue lightning shooting to his feet once again as a portal began to swirl into existence.

The trio stepped through the portal, and it vanished behind them as quickly as it appeared. Suddenly, the party appeared through the glowing blue gate, this time all three members managing to stay upright amidst the chaotic winds. Sand violently whipped up in a frenzy from the wind generated by the portal's closing.

They advanced cautiously, their forearms shielding their faces from the biting sandstorm that swirled around them. Gradually, the wind began to subside.

"Fun," Horethian remarked, brushing sand off his armour with quick swats of his hands.

A loud clicking sound pierced the air as the sand shifted ominously all around them.

"Um, Malk, where was this rune marked exactly?" Atlas asked, her grip tightening on her bow as she readied an arrow.

"Yeah, should have remembered that," Malkhia admitted, slamming his staff into the shifting sand at his feet.

As his staff penetrated the sand, it suddenly halted against something hard, eliciting a shrill shriek and an intensifying clicking noise.

The shifting sands began to retreat from the trio, leaving behind an uneasy calmness in the sandy landscape.

"You didn't answer me," Atlas said, her voice tinged with worry.

The clicking noise crescendoed, doubling in volume. Suddenly, two large pincers erupted from the ground, followed by a massive, heavily scaled body with a segmented tail, culminating in a green dripping, curved, razor-sharp point.

"Oh great, giant scorpions," Horethian muttered grimly, raising his sword and assuming a defensive stance.

"Say the word," Atlas said, her voice steady as she knocked an arrow, her anticipation palpable.

"Trea Fir," Malkhia chanted, unleashing a flaming ball towards the giant scorpion. The fiery projectile struck one of its pincers, causing the creature to recoil slightly as it shook its claw to extinguish the flames.

"I'll take that as the word," Atlas remarked, releasing her arrow. It flew through the air, finding its mark at the seam of two scaled plates on the creature's abdomen.

Meanwhile, Horethian circled the beast, preparing for a side attack. With a fierce battle cry, he lunged forward, swinging his blade overhead. The sword connected with the creature with force, chipping away some of its scaled hide but failing to penetrate.

In retaliation, the scorpion whirled around, swinging its flaming claw. The fiery appendage struck Horethian, sending him flying several meters away. He crashed to the ground with a resounding thud, rolling across the hot desert sand before coming to a stop.

With a grunt, he clambered back to his feet, his armour blackened from the flames and showing signs of numerous scratches.

Horethian broke into a sprint towards the creature, determined to regain lost ground. He lunged forward once more, his blade aimed for a vulnerable spot in the creature's armour.

His sword found its mark, driving deep into the beast's abdomen. The scorpion emitted a deafening cry of pain, thrashing about in an attempt to dislodge Horethian's weapon, firmly wedged between its scales.

"The tail!" Atlas called out, but her warning came too late. Horethian looked up just in time to see the curled point of the scorpion's tail descending upon him.

The tail struck with brutal force, piercing his shoulder and driving its sharp tip several inches deep. Green ichor spurted from the wound, staining the sand as Horethian hastily withdrew his blade, stumbling backward in pain.

As the scorpion retracted its tail from his shoulder, a mixture of green and red liquid spurted into the air. Fireballs and arrows rained down upon the creature, forcing it into a hasty retreat.

A loud shriek echoed through the desert as flames slowly engulfed the scorpion's body, its legs quivering in its failing retreat.

As the creature's legs buckled underneath it, causing it to collapse to the ground, Horethian seized the opportunity for a final strike. With a mighty leap, he plunged his sword downward between the scorpion's eyes, using his body weight and momentum to drive the blade deep into its brain.

The scorpion's movements immediately ceased, and it slumped lifelessly into the sand, a dark greenish liquid oozing from the wound inflicted by Horethian's blade.

With a grim expression, Horethian retrieved his sword from the creature's skull before stumbling backward, falling to his knees. His fingers fumbled with a bandage as he desperately attempted to stem the flow of blood from his shoulder wound.

As his head began to throb and his vision blurred, Horethian faintly heard Malkhia's chant just before he was about to lose consciousness.

"En Ril."

Suddenly, a feeling of wellness washed over him, and Horethian gradually began to see clearly again. The bandage he had applied earlier started to staunch the heavy stream of blood, which had been running down his arm and staining the yellow sand a deep red.

Horethian drove his fists into the ground, leveraging his upper body's weight to free his legs and stand upright. "I thought you'd have to rez me on that one, Malk," he quipped, brushing sand from his knees and turning to Malkhia.

"Fortunately, I didn't. I don't have enough reagents for that. We need to head into town shortly to restock," Malkhia replied, searching through a small brown leather pouch tied at his hip to the side of his robes.

Malkhia's attention snapped to the slight movement of the beast, his senses heightened by the sounds of snapping cartilage and tearing flesh. Without hesitation, he readied his staff, prepared for a sudden attack.

A spray of green liquid shot into the air, prompting a call from Atlas, who had been concealed behind the creature's corpse. "'Tis only me," she reassured them, her dagger buried deep inside the scorpion's torso.

"These scales would make some great new armour," Atlas remarked as she continued to cut away the flesh, freeing a scaled plate.

Atlas efficiently stripped the carcass of its usable scales, her dagger slicing through the flesh with precision until every scale had been removed. Once finished, she stood up, shouldering her backpack, which thumped against her back from the weight before settling against her quiver.

Her ears twitched as she detected the sound of water nearby. "I can hear water over there," she announced, turning to point in the direction of the sound.

Horethian sauntered over to Atlas, jesting, "With the state of you, you do need a bath."

Atlas turned to Malkhia, noticing him standing still with his eyes closed. "Malk?" she called out, a puzzled expression crossing her face.

"He started meditating while you were busy," Horethian explained, waving a hand in front of Malkhia's face before shrugging at Atlas's confusion.

"I know what you're doing," Malkhia suddenly said to Horethian, causing him to jump back slightly.

"How can you see me?" Horethian replied, scrutinising Malkhia's closed eyes for any sign of awareness.

"Let's go wash up," Malkhia said, opening his eyes and startling Horethian once more as his face was inches away.

The pair followed Atlas as she led the way, guided by the sound of flowing water. A hazy image began to form in the distance, revealing a picturesque oasis. Tall palms with large green fronds towered above large grey rocks clustered together. These rocks created a large circle, with crystal-clear water trickling down from the top of the central rock into a deep, round pool.

As they approached, Atlas broke into a sprint, heading directly for the now clear oasis.

"Atlas! Wait!" Malkhia called out, but she paid no heed, reaching the water's edge and stripping herself almost instantly of her weapons and clothing before diving headfirst into the pool.

Malkhia and Horethian arrived at the water's edge shortly after.

"You didn't even know if it was safe," Malkhia admonished as he looked down at Atlas, who was floating on her back, gazing at the sky.

"It's nice and cold, come in," she beckoned, floating past the pair.

"Don't have to tell me twice," Horethian replied as he started to remove his bulky armour.

Malkhia followed their lead, removing his hat and robes before neatly folding them and placing them on a nearby rock.

Loud thumps sounded to his left as he turned his head to investigate.

"You all right there?" Malkhia asked, laying his staff down onto the pile of clothes as he watched Horethian hop around on one leg, attempting to remove his heavy plate boot.

"Almost... got it..." Horethian managed to get out while he continued to hop around before falling over with a loud thud, his body hitting the sand with enough force to squash a small child.

Atlas and Malkhia broke into laughter as they watched Horethian roll around in the sandy desert.

"Got it!" Horethian exclaimed as he held up his boot as if it were a trophy.

Malkhia made his way down the mossy rocks with precision, trying not to slip over and be the next laughingstock.

He slowly lowered his body into the water up to his neck while he watched Horethian fly through the air with his legs tucked up into his chest, held by his arms.

The water exploded as the large man broke the calmness of the surface, droplets splashing onto the dry, hot sand and immediately evaporating.

Atlas and Malkhia both looked away, shielding their faces to avoid the incoming wave of water.

Horethian's head broke the surface, the sun glistening off the water droplets running down his smooth bald head. "It's not that deep, almost broke my legs," he said with a smile as he wiped the water from his eyes.

"Perfect depth for me," Atlas replied as she kicked her legs beneath her, nowhere near close to touching the bottom of the pool. Horethian swiped his hand across the surface, sending a wave into the air directed towards Atlas.

The pair went back and forth, sending wave after wave at each other. Malkhia nestled his back into the rock wall, a smile crossing his face as he watched the two enjoy themselves. He looked up into the sky and noticed a black bird circling them with a small blue speck flapping from its leg.

"Hmm," Malkhia thought to himself as he strained his eyes to focus more on the bird. Suddenly, the peace in his mind was broken as he caught a glimpse of a black and yellow blur flying through the air before coming to a stop in the trunk of a palm tree next to them.

"It's an ambush!" he yelled as he stood up out of the water.

The other two swam towards the shallower end of the oasis, the clear water rippling around them as they moved, their eyes fixed on the looming figures at the water's edge. A sense of unease settled over them as they saw the fur-clad humans, their features obscured by the shadows cast by the surrounding rocks.

Malkhia, still in the water, raised a hand to the side of his neck, his fingers grazing against something soft and feathery. A sudden, sharp sting jolted through him, and he realised he'd been struck by a small dart. His vision blurred, the world around him starting to spin as the venom or substance took hold.

As his consciousness faded, Malkhia's senses were overwhelmed by the sound of a horn, reverberating through the air from some distant point. His mind swimming in confusion, he succumbed to the darkness, his body sinking deeper into the cool embrace of the oasis.

8

"Who in their right mind would come to this dastardly place?" a stocky dwarf grumbled discontentedly, spitting out the snow that had found its way into his mouth.

"Someone who doesn't want to be found," countered a tall elf with long flowing black hair, his voice carrying a hint of mystery.

"Who is this contract for anyway? You guys are more suspicious than normal," the dwarf continued, his scepticism evident.

"Oh, please shut up, Durnek. You've done nothing but yap since we got here," a slim brunette-haired elf interjected sharply, pulling her horse to join the dark-haired elf.

The dwarf brought his hand up, opening and closing it in a mocking gesture towards the elven woman.

"How much further, Sekt?" the elven man called back to the gnome riding nearby.

The gnome replied with an outstretched arm pointing to an opening in the mountain, followed by a small grunt.

"Sylvaris, the trail is going cold. We are too far behind the group," the elven woman informed the man, her tone laced with urgency.

"Don't fret, sister. Sekt can track them," Sylvaris reassured his companion.

The group reached the opening of the mountain and observed the narrow passageway leading inside. Suddenly, the gnome dismounted and rushed towards the opening ahead of the others, his hand shooting up to stop them in their tracks.

Sekt grunted once more while kneeling down inspecting a paw print in the snow, casting a wary glance back at the others.

They all hopped off their mounts, swiftly retrieving their weapons and packs from the saddles.

"All stay," Sylvaris commanded, and the animals obediently stamped the ground in unison, understanding the directive.

Proceeding forward through the narrow passage, the group emerged into a small clearing amidst the barren, icy landscape. The frigid air bit at their skin, and the ground beneath them was coated in a layer of frost, reflecting the harsh light of the sun above. In the centre of the desolate expanse stood a solitary stone ankh, its weathered surface marred by the relentless elements. The clearing felt eerily quiet, save for the occasional howl of the chilling wind whipping through the frozen landscape.

Sekt knelt down to inspect the crimson patch of snow, looking over to a small black patch near the wall.

"They fought?" Sylvaris asked, receiving a nod from the gnome.

"I could have told you a fight happened," Durnek remarked sarcastically as he scanned the opening, his eyes catching sight of multiple patches of dry blood mingled with snow.

Ignoring Durnek's comment, Sekt walked to the black patch and bent down to inspect the ground more closely. He looked back and gestured Nymira over.

"Portal stain," she said as she bent down to join Sekt inspecting the snow.

"Can you track it?" Sylvaris inquired, striding over to the gnome.

Sekt nodded in response, his brow furrowed in concentration.

"We don't have time," Nymira interjected sharply.

"Nymira! Let him work," Sylvaris rebuked his sister, his voice firm but patient.

Durnek, meanwhile, gave Nymira a sly grin before wandering off towards the stone ankh, his curiosity piqued by the mysterious surroundings.

Durnek's eyes alighted as he noticed small engravings covering the surface of the stone. Intrigued, he stepped closer and brought his hands up to it, his fingers delicately tracing the intricate lines etched onto its surface. A sense of curiosity filled him. Yet, his fascination quickly turned to alarm as the lines he touched began to emit a bright, luminous glow. Soon, the entire surface of the ankh was bathed in a radiant yellow light, illuminating the surrounding area with an ethereal brilliance.

"What have you done!?" Nymira's voice rang out from behind, filled with a mixture of fear and urgency, prompting the others to turn their attention to the dwarf.

"I just touched it," Durnek replied, his voice tinged with disbelief as he stumbled back, putting distance between himself and the blinding stone.

An icy breeze swept through the clearing, its touch sending shivers down their spines as it carried swirling flurries of snow. The air grew colder, and the landscape seemed to shimmer with an otherworldly glow as the chunks of snow clumped together, dancing in the wind's embrace.

"Something is coming," Sylvaris declared, his voice filled with a sense of foreboding. With each word, his breath materialized in the frosty air, adding to the eerie atmosphere that surrounded them.

"Group together! Sekt, continue tracking the portal!" he commanded, urgency lacing his tone as he rallied the group to action. They huddled closer, seeking comfort and protection in their collective unity as they prepared for whatever was coming.

Meanwhile, the wind howled with increasing ferocity, whipping through the clearing with a chilling intensity. The very air seemed to hum with anticipation as the elements gathered.

As the wind intensified in front of the stone ankh, it transformed into a furious tempest, swirling with frenzied energy. A spiral of ice and snow rose from the ground, twisting and twirling in a freezing vortex of elemental power.

The group reacted swiftly, raising their forearms to shield their faces from the onslaught of the mysterious storm. Sylvaris lowered his arm slightly and squinted his eyes against the biting cold. Through the blinding flurry of snow, he caught a glimpse of a figure beginning to take shape amidst the chaos.

Emerging from the swirling tornado, a colossal, bright white torso took shape, resembling that of a muscular human. Its arms, thick with sinew and veined with frost, shot out from the torso in a familiar humanoid fashion, adding to its imposing stature.

Suddenly, an ear-piercing roar reverberated through the canyon, causing the very ground to tremble beneath their feet.

"It's an Ice elemental! Hurry, Sekt!" Sylvaris's urgent cry pierced through the chaos.

"Our weapons are useless on them," Durnek remarked, his expression puzzled as he observed the formidable figure, now fully formed before them.

"Vanc Mov," Nymira chanted, her voice resonating with power as she unleashed a bolt of energy towards the elemental's bulging torso. The creature staggered back slightly under the impact of the energy force, emitting another deafening roar in response. The tempest surrounding the elemental subsided momentarily, except at the base of the creature where the vortex continued to whip ice and snow from the ground in a frenzied swirl.

"I can't hold him back for long, Sekt," Nymira admitted, a note of urgency creeping into her voice as she prepared to unleash another bolt of energy towards the creature.

Sekt remained silent, his focus unwavering as he inspected the blackened piece of snow, despite the chaos around him.

Meanwhile, Durnek charged towards the elemental, his massive warhammer poised for a forceful strike. Yet, before he could land his blow, the elemental retaliated, sending a powerful wave of ice hurtling towards him. Durnek was sent flying back into the mountain wall, a grunt escaping his lips as the impact knocked the air from his lungs. He crashed to the ground with a resounding thud, knocked unconscious by the force of the blow.

Another deafening roar reverberated off the walls as the elemental continued its assault. Sylvaris, quick to react, raised his long-curved blade just in time to block the oncoming wave of ice. With a groan of effort, he braced himself against the onslaught, his arms trembling under the force of the impact as the wave crashed into his sword, sending him sliding backwards across the icy ground. Despite the strain, he stood firm, determined to hold his ground against the relentless assault.

"Trea Fir!" Nymira chanted fervently, her voice cutting through the chaos as she conjured fiery spheres that streaked through the frigid air towards the elemental.

The fireballs collided with the icy form of the elemental, eliciting sizzling bursts of steam as they dissolved upon impact. With each strike, patches of the elemental's muscular torso began to liquefy under the intense heat, the frozen form melting into shimmering pools of water before swiftly reforming from the surrounding ice. The elemental's resilience was unnerving, its icy form seemingly impervious to the fiery assault.

Sekt rose to his feet, grunting urgently as he attempted to scribble in the snow to relay his discovery to the others.

"SW? Solstice Wastes?" Nymira asked, looking down at Sekt's feet.

Sekt nodded in agreement.

"Understood," Nymira said, her voice firm as she retreated to the wall next to Sekt.

"Trea Ango Mov," she chanted, her voice resonating with power as she called forth ancient magic. A shimmering blue portal materialized before her, its ethereal glow casting an otherworldly light upon the frost-laden landscape.

"I've got Durnek," Sylvaris declared, determination etched upon his features as he swiftly moved to aid the fallen dwarf. He grasped Durnek's foot and began to drag him towards the portal, following the others through.

"That was too close. Wake that fool up so I can knock him out again," Nymira said between breaths, her voice tinged with frustration as she held her knees and scanned the surroundings, her eyes settling on Durnek.

"Got their trail, Sekt?" Sylvaris inquired, his focus shifting to the gnome as they regrouped in the desolate wasteland.

Sekt shook his head in response, his brow furrowed in concentration as he scoured the barren landscape for any sign of their quarry.

"What's all the commotion?" Durnek grunted, rubbing his eyes as he struggled to regain his bearings, the events of the battle still fresh in his mind.

"We're safe, no thanks to you," Nymira snapped, her frustration evident in her tone as she shot an angry glare in Durnek's direction.

"I didn't know that was going to happen," Durnek replied defensively, his tone tinged with exasperation.

"You have to touch everything," Nymira argued back in frustration, still giving the dwarf a pointed look.

Sekt interjected with a grunt, the sound cutting through the tension as he pointed towards a distant path in the wasteland.

"Lead the way," Sylvaris commanded, his tone firm as he gestured for Sekt to take the lead.

9

The serene glow of the moon cast its ethereal light upon a circular expanse of grass, creating elongated shadows beneath the towering fir trees that encircled the small clearing.

In the midst of this tranquil scene, a solitary figure cloaked in darkness stood beside an intricately carved headstone, their form slender and their head bowed in contemplation.

"Princess," a voice murmured softly from the shadows at the periphery of the clearing.

Startled, the robed figure swiftly turned toward the sound, their entire being tensing as they strained to discern the source amidst the darkness.

"It is only I, Princess, Henry," the voice reassured, as a slight, dirt-smeared boy emerged tentatively into the moonlit space. His clothing, oversized and worn, hung loosely from his diminutive frame.

"I bring tidings of the king," the boy continued, edging closer to the princess.

With a graceful movement, the robed figure lowered her hood, revealing a cascade of dark locks that spilled forth, illuminated by the moon's gentle glow. Her features, once concealed, now shone with a delicate beauty, framing her slender face in a soft radiance.

"What news do you bring, Henry?" she inquired, her voice steady as she brushed her hair away from her eyes, clearing her vision.

"The King and his party are due back in two moons, my lady," Henry responded, removing his large tweed flat cap and clutching it to his chest with both hands.

"And how certain are you of this ?" the princess queried, her tone firm.

Henry shifted uncomfortably, his gaze dropping to the ground. "I wouldn't have ventured here if I weren't certain myself, my lady," he replied nervously.

"Very well, thank you, Henry," the princess acknowledged, turning her attention back to the imposing headstone.

Henry, sensing the dismissal, began to retreat into the shadows.

"Oh, Henry," the princess called out, her gaze still fixed on the headstone. "Please relay this news to Gwen. She will reward you for your troubles. And do ask her to arrange for a tailor to fit you with proper attire."

"Thank you, my lady," Henry replied before disappearing into the darkness once more.

"Two moons. Mother, grant me the strength to fulfill what must be done," the princess murmured, her voice heavy with resolve as she knelt beside the headstone, her hand gently tracing the engraved name.

Brushing away a tear, she rose, her hood concealing her features once more as she tucked her hair into the folds of her robe.

Lifting her head toward the moon, its silvery beams casting a luminous glow upon her, she whispered, "The moment draws near," to herself before melting into the shadows of the surrounding trees.

❖ ❖ ❖ ❖

A soft, subtle knock reverberated against the imposing wooden door of Belfor's chamber, shattering his reverie as he leaned against the grand mantle, prodding at the dwindling embers with a wrought iron poker.

His hand tightly clutched a fire poker by its brown leather handle adorned with intricate silver thread. Leaning against the stone frame, a loud knock sounded from the door. "Who's there?" he called out nervously.

"It's Gwen. Open up, Belfor. We need to talk," came the urgent reply of a woman's voice from the other side of the closed door.

"Are you alone?" he queried, his apprehension palpable.

"I am. Now, quickly, open up before we're discovered," Gwen insisted, her tone urgent.

The metallic sounds of sliding bolts and clanging chains filled the air as Belfor unlatched the heavy wooden door. Peering cautiously into the dimly lit hallway, he scanned both directions, finding nothing but enveloping darkness.

"Quickly," Belfor urged, widening the door to allow Gwen swift entry into the warmth of his chamber. Gwen stepped inside, her white gown trailing gracefully behind her, skimming the ornate carpet as she moved towards the fireplace. There, she rubbed her hands together before extending them toward the flames to chase away the chill.

Observing Gwen's actions, Belfor swiftly re-latched the locks on the door, ensuring their privacy. "I sense you're aware of the prince's intentions," Gwen remarked, her gaze fixed on the flickering flames.

Belfor began pouring himself a generous goblet of wine and sank into one of the large leather armchairs positioned before the crackling fire. With a heavy sigh, he lifted the cup to his lips, took a long draught, and settled deeper into the plush cushions.

"What is it that you want, Gwen?" he asked, his tone tinged with resignation as he refilled his goblet to the brim.

Gwen met his gaze steadily, a hint of amusement dancing in her eyes. "I have a proposition, one that could prove mutually beneficial," she suggested, her voice laced with intrigue.

Belfor scoffed, downing the last of his drink before replenishing it without hesitation. "I'm a marked man, Gwen, and you know it. Otherwise, you wouldn't be here, attempting to entice me into your and the princess's reckless schemes," he retorted bitterly.

Gwen chuckled softly, gracefully taking a seat in the empty chair beside him. With a pointed gesture, she picked up another goblet from the nearby table, offering it to him with a slow shake. "All conspiracies are best discussed over a drink," she remarked, watching as Belfor acquiesced, filling her cup with a knowing glance.

"Well, at least we can find common ground on that," Belfor remarked, his tone resigned. "So, what's the plan, Gwen? What do you need from me?"

"For now, nothing. We simply need your allegiance when the time is right," Gwen replied, her hand idly swirling the wine in her goblet before she took a sip.

"And what's in it for me?" Belfor pressed, his scepticism evident.

"For starters, your life," Gwen retorted, a subtle smile playing at the corners of her lips. "The prince lacks leadership skills, and with the king's absence, we must act swiftly and decisively. I'll be in touch."

With that, Gwen rose from her seat, setting her goblet down on the table before making her way to the door.

"This is treason, Gwen. You know the consequences if we're caught," Belfor warned, turning to watch her departure.

"You're as good as dead anyway, aren't you?" Gwen countered with a smirk, opening the door and disappearing into the darkness of the hallway, leaving Belfor alone with his thoughts.

"She has a point," Belfor murmured to himself, exhaling heavily as he finished his drink, contemplating the precarious path ahead.

"**M**y Lady," Gwen greeted, gracefully holding the hems of her flowing white dress as she curtsied before the Princess.

"Ah, Gwen, just the lovely face I wish to see at this hour. Please, come and sit," the Princess invited, patting the cushion beside her on the grand three-seat couch, its royal blue upholstery inviting and plush.

Gwen approached the seat, smoothing her dress beneath her as she settled down, turning to face the Princess expectantly.

"I bring tidings regarding Belfor," she announced.

"Ah, excellent. But first, allow me to share my news. Father's return is imminent, just two moons away, as per the reports from the dock boys," the Princess responded, a smile gracing her lips.

"Two moons? Does that afford us enough time?" Gwen inquired, her expression tinged with concern.

"We shall have to expedite our plans. And what of the response to the letter you dispatched?" the Princess asked, her tone thoughtful.

"I have yet to receive any reply," Gwen admitted.

"That is rather unusual," the Princess remarked, her brows furrowing with concern as she gazed down at the floor, her mind clearly occupied with worry.

Charlotte quickly refocused, meeting Gwen's gaze with determination. "We must act swiftly now, Gwen. Time is of the essence," she declared.

"Yes, My Lady," Gwen acknowledged, rising to her feet.

"Also, has that boy, Henry, from the docks come to see you?" the Princess inquired.

"I haven't seen him yet," Gwen responded, her expression puzzled.

"When you do, please see to it that he is provided with finer attire and rewarded for the valuable information he provided to me," Charlotte requested.

"Consider it done, My Lady," Gwen pledged, executing another graceful curtsy.

"Thank you, Gwen. Please, take care," the Princess bid as she watched Gwen approach the imposing door to her chamber.

"Always," Gwen assured before disappearing through the door, leaving Charlotte alone with her thoughts.

A resounding bang echoed through the room as someone pounded vehemently against the door.

"Oh, piss off," Belfor exclaimed, his voice tinged with irritation.

"Open the door, Belfor, before I break it down," a commanding voice demanded from the other side.

"Alright, alright," Belfor grumbled, pushing himself to his feet, his movements unsteady from the effects of the copious amount of wine he had imbibed.

As he swung open the door, he was confronted by a burly figure clad in ornate bronze armour.

"Ah, Commander Sharl, to what do I owe this pleasure? Gods, you reek of death," Belfor greeted, his tone dripping with sarcasm as he raised a hand to his nose.

The imposing man ignored the remark, shoving past Belfor with heavy strides. The scent of sweat, blood, and something more acrid trailed behind him.

"Please, make yourself at home," Belfor muttered under his breath, shutting the door with a quiet click.

Sharl's sharp gaze swept the dimly lit chamber, pausing at the small wooden table. Two goblets sat upon its surface—one drained, the other still brimming with deep crimson wine. His eyes lingered there a moment longer before turning back to Belfor, unreadable beneath his hardened expression.

"Late night, Belfor?" Sharl inquired, his tone carrying a hint of suspicion.

"No later than usual," Belfor retorted, sinking back into his chair and reclaiming his wine with a nonchalant gesture.

"I'll spare you the pleasantries; the less time spent in this cesspit, the better," Sharl declared brusquely.

"Well, how unfortunate. I find your company positively enchanting," Belfor retorted with a scoff, taking another sip of his wine.

"We have a meeting scheduled for tomorrow to discuss your plans for capturing that hunting party and obtaining the map," Sharl informed him.

"You came all this way just to deliver that message?" Belfor asked, a puzzled expression crossing his face.

"Consider it more of a warning," Sharl responded gravely.

"How delightful," Belfor remarked, draining the last of his cup.

"Don't test my patience, Belfor. It's in your best interest to see this through without any further complications," Sharl warned, his stare intimidating.

"You needn't worry. I'll be there," Belfor assured him, his expression now serious.

"Is there anything else you require, Commander?" Belfor asked, refilling his glass for what seemed like the umpteenth time.

"I fail to comprehend why the King has tolerated your presence for so long," Sharl seethed with anger.

"Perhaps it's my devilishly good looks and impeccable fashion sense?" Belfor quipped with a grin, rising to his feet. Despite his smaller stature, he maintained an air of confidence that seemed to irk the commander even more.

Sharl scoffed in disgust, heading toward the door with palpable disdain. Before leaving, he cast a venomous glare back at Belfor.

"I eagerly await the day when that smug grin of yours meets the executioner's block," Sharl spat out with venom.

"Goodnight to you as well, Commander," Belfor responded smoothly, bowing low while still wearing his trademark grin, holding Sharl's gaze unflinchingly.

With a final glare, Sharl exited the room, leaving Belfor alone in the dimly lit chamber.

"Is everything all right, Commander?" one of the guards inquired, noticing the fury etched on Sharl's face as he exited.

"Has anyone passed through here tonight?" Sharl demanded, his lip curling with anger.

"Only the servants, and Gwen, passed through," the guard informed.

"I want this door under strict surveillance. Notify me of every individual who enters," Sharl ordered firmly.

"Yes, Sir," the guard responded promptly, clicking his heels together in a show of obedience.

With a nod of dismissal, Sharl strode away, his heavy footsteps reverberating off the empty stone walls of the hallway.

"Hmm, what are you planning, Gwen?" Sharl pondered to himself, his thoughts swirling with suspicion as he continued down the corridor.

10

The morning sun filtered through a gap in the light-tanned canvas of the tent, casting a warm beam directly onto Theo's face, coaxing him from slumber.

"Ughh, turn off that lantern," Theo grumbled, still half-asleep.

Jolly, his faithful companion, stirred at the noise and began to shower Theo's face with eager licks.

"Give it a rest, Jolly. Just five more minutes," Theo mumbled, half-heartedly pushing the persistent canine away.

"Fine, fine. I'm awake," Theo relented, stretching his arms out before playfully ruffling Jolly's fur.

"Why so loud?" came a groggy voice from another corner of the tent.

"Time to rise and shine, Leyla," Theo announced, emerging from his sleeping bag and deftly slipping his feet into a pair of well-worn, deep brown leather leggings.

With a grunt, Leyla rolled over, her gaze catching Theo as he dressed. His tall, athletic frame was bathed in a soft, golden glow from the glint of sunlight filtering through the tent's walls. In its gentle illumination, she couldn't help but notice the intricate web of scarred claw marks etched across his back, with two sizable bite marks on each shoulder blade. The scars spoke of fierce battles, hinting at the monstrous creatures Theo had faced.

As Theo deftly slid his arm into a crisp, long-sleeved white button-up shirt, he turned around, his gaze meeting Leyla's lingering stare. She felt a blush creep up her cheeks as she realized her eyes had been fixed on him for longer than intended, hastily turning her head to avert her stare.

"You're welcome to look, Leyla. After all, you're only human," Theo quipped with a grin as he buttoned up his shirt, adjusting a large gold medallion hanging from his neck to reach the remaining buttons.

"Pfft, seen better," Leyla retorted with a playful smirk, finally emerging from her sleeping bag.

"Mmhrm, I could see your reflection," Theo chuckled, gesturing toward a large makeshift wooden frame adorned with broken pieces of reflective glass, before turning his attention back to his morning routine.

A look of shock crossed Leyla's face, quickly followed by embarrassment as her eyes darted around the tent, searching for something to focus on.

"It's fine, Leyla, no need to stress yaself," Theo reassured her with a warm smile, grabbing his lute and swinging his pack over his shoulder before making his way out through the gap between the two loose flaps of canvas, leading to the desert. Jolly followed closely behind, his tail wagging so quickly it was almost a blur.

Leyla let out a loud sigh. "Who knew desert tribes had mirrors?" she muttered to herself as she hastily dressed and gathered her belongings, exiting the tent to join Theo.

"Couldn't bear to be away from me?" Theo teased jokingly, but the look on Leyla's face gave him the answer immediately.

"I saw they captured some adventurers yesterday. Do you know who they are?" Leyla asked, attempting to change the subject.

"Never seen 'em before. They probably took them to the same cages we were in," Theo replied casually.

"You never did fill me in on how you know the Elder here," Leyla remarked, her curiosity piqued.

"That's a long story for another time. I'm surprised he forgave me for the whole daughter thing," Theo admitted, rubbing the back of his head as he looked down.

"How hasn't a disgruntled father or husband slain you yet?" Leyla remarked, her tone edged with a mixture of incredulity and amusement.

"Explorin' day today, I think," Theo deflected, brushing off Leyla's comment. "I know there are giant scorpions in this desert, and I wouldn't mind taming one," he continued, his excitement building.

"Taming?" Leyla questioned, her curiosity piqued.

"How do you think I have all these furry friends?" Theo replied with a smirk, glancing down at Jolly, who remained faithfully by his side, his tail still wagging with enthusiasm.

Leyla shrugged and followed Theo as he began to walk into the heart of the camp.

As they passed by a large wooden cage situated near the Elder's hut, Leyla couldn't help but notice the captive figures within. An exceptionally large bald man sat facing a small, elvish blond female, while another man with long black hair and an equally lengthy beard lay sprawled out in the sand as if in deep slumber.

The hushed conversation between the captives abruptly ceased as Theo and Leyla approached, their intense gazes causing Leyla to avert her eyes, feeling their scrutiny pierce through her.

"Not a very welcoming bunch," Theo remarked to Leyla as they continued toward the outskirts of the camp.

"Well, they are prisoners," Leyla pointed out matter-of-factly.

Stepping out onto the desert sand, Theo pulled out his compass once more, pointing in what appeared to be a random direction.

"Last time we followed your broken compass, we ended up in that cage," Leyla reminded him.

"But are we in one now?" Theo retorted, striding off confidently in the direction he had indicated.

The two trekked across the sands for quite some time before Theo abruptly halted, his arm outstretched, signalling Leyla to stop.

"Shh, listen," Theo urged in a hushed tone.

Leyla strained her ears, zoning in on the faint sound of clicking.

"One is nearby," Theo murmured, readying his lute and gesturing toward Jolly, who instantly assumed an aggressive stance at their feet.

Suddenly, the sand began to shift, a large wave of moving sand rushing toward them.

Leyla swiftly threw open her robe, revealing an array of potions and throwing knives nestled within.

"No poison pots for this one, Leyla. It's immune," Theo informed her, readying his fingers on the lute's taut strings.

As large pincers lunged out of the sand, followed by a massive, armoured body, Leyla instinctively began hurling the small daggers, aiming for multiple joints in the creature's scales. With each hit, the beast let out a deafening screech that reverberated across the desert.

"I've got this one, Leyla. I want to tame it, not kill it," Theo declared as he started to play a soothing melody on his lute.

The song seemed strangely familiar to Leyla as she watched Theo's fingers dance across the strings. As he played the second set of chords, a memory stirred within her—it was the same song Theo had used to calm Ramsay, the enormous sea serpent.

Suddenly, the giant scorpion began to retreat, its pincers thrashing and its body writhing as if resisting Theo's music. Leyla felt a wave of calm wash over her as she watched in amazement. The scorpion's movements grew sluggish, its pincers dropping to the sand as if they were weightless. Finally, the creature slumped down, subdued by Theo's enchanting melody.

"That's it, calm down. I'm not here to harm you," Theo reassured the scorpion, his fingers continuing to strum the soothing chords on his lute.

"Good scorpion, I've always wanted a friend like you," he continued, his voice gentle and reassuring.

Suddenly, the scorpion raised its pincers once more, thrusting them toward Theo. With quick reflexes, he rolled out of harm's way just in time, the crash of the pincers sending sand flying in all directions.

Leyla swiftly grabbed a potion bottle filled with an orange liquid and hurled it toward the scorpion. Upon impact, the bottle exploded, causing a large group of scales to crack and peel back from the extreme heat.

Theo regained his composure and began playing the calming song once more. Once again, the scorpion slumped down into the sand, subdued by the enchanting melody.

"It's okay, we can be friends. I'll look after you," Theo reassured the creature, his voice filled with sincerity.

As he finished his sentence, the scorpion raised its body up high, keeping its large pincers pressed into the sand, this time in a much more friendly manner.

Theo cautiously pressed forward, releasing his grip on the lute so it hung at his waist from the leather strap. He outstretched his hand, attempting to touch one of the large pincers.

But the creature recoiled backward, seemingly hesitant to accept Theo's gesture of friendship.

"It's okay," Theo reassured the scorpion, his voice steady as he moved forward once more, managing to place his hand on the creature's scales. "That's it, good boy," he praised, gently patting the monster's armoured body.

Turning back to Leyla, Theo noticed the look of astonishment and confusion on her face. "Um, what just happened?" she asked, her voice tinged with disbelief.

"He is now our friend," Theo declared proudly, his grin widening.

"Do you want to name him?" he asked Leyla, his eyes shining with excitement.

"Huh, name him?" Leyla questioned, still trying to process the turn of events.

"Yeah, you can name him, and he can travel with us," Theo explained, rummaging through his pouch.

"I've never seen a giant scorpion before, let alone named one," Leyla admitted hesitantly, inching closer to the creature.

"He's fine now. He won't hurt you, well, not unless I tell him to," Theo reassured her with a laugh.

"Claws," Leyla suddenly exclaimed.

"Claws? What do you mean?" Theo asked, puzzled. But Leyla had already made up her mind, her decision firm.

"I want to name him Claws," she announced.

"Uh, yeah, okay. Claws it is," Theo agreed, his excitement matching hers as he removed a corked small purple potion from his pack.

"Claws, follow me," Theo commanded toward the scorpion. With a swift rush, the large creature bounded over to the pair. The sudden movement caused Leyla to instinctively remove two daggers from her robe, springing back into a defensive stance.

"It's okay, he's just doing what he's told. Here, I'll put him away for now," Theo reassured Leyla as he pulled the cork out of the bottle, releasing a large cloud of purple smoke.

Theo pressed the bottle to the scorpion's head, and the smoke enveloped the entire surface of the creature.

"What is happening?" Leyla asked in wonder.

As quickly as the smoke had appeared, it vanished, leaving nothing but a small figurine of the scorpion in the sand. Leyla walked up to the miniature sculpture, kneeling to get a closer look.

"This is the same as the ones you had on your shelf in the boat," she observed, looking back at Theo.

"Yup, I told you, my family," Theo confirmed as he walked over to Leyla, leaning down to retrieve the figurine from the sand before placing it into his pack.

"So, every one of those figures you have is a real live animal?" Leyla asked, her curiosity piqued.

"Yeah, just shrunken for now. Much easier to bring them all with me that way," Theo explained.

"We should be getting back. There are more than scorpions out here, especially when it's getting darker," Theo suggested, checking his compass again to find the direction back to the tribe's camp.

"It is a long walk back, and I would like to know all about your 'family,'" Leyla said, falling into step beside Theo as they ventured into the vast expanse of the desert.

Theo glanced at Leyla, noting the earnest curiosity in her eyes. "Well, where would you like to start?" he asked, a hint of amusement in his voice as they traversed the shifting sands, the distant horizon stretching endlessly before them.

11

The sandstorm raged around them, swirling grains of sand biting at their exposed skin and stinging their eyes. The wind howled like an angry beast, whipping up clouds of sand that obscured their vision and threatened to throw them off balance with every step.

"From snow to this," Durnek grumbled, his voice barely audible amidst the roar of the storm. He struggled to keep his footing, his heavy boots sinking into the shifting sands.

Sylvaris squinted ahead through the swirling sand, his gaze fixed on Sekt, who pressed on ahead, his form barely visible through the haze. "Have you still got their trail?" he shouted over the wind, his voice carrying with difficulty.

Sekt turned and nodded back to Sylvaris, his face strained against the wind as he forged ahead, his cloak billowing behind him like a tattered flag.

As the sandstorm began to relent, the landscape slowly revealed itself, unveiling a desolate expanse of dunes and rocky outcrops. Durnek shielded his eyes from the last remnants of the sandstorm, his gaze drawn to a massive form lying prone on the sand ahead.

"Is that a scorpion?" he called out, his voice tinged with awe and disbelief.

Sekt nodded in confirmation toward the dwarf.

Durnek approached the carcass cautiously, his footsteps leaving deep impressions in the sand. He crouched down beside the massive creature, examining its stripped and gnawed body with a mixture of fascination and trepidation.

"They didn't leave much behind, did they?" he muttered, his brow furrowed in consternation as he ran his hand along the creature's exposed exoskeleton.

Sylvaris joined him, his eyes scanning the surrounding landscape with a keen sense of urgency. "They took the scales," he observed, his tone grave. "They must be making armour. That could pose a problem in hand-to-hand combat."

"Sekt, let's keep moving," Sylvaris commanded, his voice cutting through the lingering echoes of the storm. "Put some distance between us and this corpse before something bigger comes looking for it."

Sekt nodded in agreement, his jaw set in determination as he led the way forward, his eyes fixed on the shifting sands ahead.

As the group traversed the vast expanse of the desert, a shimmering image materialized on the distant horizon. Durnek squinted against the harsh sunlight, brushing sand from his armour as he tried to make sense of the surreal sight.

"Is that a mirage?" he wondered aloud, his voice tinged with scepticism.

Sekt shook his head, his gaze fixed on the distant image.

The group arrived at the oasis, greeted by the sight of crystal-clear water shimmering in the sunlight and a magnificent waterfall cascading down the rocks that encircled the pool. Tall palm trees swayed gently in the desert breeze, casting dappled shadows over the water.

Sekt raised a hand, stopping the others as he observed, his sharp eyes scanning the surroundings for clues.

"What is it?" Nymira prompted, her voice betraying a hint of concern.

Sekt pointed to the water's edge. A grim look crossed his face as his gaze followed a trail of drag marks across the sand, leading from the water into the desert.

Sylvaris let out a low sigh, his brow furrowed in thought. "So, we're not the only ones," he murmured to himself, his words barely audible over the rustling palm fronds.

"Huh?" Nymira looked to her brother for clarification.

"Nothing important," Sylvaris replied dismissively, eager to press on with their mission.

But Durnek's curiosity got the better of him as he approached one of the palm tree trunks, drawn to a glint of something metallic nestled amidst the fronds.

"What's that?" he asked, reaching out a hand to investigate.

Nymira's voice cut through the air like a whip. "Something you shouldn't touch!" she snapped, her tone sharp with warning.

As Sekt stepped in front of Durnek to investigate the arrow lodged in the tree, he carefully examined the craftsmanship of the weapon. With its brown wooden shaft and bright yellow feathers, it bore the unmistakable mark of a desert tribe's handiwork.

He pulled the arrow from the tree and began scrutinizing it closer.

"Ugh, I hate desert people," Durnek grumbled as he noticed Sekt running his hand through the familiar bright feathers, his disdain evident in his voice.

Nymira rolled her eyes at Durnek's remark. "Did the desert tribe take the party?" she inquired, her tone laced with concern.

Sekt nodded, his gaze still fixed on the arrow in his hand.

"Well, looks like we need to find them," Nymira declared.

Sylvaris's sharp eyes caught movement in the distance, and he observed a lone figure stealthily approaching them from afar. "Looks like they already found us," he remarked, his tone calm but alert.

"How many?" Nymira asked, her eyes scanning the horizon for any further signs of danger.

"Looks to be only four. I don't think they were ready for a second lot of guests," Sylvaris replied, his gaze unwavering as he assessed the stranger's movements.

As Sekt stealthily slipped away behind the rocks, the others continued on, seemingly oblivious to the imminent threat closing in on them.

"Two behind, one left and one right," Sylvaris murmured, his voice calm and composed as he knelt by the water's edge, splashing his face with handfuls of cool water.

Meanwhile, Sekt deftly retrieved two sturdy bolts from a small quiver at his waist and methodically loaded them into his crossbow.

Suddenly, a feathered dart hurtled toward Sylvaris, but he reacted with lightning-fast reflexes, snatching the dart out of the air with a deft movement of his hand. With a quick smile of acknowledgment, he watched as Sekt swiftly pressed one of the triggers on his dual crossbow, sending a bolt hurtling toward their assailant. The projectile found its mark, striking the man squarely in the chest and sending him crashing to the ground.

Meanwhile, Nymira's voice cut through the tension as she chanted, "Mov Agi Fie." In response, a bolt of lightning streaked down from the sky, slamming into the head of the man on the left with a deafening crack, leaving him charred and smoking in its wake.

Sekt swiftly pulled the second trigger, sending another bolt hurtling past Sylvaris and grazing the skin of the tribeman's shoulder. A sharp cry of pain escaped the assailant as he staggered backward, clutching his wounded arm.

Meanwhile, Sylvaris seamlessly began his advance, his movements fluid and effortless as he glided across the ground with uncanny grace. His curved blade gleamed in the sunlight, poised and ready to strike with lethal precision.

With a forceful slash, Sylvaris cleaved through the air, his curved blade slicing through the man's flesh like a scythe through wheat. He landed gracefully behind the now mortally wounded assailant, holding his blade high as he paused, allowing droplets of blood to drip from the gleaming edge and splatter onto the yellow sand below.

The man gasped in shock and agony as his body began to shift, a deep diagonal cut running from his waist to his opposite shoulder, oozing crimson with each passing moment. Slowly, the top half of his body started to slide downward, leaving a trail of blood in its wake until it crashed onto the sand with a sickening thud, staining it a dark red hue.

"One left!" Sylvaris called out, turning to Durnek.

"I got him," the dwarf responded, his voice echoing with resolve as he leapt through the air, his hammer raised high above his head.

The remaining assailant, frozen with fear amidst the chaos, barely managed to flinch before Durnek's hammer came crashing down with thunderous force. The sound of bones crunching and breaking echoed through the desert as the man's body crumpled beneath the weight of the powerful blow.

"Is that it?" Durnek asked, nonchalantly throwing his hammer onto his shoulder as he turned to face the rest of the group, his demeanour betraying the violence of the scene that had just unfolded.

"For now," Sylvaris said, his voice calm yet authoritative, as he slid his sword over his shoulder, wiping the blood away with a practiced motion before returning it to its sheath.

"Sekt, lead the way," Sylvaris commanded, and the group fell back into formation behind the gnome.

Sekt nodded and began forging ahead once more.

As they marched into the desert, leaving the scene of carnage behind them, Durnek's stomach growled audibly. "I'm getting hungry," he remarked.

"How unusual," Nymira retorted, her sarcasm evident in her tone.

Durnek's patience snapped. "I don't know why you don't like me, Nymira, but I've had just about enough of it," he retorted.

Nymira's anger flared. "How could you not know why?!" she fired back, her frustration evident in her voice. "You are a fumbling idiot!"

Sylvaris intervened before their bickering escalated further. "Enough!" he commanded sternly. "We are a team for the time being. Once we finish this job, we can go our separate ways. But for now, no infighting, or we won't stand a chance."

The pair grumbled in response, turning away from each other in a huff as Sylvaris strode off to catch up with Sekt.

Sekt stopped mid-step and began pointing forward, leading the group to a large rocky outcrop.

As they reached the summit, they peered over the edge to behold a small village nestled in the valley below.

"This must be where they are," Sylvaris observed.

"Look there," Nymira pointed out, directing their attention to a wooden cage situated on the outskirts of the town.

"That's them," Sylvaris confirmed, his gaze fixed on the three captives confined within the wooden enclosure.

"We wait until dark," he decided, turning around and pressing his back against the rock wall.

"There are two more, these ones aren't prisoners," Durnek added, gesturing to a man and a woman entering the village from the desert.

"We only want the three, keep watch" Sylvaris asserted, tilting his head back and beginning to close his eyes.

"Fine, I can wait," Durnek grumbled, dropping his body into the sand to await the cover of darkness.

12

orethian's eyes cracked open with a loud grunt, his heavyset frame springing to life as he swiftly sat up, taking in his surroundings with frantic intensity. His vision was clouded, struggling to pierce through the lingering haze of the narcotics pulsing through his bloodstream.

Through his hazy vision, he spotted Atlas lying motionless on the dirt floor, mere meters away, her form pressed against the thick, rigid wood bars enclosing them in the small cage. With a surge of urgency, Horethian scrambled to his knees, his movements frantic as he crawled over to Atlas, shaking her shoulders in a desperate attempt to rouse her.

"Ughhh," Atlas groaned in response as Horethian continued to shake her awake, his heart pounding in his chest with a mix of fear and relief.

As Atlas's eyes began to flutter open, Horethian drew in a deep breath, exhaling a sigh of relief that echoed through the cramped confines of their prison.

"You're alive!" Horethian exclaimed with palpable relief.

"I feel like death though," Atlas replied, her words muffled as she rubbed her foggy eyes, still struggling to shake off the effects of the sedative.

As Horethian's eyes began to focus more clearly, he spotted Malkhia lying on his side at the other side of the cage. Despite his efforts to stand, Horethian found his legs unresponsive, refusing to obey his commands. With a frustrated grunt, he resigned himself to crawling over to Malkhia's side.

"Malk!" he called out, shaking the man as he had done with Atlas.

"I'm okay, Horethian," Malkhia reassured him, his voice strained. "Let me rest a little longer so my mind is clearer to find a way out of here."

Horethian crawled back to the side of the cage where he had initially woken up, thumping his rear down as he rested his back against the unyielding bars. They stood firm against his weight, offering no hint of give.

"Sturdy bars," he remarked to Atlas, who was now sitting up, still rubbing her eyes in an attempt to shake off the remnants of sleep.

"Where even are we?" Atlas asked, her voice tinged with confusion.

Horethian shrugged, his gaze sweeping over the campsite surrounding their cage. "They've been here awhile though, judging by how built up this camp is," he observed.

Their conversation was interrupted as they noticed a man and a woman, dressed differently from the rest of the camp, walking towards their cage. Horethian regarded them with a curious gaze, but the woman caught his stare and quickly averted her eyes, murmuring something to the man.

"They're definitely not from the tribe," Horethian remarked to Atlas once the pair was out of earshot.

"I wonder what they're doing here," Atlas pondered aloud.

Before they could delve further into speculation, Malkhia, who had been roused by their conversation, interjected.

"You both need to talk a little louder. I don't think the people on the other side of the desert heard you," he remarked, sitting up and stretching his arms wide with a yawn.

"Ahh, did we wake you, little Malky?" Horethian teased with a smirk.

"Ha ha," Malkhia replied dryly, rolling his eyes at the nickname.

"Anyone noticed any chief figure around the village?" Malkhia asked, breaking the silence that had settled over them.

Both Atlas and Horethian shook their heads simultaneously.

Malkhia stood up and walked over to the front of the cage. He called out to one of the tribe members, who approached the edge of the cage with wariness in his eyes.

"Can we speak to your chief, please?" Malkhia requested, his voice firm and resolute.

The tribe member looked at him with evident confusion, prompting Horethian to offer a suggestion. "Maybe he doesn't speak our language," he speculated.

"Chief? King? Elder?" Malkhia tried again, his tone growing more insistent.

The man's expression shifted at the word "Elder," prompting Malkhia to press on. "Yes, Elder. I must speak with him."

With a nod of understanding, the tribe member hurried off towards a nearby house adjacent to their wooden prison.

"I think he understood," Malkhia remarked, turning back to Atlas and Horethian, who remained seated against the bars.

Moments later, the man returned, accompanied by another older tribe member. This man was well-fed, adorned with an intricately carved wooden staff topped with a large bird skull. Upon his head rested an ornate crown made of small bones and feathers, marking him as the Elder.

Malkhia turned around to face the two men, his hands gripping the bars tightly as he steadied himself against the lingering effects of the tranquilizer.

"We mean you no harm. We are just a group of adventurers seeking gold and valuables from only the monsters in this desert," Malkhia explained to the man, his voice firm yet respectful.

The man nodded in acknowledgment, lifting his staff above his head before bringing it down forcefully into the soft yellow sand with a resounding thud. The skull atop the staff rattled back and forth, gaining momentum as the man muttered what sounded like an incantation.

Sensing danger, Malkhia released his grip on the bars and stumbled backward, his warning echoing through the cage. "Get back!" he exclaimed urgently to the others, his eyes wide with alarm.

Atlas and Horethian sprang to their feet, joining Malkhia as they pressed themselves against the back of the cage, their hearts pounding with a mixture of fear and anticipation.

A gold glowing line began to materialize at the top of the cage in front of the Elder, capturing the attention of the captives. Slowly, the line expanded, tracing a rectangular shape in the bars, forming a doorway-sized opening.

A loud crack reverberated through the air as the bars shook with intensity. Abruptly, the golden line dissipated, leaving behind a small seam that followed its path. Without hesitation, the young man standing beside the Elder reached out, grasping one of the bars and pulling it toward him. To the captives' amazement, the cage began to open like a door along the newly created seam.

"The Elder has agreed to free you for trial. If you pass, you will be free to go," the man informed them.

"Trials?" Malkhia exclaimed, his voice laced with puzzlement.

"He knew our language the whole time," Horethian exclaimed, his surprise evident.

The Elder nodded toward the man holding the door open before turning and walking back toward the hut next to the cage.

"Come with me. We will begin immediately," the man instructed, gesturing for the trio to follow him as he moved his arm outward, indicating the direction they should head.

"Malk, what should we do?" Atlas asked, her voice tinged with uncertainty.

"What they say. We don't want to fight them if we have no reason to," Malkhia replied, his tone resolute as he took a step forward.

Hesitantly, the party walked toward the man and out of the cage's door. They followed the tribe member into the village centre and saw three large seats atop a makeshift platform.

"Be seated," the man said, waving his arm once more toward the seats.

As the three adventurers took their seats, they noticed the village people gathering in the opening in front of them, standing in a perfect line with the children up front.

The Elder took his place at the front of the platform, using his staff to support his weight as he ascended the small steps.

"The trials shall begin," the man who led them to the chairs announced before joining the rest of the village.

A loud thud echoed from the wooden staff hitting against the platform, and a golden light shot from the eyes of the skull, instantly forming a circle above where Atlas was seated.

As Atlas watched, her heart pounded with anxiety, her eyes darting between Malkhia and the glowing light above her.

Malkhia maintained his composure, his expression unreadable as he observed the unfolding events.

Suddenly, the golden light above Atlas began its transformation, shifting from its initial hue to a mesmerizing blend of green and red before finally settling into a vibrant shade of green.

A collective sigh of relief escaped the villagers as they witnessed the colour stabilize. Their eyes remained fixed on the scene, anticipation hanging in the air like a tangible presence.

With a solemn gesture, the elder raised his staff once more, the weight of authority palpable in the air. As the staff descended, the light shifted its focus to Horethian, seated at the far end of the platform.

Again, the light danced and wavered, teasing with different hues before ultimately settling on green. The villagers exhaled in unison, their tension easing slightly with this reassuring sign.

The elder's next strike against the platform was more forceful, sending a shiver through the wooden structure. A spark leapt from the skull atop his staff, bridging the gap between him and the golden light above Horethian. In response, the light took on a rich, golden hue.

With a sense of solemnity, the light then moved to the middle chair, hovering directly above Malkhia. This time, its transformation was swift and dynamic, cycling through a kaleidoscope of colours before finally coming to rest on a deep, calming shade of blue.

Horethian's brow furrowed as he tried to make sense of the glowing orb. "Blue? What does that mean?" he asked again, seeking clarification from Malkhia.

Malkhia shook his head, his expression mirroring Horethian's confusion. "I have no idea," he admitted, his thoughts swirling with uncertainty.

The elder's booming voice interrupted their exchange, announcing the outcome of the trial to the jubilant crowd. "The light has spoken; the truth was shown. They shall be freed, as so it should be," the elder declared, his words carrying across the village square.

A wave of cheers erupted from the villagers, their relief palpable as they dispersed and returned to their daily tasks. With the commotion subsiding, the elder turned to Malkhia, beckoning him to follow.

"Come with me, we have much to discuss," the elder said, his voice grave yet inviting. He leaned on his staff for support as he made his way towards the small hut adjacent to their former prison.

Malkhia nodded in acknowledgment, a sense of apprehension mingling with curiosity as he fell into step behind the elder. Horethian and Atlas exchanged uncertain glances, watching as Malkhia disappeared into the hut with the elder.

"Umm, that was weird. What do we do now?" Horethian asked, rising from the chair and turning to Atlas, his brows furrowed in confusion.

Atlas shook her head, a puzzled expression mirrored on her face. "No idea," she replied, her voice tinged with uncertainty.

As they exchanged uncertain glances, a tribe member approached, his demeanour calm and reassuring. Stepping onto the platform, he gestured for them to follow.

"This way," he said, before turning and walking off.

"Well, I suppose we should follow him," Horethian said to Atlas, his tone hesitant.

Nodding in agreement, Atlas stepped beside him as they trailed after the tribe member. Entering a large rectangular tent, they found themselves confronted with a long table adorned with intricately carved wooden cutlery and dishes.

At the head of the table, the man bent over a large silver chest, unlocking it with practiced ease. As he swung the lid open, he gestured toward the contents within.

"Your belongings," he announced, stepping back to allow them access.

The adventurers quickly gathered their gear, the familiar weight of their weapons and armour comforting in their hands.

"I missed you," Horethian murmured, pressing his lips against the hilt of his sword.

Atlas arched an eyebrow. "That's not weird at all," she remarked dryly as she slid her quiver and bow over her back.

Exiting the tent, they made their way toward the village centre. Already, the platform had been dismantled and replaced with carts laden with chopped logs and piles of raw ore.

"They don't mess around here," Horethian commented, observing the industrious activity around them.

"Hey, look over there," Atlas said, her gaze shifting toward the outskirts of town.

Curious, Horethian followed her gaze, spotting the pair who had walked past the cage earlier. The woman appeared buzzing with excitement, her movements restless and her voice animated.

"Excuse me, who are those two?" Atlas asked a passing villager, who was laden with arms full of fresh linen.

"Friends of the elder," the villager replied before hurrying on.

Atlas spotted Malkhia emerging from the elder's tent, now clad in his usual blue robes, his hands brushing dirt from the front.

His gaze lifted, catching sight of the pair standing in the village centre, and he approached them with a nod. "Ahh, I see you guys have got your stuff back," Malkhia said, adjusting his pointed hat.

"What was the talk about?" Atlas inquired.

"Enough time for that later. Right now, we must head to an old burned village nearby. There is someone there who could help us decode this map," Malkhia replied.

Horethian and Atlas exchanged puzzled looks. "Hmm. But you will tell us?" Atlas pressed.

"In due time, my friend," Malkhia replied, his voice carrying a calm assurance, as he lifted his head to survey the black bird circling the village. Its presence stirred a familiar sense of responsibility within him. "What news does she bring?" he thought, eyeing the avian messenger with a hint of curiosity.

"Go eat and drink, we leave in the morning," Malkhia instructed Atlas and Horethian, his words punctuated by a subtle urgency. He watched as Horethian wasted no time, hastening toward the scent of freshly brewed ale like a moth to flame.

"Don't need to tell me twice," Horethian quipped, his departure swift, leaving Atlas to call out after him with a mix of exasperation and amusement.

"Wait up, you big oaf!" Atlas's voice trailed after Horethian as she followed him through the tent opening.

Meanwhile, Malkhia found solace on the outskirts of the village, seeking out a secluded spot where he could be alone with his thoughts. His gaze lifted skyward, meeting the bird's circling flight with a knowing look. With a practiced whistle, he called the creature down, marvelling as it executed a graceful descent, delivering a rolled parchment with such precision.

Malkhia's fingers deftly broke the red wax seal, his movements methodical yet tinged with a sense of anticipation. With care, he untied the blue ribbon that bound the scroll, unravelling the note.

"My dear M,
I hope this letter finds you well.
It is almost time to implement my plan, so please tell me you are safe and have the map in your possession.
I can't say too much in-case this letter does not reach you and falls into the wrong hands.
Just know multiple search parties have been sent out to look for you and the map, I truly hope they are yet to find you.
Stay safe my love.
Always yours
C"

Malkhia carefully rolled the note back up and tied the ribbon securely around it before stowing it away in his pack. With a frustrated sigh, he rummaged through his belongings, his hand seeking out the familiar feel of a feathered quill.

He found a suitable spot against the side of a nearby tent and flattened out the parchment, the surface smooth against his palm. With a steady hand, he began to write, the feathered quill gliding effortlessly over the parchment as his thoughts took fading ink.

"Blasted ink," he muttered under his breath, shaking the quill in an attempt to coax the stubborn liquid down its tip. Frustration mounting, he muttered to himself as he delved deeper into his pack, searching for the small vial of ink nestled within.

Finally finding it, Malkhia uncorked the bottle and dipped the feather quill into the dark liquid, the ink coating the tip smoothly as he began to write.

Once his message was complete, Malkhia carefully rolled up the parchment and sealed it with a small wax ball retrieved from his bag. Pressing one of his ornate rings into the melting wax, he imprinted the emblem onto the seal, ensuring its authenticity.

"That'll do," he murmured to himself as he wrapped the note in the loose blue ribbon salvaged from his pack.

Returning to the open space outside the village, Malkhia tilted his head back, his gaze scanning the expanse of blue sky above. With practiced precision, he placed his fingers to his lips and let out a piercing whistle.

In response, the black bird answered with a shrill call, diving swiftly towards him. Anticipating its approach, Malkhia tossed the note into the air just as the bird swooped down to meet it. With a deft movement, the bird caught the parchment in its talons and soared off into the distance, disappearing into the horizon.

Watching the bird fly off into the air, Malkhia murmured softly, "I hope that finds you," before turning back towards the village, his mind already shifting to the tasks ahead.

❖ ❖ ❖ ❖

"Isn't that one of them?" Durnek's gruff voice broke the silence as the group observed the outskirts of the village from behind the rocky outcrop.

"It is," Sylvaris confirmed, his gaze fixed on the robed figure as it released a parchment into the air, a raven swooping down to catch it in its talons.

"Nymira, that scroll," Sylvaris instructed his sister, who responded with a quick nod of understanding.

"En Ren Mov," Nymira chanted, her voice resonating with power as she cast a spell towards the bird. In an instant, the raven froze mid-flight, plummeting from the sky to land in Sylvaris's waiting hands.

Sylvaris untied the blue ribbon and broke the seal, his eyes quickly scanning the contents of the note. A grin spread across his features as he rolled the parchment back up, securing it with the ribbon before returning it to the bird's grasp.

"En Agi," Nymira chanted once more, her hands outstretched towards the now-revived raven. With a sudden jolt, the bird sprang back to life, fluttering around before taking off into the air once more, still clutching the note tightly.

"We know where they're going," Sylvaris declared, a wicked grin playing on his lips as anticipation built within the group.

13

The dim glow from the oil-slicked torch danced upon the cave walls, reflecting off the slow trickling water that adorned its surface.

"There's an opening up here, my lord!" a man in scuffed silver armour called out, his voice echoing through the cavern as he peered back at the group of men.

Stepping into the aperture, the man lifted his torch high, illuminating the expanse of the cavern. Rivulets of thick oil cascaded down the torch's wooden handle, glistening in the flickering light as they dripped onto the thin plate metal gauntlet encasing the man's hand.

"This will serve as our camp for tonight, men," declared a large figure among them, adjusting the emblem-branded plate mail tunic that hugged his sturdy frame, the emblem of a sinuous snake glinting in the torchlight.

As the troupe of men ventured into the cavern, their footsteps echoed against the rugged wet walls. They began to unload their heavy packs, the clatter of equipment mingling with the subdued sounds of the underground.

Amidst the dim light from the torches, two men broke away from the group. Wielding their axes, they started slicing through the thick vines that coiled around the cavern walls like serpents, their efforts accompanied by the rhythmic thud of metal against wood echoing throughout the cavern.

With a loud grunt, one of the men landed a hard blow with his hatchet, the blade glinting in the dim light of the cavern. As he delivered the second blow, his words cut through the air, "These are rather green," his voice echoing softly against the stone walls.

The hatchet sliced through the thick vine, sending droplets of sap scattering into the air, sweat beginning to pool on the man's brow.

As he bent over to scrutinize the vine, his eyes caught a glint of something unusual—a viscous green ooze trickling from the fresh cut. Intrigued, he extended his fingers toward the liquid, drawn by a strange allure.

With curiosity, he dipped his fingertips into the mysterious substance, feeling its warmth through his leathered hand. Raising it to his face, he observed the vibrant hue, mesmerized by its iridescence.

Slowly, he rubbed his fingers together, gauging its viscosity, his mind buzzing with uncertainty.

"Strange," he murmured to his companion, who remained absorbed in hacking away at his portion of the creeping vine.

In an instant, a vine burst forth from a crevice in the cave wall, swiftly entwining itself around the man's ankles. With a sharp yank, it pulled him off balance, sending him tumbling to the rocky floor below.

He swung his hatchet wildly, desperately trying to free himself from the tangled mess encircling his feet. The other man, sensing the urgency, swiftly turned to assist him, springing into action to lend a hand.

Raising his hatchet high above his head, he brought it down with a forceful thud, cleaving through the green, wooden limb-like branch with deadly precision.

The man on the floor panicked, his movements frantic as he scrambled backward, desperately seeking distance between himself and the looming danger. As he retreated, he watched on as a horrifying sight unfolded before him.

A massive green plant-like torso emerged from a gaping crack in the cave wall, with a monstrous mouth, grotesquely wide and lined with rows of jagged teeth, dominating the top of the torso. Each tooth, like a dagger, sharp and menacing, was all encircled by large, deep red leaves dripping with a green ichor.

The malformed plant cast an eerie, elongated shadow on the wall in the dimly lit chamber. "It's a corpse eater!" the man exclaimed, panic etched across his face, his spine stiffening with terror.

A small dwarven man, with his meticulously braided black beard adorned with gold bands, noticed the commotion and swiftly reacted. With a decisive snap of his head, he focused on the creature causing the chaos. Dropping his heavy pack to the ground with a resounding thud, he grabbed the pickaxe from its looped holders and let out a primal roar before charging towards the creature.

As the dwarf closed the distance, the creature emitted a loud shriek, its attention now fixed on the oncoming threat. Vines shot out from its midsection towards the dwarf, but he reacted with lightning-fast reflexes. With precise movements, he deflected the vines away with swift blows from the pickaxe.

Within seconds, the dwarf was upon the creature, the blackened head of the pickaxe poised for a devastating strike. With a mighty heave, he swung the weapon towards the creature's centre mass, using the weight of the pickaxe and his own strength to deliver a powerful blow.

Another ear-piercing shriek reverberated off the cavern walls, drawing the attention of every member of the party to the flailing vines of the creature. The dwarf, undeterred by the spray of green fluid from the wound that covered him and the surrounding floor, withdrew his pickaxe.

With a swift and powerful swing, he struck the creature once more, the force propelling the pickaxe straight through its deformed body and out the other side. Sticky green fluid gushed from the open wound, splattering against the wall behind the creature. As the creature's life force began to fade, its vines dropped one by one onto the ground.

The dwarf wiped his bushy dark brows with a muscular, stumpy forearm, collecting sweat and the creature's blood in the thick arm hairs as he did. Despite the intense battle, his demeanour remained resolute.

"Th... th... thank you," the man uttered from his back while still frozen with fear.

"No need to thank me, laddy," the dwarf said gruffly, placing a thick fur boot on the corpse to help lever out his pickaxe. With a practiced motion, he swung the pickaxe around before resting it on his shoulder.

"Aye, it had been a while since this thing had seen any action," he remarked to the man, shooting him a sly wink.

The dwarf then extended a fur-gloved hand to the man, helping him to his feet with a sturdy grip.

"Let's get that fire going, eh?" the dwarf suggested, flashing a reassuring smile at the still-petrified man, attempting to ease his nerves.

"You enjoyed that, didn't you, Eric?" a large man remarked with a grin as the dwarf returned to his pack.

"Ay, my king, been too long in these damn tunnels," the dwarf responded as he rested his pickaxe against his bag before dropping down next to it.

"Well, hopefully not too much longer. The scouts say we're close. I do miss my bed, though," the king remarked, lowering himself onto the wet floor beside Eric.

"This ore deposit, is it real?" Eric questioned, directing his gaze towards the king.

"Losing trust now, Eric? After all we've been through?" the king jested, though a hint of concern slipped through his tone.

"Nay, my lord, I know the tales. But are they just tales, is all," Eric responded with a deep sigh, sliding further down his pack and resting his head on a bulging pocket.

"Let's hope not, Eric, for all our sakes," the king replied, his voice tinged with a hint of anxiety.

"My lord, sorry to interrupt," a heavily armoured man spoke up, his legs clanging together as he saluted, bringing his hand to his forehead.

"We are running low on rations," the heavily armoured man continued, resting his arm back to his side and relaxing his legs.

"Water levels?" the king inquired.

"On par with the food, my lord," the man replied.

"Filter what you can from the floors and walls for water. As for food... Have you ever eaten a corpse eater?" the king asked with a curious tone, turning to Eric.

"Can't say I have, mi lord. Always willing to give it a go," Eric responded, returning the curiosity.

"See what you can salvage from that corpse. If we cook it enough, it should be safe to eat," the king said, shifting his weight to find more comfort on the cold, hard stone floor.

"Uhh, yes, my lord," the man acknowledged, clinking his heels together and saluting one more time before walking off towards the dead creature.

"Should we inform the men about the dwindling supplies?" Eric inquired, turning towards the king.

"Not yet. We are so close. I don't want to incite panic," the king replied, rising to his feet and striding towards the campfire.

A soldier, burdened with large pieces of the monster, headed towards the fire, green blood dripping from the slabs of meat covering his armoured hands, leaving a trail in his wake.

"What are we doing with that?" another soldier asked, turning to his companion.

"No idea," the other man replied with a shrug.

With a wet thump, the meat hit the ground next to the campfire. Another man, wearing a large apron, approached the pile, running a knife back and forth across a sharpening block. He delivered quick, precise strokes with the sharpened blade, making the butchering of the hunks of meat look effortless, producing large, well-portioned steaks. They would have resembled cuts from a cow if not for the dripping green fluid.

The scent of sizzling meat filled the cavern as the man began to toss each steak onto an oversized flat plate, the sound echoing off the walls as the steaks seared to a deep brown.

"Are we going to eat that?" the soldier who had questioned earlier inquired.

"Looks like it," his partner replied.

"Do we even know if it's safe?" the man questioned, concern evident in his tone.

"I'll try it first," the King interjected, overhearing the conversation.

"Nay, my lord. I cannot let you risk it," Eric cut in, dismissing the King's objections. "Anyone can mine and smelt ore," he continued.

Eric delicately retrieved a small dagger from his belt, its glint catching the flickering light of the campfire as he reached over, piercing a perfectly seared steak. His scrutiny intensified as he inspected the meat, its aroma wafting enticingly. With a casual shrug, he brought the morsel to his lips, his teeth sinking into the succulent flesh.

"How long do we wait?" a soldier inquired.

"Depends. If it's poisoned, then what type of poison and how swiftly it acts," Eric responded, his tone laced with a hint of caution.

Beads of sweat formed on Eric's brow as he observed the group gathering around him, their eyes fixed on him, awaiting any sign of distress. Time seemed suspended, each moment stretched to its limit until the silence was finally broken by the chef.

"Well, it's been twenty minutes. We either indulge now or risk these turning as tough as leather," he declared to the group, rising gracefully to his feet.

The men formed an orderly queue, eagerly snatching up the steaks from the fire. The cavern fell into a hushed reverence, interrupted only by the rhythmic sounds of chewing and occasional grunts of satisfaction.

"Not bad," the king remarked, turning to Eric with a nod of approval, observing as Eric settled onto his pack, his hands resting on his contented stomach.

"Aye, my lord, and still very much alive," Eric quipped back, a wry smile playing on his lips.

"I'd hope so," the king jested lightly, before taking another hearty bite of his meal.

The warm glow of the fire cast dancing shadows against the cavern walls, enveloping the men as they settled into their makeshift beds for the night. Two guards, stationed at each entrance, stood vigilant, their eyes scanning the darkness for any signs of danger.

"Here's to another eventful day," the king remarked to Eric, arranging his pack for a makeshift pillow.

"Aye, goodnight, my lord," Eric replied softly, closing his eyes.

As the night wore on, Eric awoke to find the party still immersed in slumber. Gently rubbing the sleep from his eyes, he stifled a yawn before rising to his feet. With cautious steps, he navigated towards the far entrance of the cave, careful not to disturb the sleeping figures.

"Tut, tut, tut," he murmured, clicking his tongue softly against his teeth as he approached the guards, who were sound asleep at their posts.

Placing a firm yet gentle hand on one guard's shoulder, Eric roused him from his slumber with a subtle shake. The guard startled awake, his eyes wide as he looked up at Eric, who placed a finger to his lips in a hushing gesture.

"Wake your friend and resume your duty," Eric whispered in a low tone.

"Yes, sir. Apologies, sir," the guard responded quickly, scrambling to his feet to awaken his comrade.

Eric strode down the unexplored path, his senses keen to the mysteries lurking in the dark tunnels. The walls, cloaked in moss, exuded a dampness that clung to his fingers, the warmth within eerily unsettling.

As the tunnel narrowed sharply ahead, Eric was forced to contort his body sideways to press on. With each careful shuffle, he navigated the tight space, the passage seemingly stretching on endlessly.

Focused on the path ahead, he caught a glimmer of sunlight piercing the darkness. Step by step, he continued, anticipation mounting until the tunnel finally yielded to a roofless expanse. Lush green grass carpeted the ground, encircled by towering trees that scraped the sky.

Taking in the scene around him, Eric's gaze lifted to the cloudless blue sky through the cavernous opening.

"Ah, it's been a while," he murmured to himself, a sense of nostalgia tugging at his heartstrings.

His attention drifted to the majestic trees, where a glint of vibrant purple caught his eye. With a swift stride, he hurried over to investigate, darting behind the massive trunks to uncover vast deposits of glistening purple ore.

"This is it!" he exclaimed, a surge of excitement coursing through him. "Amethystite! It's real."

14

" **Y** our majesty," Commander Sharl said with a reverent bow towards the prince.

"Why must we wear such cumbersome armour for a mere hunt?" the prince argued, his tone tinged with impatience, as a servant struggled to adjust his chest plate, the metal clinking softly.

"It is for your utmost protection, my liege," Commander Sharl responded.

"I am the prince; no one dares to lay a hand on me," the prince retorted, a haughty smirk playing on his lips, his arrogance unmistakable.

"Indeed, your highness, but as a precaution," the commander said, his voice calm and composed, masking an underlying concern.

"Your helmet, sir," one of the servants interjected, presenting a grand bascinet helmet adorned with gleaming gold plating along its sides.

"Very well, let's proceed, Sharl," the prince said, his frustration evident in the furrow of his brow and the tightness of his jaw.

As the pair strode out of the prince's opulent bedchambers, they navigated the labyrinthine corridors of the castle, their footsteps echoing against the ancient stone walls, until they emerged through the imposing main doors onto a spacious clearing near the bridge. Here, a formidable assembly of armoured knights on horseback, accompanied by a pack of eager bloodhounds, stood at the ready, their presence imposing against the backdrop of the castle's towering silhouette.

Sharl rode at the forefront of the procession. With a quick nod to the party leader, he silently conveyed his approval, prompting the man to unleash a resounding blast from a large horn, its echoing call slicing through the crisp air and signalling the commencement of the hunt.

As the reverberations of the horn faded into silence, the group erupted into a primal roar of anticipation, a symphony of raw energy and excitement. The bloodhounds, keen senses ablaze, surged forward as one, their nostrils flaring with the scent of their quarry, while the knights, a formidable force clad in gleaming armour, followed in swift pursuit.

The prince urged his majestic pearl white thoroughbred onward with a sharp kick of his heels, the creature responding with a burst of speed that threatened to unseat him. With a startled gasp, the prince grappled with the reins, his armour rattling loosely against his frame as the horse galloped fiercely beneath him, each pounding hoofbeat sending tremors through his body and causing the unforgiving metal to bite into his tender flesh.

"Are you okay, my lord?" a knight called out, riding up alongside the prince.

"Of course," the prince retorted sharply, his voice laced with irritation, his grip tightening on the reins.

The hunting party plunged deeper into the dense woods that cloaked the rear of the castle grounds, their pursuit relentless as they followed the distant baying of the bloodhounds, still far ahead. Suddenly, the hounds veered in a new direction, their collective bark ringing out with a fierce growl that reverberated through the forest.

"They've caught the scent," the lead rider announced.

"They didn't get too far," the prince jested, a smirk playing on his lips as he relished the anticipation of the chase.

A knight broke from the flow of the group, wheeling his horse around to position himself between Sharl and the prince.

"My prince, the prey is cornered," he informed the prince urgently.

"Very well, onward!" the prince commanded, his voice ringing out with determination as he urged his horse forward once more, the steed responding eagerly to his master's command, its powerful muscles rippling beneath its sleek coat.

The prince charged toward the source of the growling, the encircling knights parting seamlessly to allow his passage. In the distance, his prey came into view, and he spurred his horse onward, his grip tightening on the spear held firmly in his grasp.

With a swift and practiced motion, he raised the spear high above his head, the glint of determination in his eyes matching the gleam of the weapon's tip as he closed the distance. With a forceful thrust, he released the spear, a primal roar of triumph escaping his lips as it found its mark with accuracy.

A guttural cry of agony echoed through the air as the spear struck true, causing his prey to falter momentarily. Seizing the opportunity, the prince deftly manoeuvred his horse, preparing for another decisive blow.

"Treasonous vermin!" he bellowed, his voice carrying across the field as he hurled a second spear, his aim unwavering. The projectile found its target with chilling precision, striking its intended victim square in the chest.

With a tug of the reins, the prince brought his horse to a halt beside the fallen woman, now kneeling in the soft grass, the shaft of the spear pinning her to the ground. The prince regarded her with a mixture of contempt and triumph, his features twisted in a mask of hatred.

"Please, Eron," the woman pleaded, her voice strained with desperation, each word tinged with fear and urgency, as the crimson stain of blood began to mar her once pristine white gown.

The prince dismounted with a heavy thud, the weight of his armoured form bearing down on the ground as he drew his great sword from its sheath, the metal gleaming in the dim morning light.

"Have mercy," the woman implored, her words barely a whisper against the backdrop of impending doom.

A cruel smile twisted the prince's lips. "There shall be no mercy for treason, Gwen," he declared with chilling resolve, his voice low and menacing, as he thrust his sword forward.

The blade sliced through the air with deadly intent, the prince's movements swift and precise. With brutal efficiency, it found its mark, piercing Gwen's throat. A gurgled gasp escaped her lips as crimson spilled forth, staining the prince's armour with a macabre hue.

"How dare you!" the prince snarled, his voice laced with righteous indignation, as he withdrew his blade, preparing for another strike.

In the midst of the escalating violence, Commander Sharl arrived on the scene, his presence a beacon of reason amidst the chaos. "I'd say she's suffered enough," he interjected, his voice firm but tempered with restraint, as he attempted to intervene.

"I'll decide when she's had enough," the prince retorted, his grip tightening on the hilt of his sword, his gaze ablaze with unchecked fury.

With a swift and decisive motion, the prince swung his sword once more, the blade slicing through flesh and bone with a sickening crunch, severing the head from the neck in a gruesome display of brutality.

"She's had enough," the prince declared, his voice cold and final, as he sheathed his blade and mounted his steed once more.

"Take the head as a warning," he commanded, his voice cutting through the tension like a blade. "Clean this up, and hunt me a boar," he continued, addressing one of the knights who had ridden ahead to join Sharl. His tone brooked no argument, carrying the weight of his authority and the finality of his decree.

The prince galloped off with a large, sickening grin etched on his face, a cruel testament to the satisfaction he derived from his actions. Shortly thereafter, Commander Sharl joined him.

"We need to find Charlotte," the prince asserted.

"The men are already on it," Sharl responded swiftly, his words a reassuring promise of action.

"And Belfor?" the prince inquired, his curiosity tinged with a hint of impatience.

"They have him already," Sharl confirmed.

"Good work," the prince acknowledged smugly, a self-satisfied smirk playing on his lips as his horse slowed to a canter, the rhythm of their movement mirroring the calculated pace of his thoughts.

"My mother hit me harder," Belfor retorted defiantly, his words punctuated by a spurt of blood and teeth ejected from his battered mouth.

Undeterred, the guard brought down his heavy armoured hand once more, the force of the blow echoing through the air.

Belfor let out a laugh, his voice laced with defiance. "Is that all you've got?" he taunted, his tone mocking and teasing despite the pain coursing through his battered frame.

Suddenly, the guard let out a painful grunt, his hands clutching his thigh as blood sprayed onto the stone floor of Belfor's chambers. Belfor watched in astonishment as a small, ragged boy leapt onto the guard's back, plunging a dagger into the side of his neck. The guard's body went limp, crumbling to the floor in a lifeless heap.

"Who are you?" Belfor asked, spitting out more blood as it began to pool beneath him.

"It's time to show your allegiance," the boy declared, his voice firm and determined, as he swiftly cut the bindings holding Belfor's hands behind his back, freeing him from the wooden chair.

Struggling to his feet, Belfor eyed the boy warily as he stood in the doorway, a silent sentinel of unknown intentions. The boy then placed his fingers to his mouth and released a loud whistle.

A returning whistle echoed through the stone hallway, prompting urgency in their escape. "Hurry," the boy beckoned Belfor, who wasted no time in following him out into the corridor.

"Make your way to the cellar and wait for us there," the boy instructed Belfor, who responded with a nod of agreement. With a shared understanding, the pair parted ways, each heading in opposite directions down the hallway.

A short, quick whistle pierced the air, signalling a coordinated effort. The boy sent a returning whistle back as he sprinted up the hall, his movements swift and silent, his breath controlled despite the urgency of their mission.

"Did you get him?" another boy, dressed in much finer and well-fitted clothes, inquired as the raggedly dressed boy approached.

"He's on his way to the cellar," the ragged boy replied, his voice steady despite the tension in the air.

"Good. You go keep an eye on him and make sure he makes it. I'll get Charlotte," the well-dressed boy declared.

"Got it," the ragged boy responded, his resolve unwavering as he darted back down the hallway, following in Belfor's footsteps.

The well-dressed boy navigated the winding corridors of the castle with practiced ease, his movements calculated. Ahead, he spotted two guards hastening towards the entrance to Charlotte's room.

Quickly assessing his surroundings, the boy's keen eyes caught sight of a loose stone in the castle wall. With deft fingers, he pried it off, steadying his aim as he prepared to create a diversion.

With a swift and decisive motion, he released the stone, sending it hurtling down the hallway towards the guards. The small projectile flew past them and crashed into a wrought iron candelabra, illuminating the darkened corridor. The impact caused the holder to fall, extinguishing the flame and shrouding the area in darkness.

Reacting instinctively, both guards drew their swords and pivoted towards the noise, their backs turned towards the boy.

With silent footsteps, the boy rushed down the hallway towards the guards. Drawing a small dagger from his belt, he braced himself against the wall, using it as a foothold to propel himself upwards, gaining height in a single fluid motion.

Meeting one of the guards' throats with the dagger, the boy struck with deadly accuracy. Blood sprayed as the guard's hands shot up to his throat, desperately attempting to stem the flow before stumbling forward and collapsing to the ground, his life slipping away.

The other guard pivoted around to face the boy, but he had already rolled back, creating distance between them in a calculated manoeuvre. With a steady gaze and poised stance, the boy prepared for the next move.

"You little shit," the guard spat, his voice seething with rage as he raised his sword and advanced towards the boy. But before he could make a move, a blur streaked through the air towards him, catching him off guard.

A loud gasp escaped the guard as his breath was knocked from his lungs. With a startled glance down, he saw the glint of a small silver handle protruding from his chest, the blade buried deep within. Clutching at the handle, his clumsy hands failed to dislodge the dagger as he staggered, dropping to his knees in a futile attempt to fight off the inevitable.

The boy approached him slowly, a silent observer of the guard's desperate struggle. With a calculated step, he placed his foot on the guard's chest, his eyes locked on the dying man's face as he began to pull the dagger free. As he did, he twisted his wrists ever so slightly, eliciting a pained cry from the guard before he succumbed to his wounds, collapsing to the ground beside his fallen comrade.

He slid his dagger back into his belt and stepped over the bodies, his demeanour unchanged by the violence he had just witnessed. He continued down the corridor until he reached a large wooden door.

Slowly, he cracked the door open, the hinges protesting with a loud creak that echoed through the room. Peering inside, he saw nothing but shadows dancing on the walls, illuminated by the flickering candlelight.

Stepping cautiously into the darkness, he heard sudden movement towards the bed. "My lady, it's Henry. I'm here to get you out of here," he announced, his voice strained with urgency as he squinted at the shadowy figure standing at the room's edge.

"Henry? What's happening?" the princess inquired, her voice tinged with apprehension.

"We need to leave now. The prince knows," Henry explained tersely, his tone brooking no argument.

"Where is Gwen?" the princess asked, her expression clouded with worry.

"I'm sorry, my lady, but the prince got to her before we could," Henry replied solemnly, his words heavy with regret.

"You mean... Gwen's dead!?" the princess exclaimed, her voice cracking with sorrow, her heart heavy with grief at the loss of her loyal companion.

"I'm sorry, princess, but we must leave now," Henry insisted.

The princess joined Henry by the door, her eyes scanning the dark hallway as Henry gave her a quick wave, signalling the all-clear. With cautious steps, they made their way back through the corridors, past Belfor's room.

"What about Belfor?" the princess asked, her voice tinged with concern as she looked at his chamber door.

"We already have him, princess. Don't worry," Henry reassured her, his tone steady despite the gravity of their situation.

As they neared the throne room, Henry raised his hand abruptly, signalling for Charlotte to stop. Pressing their backs against the cold stone wall of the opening, they concealed themselves behind the arching doorway.

"Belfor escaped somehow," a guard rushed past, his voice tense with urgency.

"I don't know what the prince is planning, but this is madness," another guard replied, his tone filled with apprehension.

"Don't let him hear you talking like that, or you'll end up like Gwen," the first guard warned, their voices fading as they hurried towards the entrance to the throne room.

"Okay, it's clear," Henry whispered to Charlotte, his voice barely audible in the quiet of the corridor.

The pair continued through the throne room, passing by the three elegant thrones on the small stage, illuminated by the morning sun streaming through the stained-glass windows behind them.

"Where are we going?" Charlotte asked in a hushed whisper, her eyes darting nervously around their surroundings.

"The tunnels," the boy replied tersely, his tone leaving no room for further questioning.

"Tunnels?" Charlotte questioned, her confusion evident.

"I will explain later. We need to get out," the boy said firmly, shutting down the conversation as they pressed on.

They continued through the opposite opening of the throne room and down a long corridor towards the scullery.

"Through here," the boy beckoned, leading Charlotte into the kitchen.

Large meat-drying racks lined the walls neatly, while a pile of used plates and goblets sat next to a large sink.

Henry pushed one of the drying racks aside to reveal a small stairway leading down. "Down here," he said, taking a step into the darkness.

"The cellar?" Charlotte questioned, her uncertainty palpable.

"Just follow me, Princess," the boy insisted.

He placed his fingers in his mouth and let out a loud, quick, sharp whistle. Suddenly, a response echoed from deep within the darkness.

"Okay, it's safe," the boy said, his voice calm yet urgent, as he led Charlotte down the narrow, steep steps and into the cellar.

"Henry, the entrance is over here," the ragged boy called out as they walked towards him.

"My Lady," Belfor greeted the princess with a respectful bow.

"This leads to the sewers. We can use them to get to the docks and you two to safety," Henry explained swiftly.

"Quick, I saw them go through here!" a voice echoed off the wine barrels from the kitchen, signalling the approach of their pursuers.

"They're coming, go!" Henry urged.

The group sprinted down the cellar, passing the wine barrels and sacks of grain, their breaths quickening with each step. At last, they reached a large piece of battered wood propped up against the corner of the wall.

Henry shifted the wood slightly, creating a gap and revealing a deep, narrow tunnel hidden behind it.

"In, quickly," he urged, his voice breaking as he watched Charlotte, Belfor, and his friend slide through the gap and into the tunnel.

Peering back into the darkness, Henry spotted lit torches making their way down the stairwell towards them. With swift movements, he slid behind the wood, repositioning it over the opening before rejoining the group in the tunnel.

15

The sun began to set over the desert, casting long shadows and bringing with it a cold, chilling breeze that enveloped the small desert village.

"That tent sounds like fun," Leyla remarked to Theo, her gaze drawn towards a large tent bustling with villagers.

"Well, let's go have a look," Theo agreed with a nod.

The pair entered the tent through its open entrance, greeted by the sounds of laughter and lively conversation. A small group sat in the corner, playing their instruments with skill, providing the patrons with joyful background music.

"At least there's music," Theo observed with a smile, appreciating the lively atmosphere.

"Let's get a drink," he suggested, gesturing towards the bar stocked with fresh ale.

As they approached the bar, Leyla's eyes widened as she spotted the prisoners seated at a nearby table. The small blonde elf laughed merrily while watching the large man take on the locals in arm wrestling competitions.

"Hey Theo, that's those prisoners we saw this morning. Seems they also got out," Leyla remarked, her tone tinged with surprise and curiosity.

"They must know the elder as well," Theo chuckled, amused by the unexpected turn of events, as he gestured for the bartender's attention.

"Two ales, please," he requested once the bartender finally caught his gaze, the anticipation evident in his voice.

The bartender smiled and promptly placed two large wooden jugs down, brimming with a golden liquid.

"How much?" Theo inquired, but his question was met with a dismissive wave of the bartender's hand before he moved on to serve the next thirsty customer.

"Must be free," Theo remarked with a shrug, picking up the jugs and handing one to Leyla.

"We should go say hi," Leyla suggested, taking a sip of her ale while her eyes remained fixed on the two outsiders.

"I suppose. We outsiders should stick together, plus I reckon I could beat him," Theo said with a laugh, taking a large drink from his ale as well.

The pair walked towards the others, the elvish woman catching them in her gaze as they approached.

"Who's next?" Theo asked the large bald man, his tone friendly and casual, eager to join in the camaraderie of the moment.

"You are," the large man responded with a hearty smile, his enthusiasm evident as he gestured for Theo to take a seat.

"Here, hold this," Theo said, passing his jug to Leyla as he settled in at the small wooden table.

"I'll go easy on your boyfriend," the large man said, turning to Leyla with a friendly grin.

"Oh, he's not my boyfriend. Go as hard as you please," Leyla responded, shooting a playful smirk towards Theo.

"Righto, let's get it over with," Theo said, rolling up the sleeve on his right arm and placing his elbow on the table, ready for the challenge.

"Don't worry, he won't hurt your friend," the blonde woman reassured Leyla, motioning for her to take a seat beside her at the bar.

"I'm Atlas, and this brute is Horethian," Atlas introduced herself as Leyla settled into her seat and adjusted her robe while placing Theo's jug down on the table.

"I'm Leyla, and that's Theo. Pleasure to meet you," Leyla replied, taking a sip of her ale.

"Where are you from?" Atlas inquired, her curiosity piqued as she leaned in to hear Leyla's answer.

"We came from Serpentia," Leyla said, her voice tinged with a hint of bitterness. "But I don't want to go back anytime soon."

"Ahh, don't blame ya. Spent some time there. That Prince Blackscale is a right twat," Atlas remarked, taking a large gulp of her beer.

"Totally agree. His guards can be on the heavy-handed side," Leyla agreed, nodding in solidarity.

"What about you two?" Leyla inquired, shifting the conversation towards their new acquaintances.

"We don't really have a home per se, just passing through," Atlas responded cryptically, not divulging much about their background.

"Judging by your outfit, you're a thief, am I right?" Atlas continued, eyeing Leyla up and down with curiosity.

"I prefer the term rogue," Leyla retorted with a hint of snarkiness.

"Whoa, didn't mean to offend. Rogue it is. My apologies," Atlas quickly responded, realizing her misstep and trying to amend any harm done.

"No offense taken. Ranger, I presume?" Leyla countered, attempting to lighten the mood.

"Right you are," Atlas confirmed with a nod of her head.

"Where are you guys heading?" Leyla asked, eager to change the subject and steer the conversation towards more neutral territory.

"Not too sure, our party leader hasn't told us yet," Atlas replied casually.

"Party leader? Horethian?" Leyla inquired, her curiosity piqued.

Atlas almost spat out her drink in laughter. "Horethian won't be able to find his way out of this tent, let alone lead us. Our leader isn't here right now. He may join us, but I doubt it."

"He says ale clouds his mind. I don't see the problem, as that's what it's meant to do. But you know, each to their own," Atlas continued, raising her drink in the air before taking another swig.

"That must be the third man we saw in the cage," Leyla thought to herself as she followed Atlas's lead and took a drink.

"You two still going?" Atlas asked, shifting her gaze towards Horethian and Theo, her tone light and casual.

A look of strain crossed Theo's face as he struggled to keep his arm upright, veins beginning to pop from his forearm as the blood rushed to it. Meanwhile, Horethian sat quietly, drinking from his mug, a large grin spread across his face as he watched Theo's struggle.

Suddenly, a loud crash reverberated through the tent as Horethian slammed Theo's hand down onto the table with such force that the wood cracked and plates and mugs fell to the floor in a clatter. Horethian let out a triumphant cheer, lifting his arms high in the air, with Atlas following suit, her legs and arms shooting out of the chair in excitement.

"Good try," Horethian said, extending a friendly hand towards Theo, who was caressing his now tender shoulder.

"I'll get you next time," Theo responded with a smile as he grasped the man's hand, shaking it in a show of sportsmanship.

"You must be Theo," Atlas said as Theo walked over to the table to retrieve his mug.

"The one and only," Theo replied with a small bow before taking a large drink.

"I'm Atlas, and this is Horethian," Atlas introduced, pointing towards the large man.

"Pleased to meet ya. Sorry about the shoulder," Horethian said, noticing Theo still nursing his injury.

"Eh, it'll be right," Theo shrugged it off.

"Not a bad spot, this," Theo continued, his eyes scanning the tent.

"Better spot than where we were this morning," Horethian chuckled lightly.

"That cage isn't too bad. We spent the first morning in there, too," Theo remarked.

"Oh, so you guys had the light show also?" Atlas asked, her curiosity piqued.

"Light show?" Leyla questioned, intrigued by the mention.

"I guess not," Horethian added with a shrug.

"Never mind. Anyways, where are you two off to? Leyla was just telling me you came from Serpentia," Atlas said, steering the conversation towards their plans.

"Indeed, we did. Not too sure where we're off to. Any ideas, Leyla?" Theo turned to Leyla, seeking her input.

"I'm in no rush to be anywhere," Leyla replied nonchalantly.

"You should join us!" Horethian interjected, excitement evident in his voice.

Atlas swatted her hand, playfully slapping Horethian on the back of the head.

"What was that for? Just because you're on a stool and can reach my head," Horethian exclaimed, rubbing the spot where Atlas's hand had made contact.

"Sorry, you'll have to forgive my friend. We would gladly accept your company, but we need to run it past the rest of our team," Atlas explained, her tone apologetic.

"Malkhia won't care, the more the merrier," Horethian insisted, ducking another swipe from Atlas with a grin.

"Well, we don't want to intrude. What do you think, Leyla? If it's all good with this Malkhia person," Theo asked Leyla, seeking her opinion.

"Fine by me. Sounds like fun," Leyla replied with a smile, her excitement evident.

"It's a plan then. Drinks on me!" Horethian declared cheerfully as he strode through the crowd to the bar, ordering four more jugs with a generous wave of his hand.

Horethian returned to the table, slamming down the four jugs with a hearty thud, causing some of the liquid to spill over the rim.

"Here's to new friends!" he declared, raising his drink high as the others followed suit.

"Here, here," Theo agreed, lifting his jug to his lips for a drink.

"Dance with me," Leyla insisted, tugging on Theo's hand once more, determined to pull him away from the table.

"I'm not a good dancer, even when sober," Theo protested, but Leyla's tugs became more insistent, forcing him to reluctantly set his drink down.

She dragged him through the crowd to the front of the band, where she started to dance in front of him. Theo awkwardly attempted to join in, earning small laughs from Leyla as she watched his moves.

"Don't laugh, I told you," Theo said with a smile.

"I mean, those are some real good dance moves," Leyla teased sarcastically.

Meanwhile, back at the table, Horethian sat down next to Atlas. "So, what do you think?" he asked.

"They seem genuine, could come in handy also," Atlas replied thoughtfully.

"Reckon Malk will agree?" Horethian wondered aloud.

"Who knows? Since we got that map, he hasn't been himself," Atlas responded, her brow furrowing in concern.

As she finished her sentence, the pair noticed a shadowy figure standing in the entryway to the tent, the silhouette of a man in long robes with a pointy hat.

"Speak of the devil, Malk!" Horethian yelled out, managing to be heard over the noise of the band.

Malkhia walked inside the tent and over to the pair, a small smile gracing his lips. "I see you're having fun," he said, his voice calm yet authoritative. "Just came to check in and remind you we are leaving in the morning," he continued, his gaze sweeping over the gathering.

"We found some people to join us," Horethian said, attempting to stop the slur of his words.

"How much have you let him drink?" Malkhia asked Atlas, a mixture of concern and amusement evident in his tone.

"You know what he's like around free ale," she responded with a knowing smile.

"Free? If I had known that I wouldn't have let you two off on your own," Malkhia said with a chuckle, his eyes twinkling with humour.

"So, about these people you found, you want them to join us?" Malkhia continued, his tone thoughtful.

"I've been sussing them out, they actually might be a good fit. One's a rogue and the other looks to be a bard," Atlas replied, her eyes following Malkhia's gaze toward the front of the tent.

"Hmm, rogue and a bard. They could come in handy. Trustworthy?" Malkhia asked, his brows furrowing in contemplation.

"They seem so. That's them there," Atlas said, pointing over to the band where Theo and Leyla were dancing.

"The man and woman at the front," she clarified.

"Hope he's a better bard than he is a dancer. What is he doing?" Malkhia said in confusion, his lips twitching with amusement.

"If you two agree, then I have no worries. I'm off to bed. Don't stay up too late, and please, Atlas, keep an eye on this one," Malkhia said, nodding towards Horethian, who was lifting two women high above his head while they were still seated in their chairs.

"Night, Malk. I'll do my best," Atlas said, watching Malkhia turn and walk out of the tent.

Leyla and Theo rejoined the others, Leyla still laughing as Theo attempted to explain his dancing.

"Good news, you two. You're welcome to join us if you still want," Atlas said, her voice warm and inviting.

"Yay!" Leyla exclaimed; her words punctuated by a loud hiccup. She quickly covered her mouth with her hands, her cheeks flushing with embarrassment.

"That would be a yes," Theo confirmed with a chuckle.

"Well, you should probably get some rest then. We leave first thing," Atlas advised, her gaze shifting to Leyla's inebriated state.

"Yeah, probably should get this one to bed," Theo agreed, his smile affectionate as he reached out to steady Leyla, who seemed to have lost her footing while still swaying to the band's music.

"See you tomorrow then," Theo said, gently steering Leyla toward the front of the tent.

"That you will," Atlas agreed, raising her drink in acknowledgment as she watched them leave.

"They're nice people," Leyla said to Theo as she propped herself up, leaning on him for support as they made their way toward the fresh outside air.

"They seem it," he agreed with a smile.

"I want to dance and drink more," she declared, attempting to break free from his grasp.

Theo managed to maintain his hold on her, chuckling softly. "We need to sleep."

"Don't get any ideas. I'm not sleeping with you," she retorted sternly, though her body gave out, leaning heavily on Theo's arms.

"Let's get you to bed. We have a new adventure tomorrow," Theo said, leading Leyla into their tent.

"We're home, Jolly!" Theo announced as they entered, causing their dog to stir from his nap and wag his tail in greeting.

"Alright, in you get," Theo said, trying to gently lay Leyla down, but she resisted, still fighting against him.

"Can't sleep in this!" she declared with a slur, quickly beginning to disrobe.

Theo tried to avert his gaze, but it was drawn back by the mesmerizing sight before him. The robes slipped down Leyla's figure, tracing the delicate contours of her body, revealing the gentle curves of her hips and the enticing softness of her skin. He couldn't help but feel a flutter of warmth in his chest as he watched her movements, his breath catching in his throat.

As she shimmied, the robes cascaded to the ground, pooling at her feet, and Theo's eyes followed the graceful motion, captivated by her every movement. Just as she began to lose her balance, Theo reacted instinctively, reaching out to steady her. His hands found her waist, the warmth of her skin sending a jolt of electricity through him.

In that moment of contact, time seemed to stand still. Theo found himself lost in the depths of Leyla's emerald-green eyes, a silent exchange passing between them. His heart raced, his senses heightened by the closeness of her presence. For a fleeting moment, he entertained the notion of leaning in, of tasting the sweetness of her lips.

But before he could act on his impulse, a sudden bark pierced the air, shattering the fragile spell. Theo blinked, shaking himself out of the reverie, realizing the precariousness of the situation. With a gentle sigh, he released Leyla, stepping back and offering a sheepish smile, trying to regain his composure in the wake of their shared moment.

"Alright, time for bed," Theo said gently, guiding Leyla onto the sleeping bag and tucking the cover snugly around her.

With a weary sigh, Leyla murmured, "Hey, Theo."

"Yes?" he responded, attentive to her every word.

"Thank you," she said softly, her eyes closing as sleep beckoned.

"Anytime, Leyla," Theo replied warmly, watching over her as she drifted into peaceful slumber.

16

"My king!" Eric's voice echoed through the cavern, startling the group from their slumber. He bounded into the chamber, coming to an abrupt stop before the king, hands on his knees as he struggled to catch his breath.

"I don't think I've ever seen you run," the king remarked, sitting up to assess the situation.

"It's real!" Eric managed to gasp between breaths.

"Missing a bit of context there, Eric," the king replied, his eyes still adjusting to the sudden disturbance.

"Amethystite. I found the vein. A large one too," Eric explained, his voice brimming with enthusiasm.

The king's eyes widened, suddenly fully alert. "You found it! My God, man, show me the way," he exclaimed, leaping to his feet.

Eric wasted no time leading the king down the dimly lit passage to the narrow tunnel beyond.

"It's just through here. Oh, boy, you should see how pretty it is. More than the tales say," Eric gushed, his voice tinged with joy.

"Well, lead on," the king responded eagerly, anticipation evident in his voice.

The pair carefully manoeuvred their bodies sideways as they shuffled through the narrow tunnel, their footsteps echoing softly against the rocky walls. Finally, they emerged into the open, verdant-filled cavern.

"It's just behind those trees," Eric said, pointing to the massive trunks looming ahead.

The king strode in the direction Eric indicated, inspecting the wall behind the towering trees. His keen eyes caught the glint of a deep purple flicker amidst the earth and stone.

"You did it, Eric!" the king exclaimed, turning back to the dwarf with a proud smile.

"Nay, we all did it," Eric responded humbly, his gaze fixed on the glittering amethystite.

"Men! Gather the pickaxes. The carts can be positioned just before the narrow tunnel, and we can load them through here," the king commanded, raising his voice to be heard by the guards who had followed.

"Yes, my lord," the lead guard acknowledged, turning to relay the orders to his companions.

In no time, the group had organized themselves into a construction line. Some set to work with forceful strikes of their pickaxes, chipping away at the ore, while others gathered it and tossed it into sacks to be dragged down the narrow tunnel and loaded into the waiting ore carts.

"I thought we lugged these carts down here for nothing," Eric remarked to the king, a mix of incredulity and relief in his voice.

"I was beginning to think the same," the king responded, his smile still broad and unwavering.

"So, you're sure you can smelt and work this?" the king inquired, his eyes fixed on Eric with a hint of doubt.

"Aye, ore is ore, especially if you have the skill," Eric replied confidently, his demeanour resolute.

"And that you do, old friend, that you do," the king acknowledged warmly.

The sound of metal hitting stone reverberated off the cavern walls as the men continued chipping away at large chunks of the purple ore embedded in the rock.

"How deep do you think this goes?" one of the men queried, pausing to wipe the sweat from his brow.

"No idea, but at least we can go home soon," another man responded, his voice tinged with relief at the thought of completing their task.

"You two, stop chin-wagging and keep going. I want to go home also," another voice cut in sharply, its tone urging the men to focus on their task.

"If the ore is real, do you think the rest of the myth is?" Eric asked, his expression filled with concern as he glanced at the king.

"For our sake, I hope not," the king responded solemnly, his gaze thoughtful.

"We should prepare, just in case," Eric suggested, his voice tinged with urgency.

"Good idea. I'll leave that one up to you. You've read more about this myth than anyone I know," the king replied, acknowledging Eric's expertise on the matter.

"I'm no fighter, plus it only speaks of 'em. Not how to kill 'em," Eric said, worry evident in his expression.

"From your display yesterday, you can hold your own. I trust you," the king reassured him.

"Aye, my king. Leave it with me," Eric said resolutely as he strode off to confer with a nearby guard, his mind already turning to plans for what might lie ahead.

As the king explored the cavern, a sense of triumph filled his thoughts. "We finally found it," he said to himself, his voice echoing softly in the vast chamber. His gaze was drawn to the sight of water cascading down the rocks into a serene pond, where large fish swam gracefully, adding to the tranquil scene. However, he quickly dismissed the idea of indulging in fishing while his men toiled away.

"Yes, sir," a guard acknowledged behind him, prompting the king to turn around as the guard left the cavern after conferring with Eric.

"All sorted?" the king queried as Eric approached him by the pond.

"It is, my king. Oh look, fish," Eric remarked, gesturing excitedly towards the aquatic life. "We should do a spot of fishing," he suggested.

The king responded with a playful jab. "Now, Eric, what kind of image does that show the men?"

Eric chuckled in agreement. "You're right, maybe not a good idea."

"Wait here a moment, I must show you something," the king continued.

He swiftly retrieved something large from his pack and walked back to Eric, his arms held behind him. With a mischievous glint in his eye, the king produced a makeshift fishing rod. "I didn't say it wasn't a good idea, just not a good image," he quipped, sharing a grin with Eric.

"Whoever complains can eat the rest of that corpse eater while we dine on fish," the king said with a wry grin as he cast his line into the pond, the makeshift fishing rod cutting through the calm surface.

Eric's hearty laughter echoed through the cavern as he clapped the king on the back. "I'll leave you to it then," he chuckled, turning away to join the group of guards gathering in the centre of the cavern.

"Now, men, there is a tale about this ore. It is protected. We need to be aware in case it is true, and we get ambushed," Eric addressed the group, his voice carrying a note of caution.

Curious glances were exchanged among the guards. "Any idea by what?" one of them ventured, his brow furrowed in concern.

"An elemental, not the normal kind either. As you know, they take the makeup of the ore they're built from, so this one will be unlike anything we have ever seen before," Eric explained, his words laden with solemnity.

"How do we kill it?" another guard asked, his tone tinged with apprehension.

"That I do not know," Eric admitted, his gaze falling to the ground momentarily, uncertainty flickering in his eyes. He mentally lamented not recruiting the magic users from Helge. "I do have a plan, though," Eric continued, lifting his head back up high, hoping the morale hadn't dropped.

The guards nodded in agreement as Eric meticulously went through every fine detail multiple times, ensuring the men understood what needed to be done. After a lengthy explanation, he asked, "Got it?"

"Yes, sir," they responded in unison.

"Alright, well you two start on the rope," Eric said, pointing to two of the men, "and the rest of you gather what you need for the forge," he continued, addressing the remaining guards.

"Yes, sir," they all echoed once more before dispersing from the circle to begin their assigned tasks.

"Men!" a voice called from the edge of the cave, drawing everyone's attention. "Time for a break!" the king yelled. His words reverberated through the cavern, bringing an abrupt halt to the clinking of metal against stone as the sound of hessian bags thudding against the floor filled the air.

"Chef, cook this up for the men," the king continued, gesturing to a large pile of fresh fish nearby.

"Nice haul, sire," Eric remarked as he walked over to the king, admiring the pile of fish at his feet.

"They seemed to love the corpse eater," the king said with a smile.

"Give us a hand," the chef said to a nearby man, who followed him and grabbed armfuls of the fresh fish, carrying them back to the fire pit.

"You have a plan?" the king asked Eric as they began to walk towards the campfire.

"Aye, a risky one, but no one's faced one of these before," Eric responded.

"I have faith, and hopefully the plan isn't needed," the king reassured Eric, his voice carrying a hint of optimism as they strolled towards the campfire.

"How do you think the prince is going?" Eric probed, his tone filled with genuine concern.

"I truly don't know. I don't think he's ready to lead. Hopefully Belfor and Sharl can help remedy that," the king replied.

"And Charlotte?" Eric persisted, shifting the conversation to the enigmatic princess.

"If she hasn't killed her brother yet, I'd be surprised," the king chuckled, a warm smile playing at the corners of his lips. "She has Gwen to keep her in line, though," he added.

"Aye, strong-willed, that one," Eric remarked, a wistful edge to his tone as he recalled past encounters with the fiery princess.

The king's laughter rumbled through the cavern, blending harmoniously with the crackling of the fire. "Got that right. I blame her mother," he jested, a twinkle of fondness in his eyes as he reminisced about the queen's indomitable spirit.

"That smells good, chef," the king complimented, inhaling deeply as the rich aroma of fire-roasted fish wafted through the cavern, mingling with the earthy scent of the underground.

"Thank you, my liege. It's almost ready," the chef replied with a respectful nod, his movements methodical and practiced as he tended to the fish sizzling over the open flames.

The men gathered eagerly around the fire, their faces illuminated by the warm glow as they each selected a fish, their appetites whetted by the tantalizing aroma.

"Wish there was some mead left," one of the men mused wistfully, his gaze lingering on the dwindling flames of the fire. Another nodded in agreement, his mouth still occupied with a sizable fillet of fish, his expression conveying a shared longing for the honeyed drink.

As the group finished their meals, they tossed their picked-clean skeletons, skewered on branches, into the fire, igniting a burst of flames that danced and crackled with renewed vigour, casting long shadows across the cavern walls and bathing the space in a warm, flickering glow.

"I'm going to go check on the carts," the king announced, his movements somewhat stiff as he rose to his feet, his joints protesting the sudden change in position. With a low groan, he began to make his way towards the narrow tunnel leading to the surface.

"Sir, the forge is complete," a man informed Eric, breaking the silence that settled over the group in the king's absence.

"Ah, good. Fetch me some ore, and we shall see how it smelts," Eric responded, his voice tinged with a blend of excitement and anticipation. With practiced efficiency, he began to prepare the forge, stuffing it with charcoal embers from the fire pit and carefully adjusting the small bellows to direct the airflow.

With only a few pumps of the bellows, the forge sprang to life, the embers glowing a brilliant shade of orange as they heated up the chamber.

"Here, sir," the man returned, bearing a large sack of amethystite, the precious ore glinting in the firelight as it spilled from the sack.

"Wonderful," Eric murmured, his gaze fixed intently on the glimmering purple hue of the amethystite as he opened the sack, his fingers sifting through the precious ore with reverence.

Rummaging through his pack, he retrieved a large crucible, its surface gleaming in the firelight as he filled it to the brim with the ore before carefully placing it inside the roaring forge.

With each pump of the bellows, the embers glowed brighter, heat radiating outwards as the ore began to liquefy within the crucible. Eric added more chunks of amethystite, watching intently as the molten liquid rose.

"Find me some soil, if possible," Eric instructed the man, who nodded in understanding before darting off to fulfill the request.

Returning swiftly, the man carried a wooden bucket filled to the brim with dark, dry dirt. "Will this work?" he asked, setting the bucket down beside Eric for inspection.

"Perfect," Eric confirmed with a nod of approval, his hands diving into the soil to scoop out handfuls, which he began to shape on the ground next to the forge.

Using branches as makeshift tools, he compacted the soil and moulded it into a deep rectangle, his movements methodical and precise. "This ought to do," he declared, satisfied with the result.

Retrieving a large set of tongs, he carefully extracted the glowing crucible from the forge, the molten liquid shimmering within. With steady hands, he poured the searing liquid into his newly created moulds, each pour filling the air with a hiss and sizzle as it met the cool earth.

"Look at the colour of that!" Eric exclaimed, his voice filled with awe as he watched the vibrant purple hues break through the golden glow of the freshly poured ingot, the metal beginning to cool.

"Get me the smoothest rocks you can find," Eric commanded, turning to the guard standing beside him.

Without hesitation, the guard scurried off, quickly returning with flat, smooth rocks gathered from the walls of the cavern, placing them at Eric's feet.

Eric meticulously piled the rocks on top of each other, giving the structure a firm shake after each layer to test its stability. Retrieving a small, flat piece of thick metal from his pack, he carefully placed it atop the makeshift anvil, the guard observing with a puzzled expression.

"Head back to that corpse eater and see if you can gather up some of its vines," Eric instructed the guard, glancing up at him after giving the makeshift anvil a final test.

"Yes, sir," the guard responded promptly, hurrying off down the tunnel to fulfill Eric's request.

With the set of tongs firmly in hand, Eric placed the ingot into the forge, the intense heat radiating around him as he rhythmically pumped the bellows with his foot. As he continued to stoke the flames, he reached into his pack and withdrew a large, exquisitely crafted smithing hammer.

Eric deftly retrieved the now glowing ingot from the forge, resting it onto his anvil. He began the arduous task of shaping the metal. Blow after blow, he hammered away at the ingot, manoeuvring it back into the forge every so often to reheat it.

The rhythmic clang of metal against metal drew the attention of the group, who paused their own tasks to gather around in amazement. Purple sparks danced in the air as Eric's hammer struck the ore with precision and force.

Wiping the sweat from his brow, Eric placed the now large, flat, curved piece back into the forge for its final heating. As it glowed a deep yellow, he retrieved it and strode purposefully towards the pond at the edge of the cavern. Plunging the piece into the cool water, steam rose in wisps as the metal hissed and sizzled, quenching the heat.

Examining the final product under the light, Eric scrutinized it with a keen eye. "No fractures," he declared before grabbing a rock from the ground and sliding it along the edge. "Hardens well too," he continued, satisfied with the result as he made his way back to the forge.

"Here's the vines you requested," the guard announced, returning with his arms laden with branches and vines of all sizes and lengths.

"Great timing," Eric responded, his hands deftly sorting through the pile as he selected a long, straight branch and multiple small whip-like vines. With focused determination, he attached the branch to his piece of amethystite, fastening it tightly with the vines in intricate patterns. Yet, a nagging feeling of incompleteness tugged at him as he studied his work.

"Ah ha," he exclaimed, a spark of realization igniting within him. With quick motions, he set the piece down and grabbed a small knife from his belt. Carefully, he cut a strip off the bottom of his apron before wrapping it around the base of the branch.

"What's this, then?" the king inquired, joining the men who watched in awe.

Eric smiled with pride as he held up the completed weapon, a large, sturdy battle-axe. Its surface boasted a mesmerizing deep purple hue, adorned with elegant streaks of black that seemed to dance across the steel. The handle was a perfect complement, adorned in rich, mahogany brown hues, meticulously wrapped in vibrant green vines. The finishing touch: a supple tan leather handgrip.

"Exceptional work, Eric," the king said with a hint of jest, his eyes filled with admiration as he surveyed the craftsmanship of the battle-axe. "Now you need to make yourself one."

17

Charlotte's legs carried her through the dark, sodden maze of the sewers as she followed Belfor, Henry, and the other dock boy, her footsteps muffled by the pounding in her chest. Thoughts of her dear friend Gwen lingered in her mind as she wiped away a falling tear.

Henry looked back and noticed the princess falling behind. "Not much further, my lady," he called back, receiving only a nod in response.

"I will destroy Eron for this," Charlotte vowed silently as she came to a stop behind the trio. Henry turned to address them, his voice cutting through the damp air. "The opening to the dock is just up ahead; we have a ship waiting to take you to safety."

"Where are we going?" Belfor asked.

"Tryn is the closest city with a port, and we have friends there. It'll be safe for now," Henry replied, his tone reassuring.

"Any place is better than Serpentia at the moment," Belfor remarked, casting a concerned glance at Charlotte, who remained lost in her troubled thoughts.

"How did you know the prince's plan?" Charlotte asked as she looked up at Henry.

"Gwen got the word out. She had been watching Sharl, who unfortunately was also watching her," Henry replied, his expression reflecting a mixture of regret and sorrow.

"As soon as we heard, we tried to get to her, but we were too late," he continued, his head hanging low, a shadow passing over his features.

"I can't leave. I must take back what is mine," Charlotte asserted, determination flashing in her eyes.

"It is too risky at the moment, Princess. We need to get you to safety and strategize our next move," Henry cautioned.

"We have already begun preparations. A ship set sail only hours ago with a full crew to establish a refuge in Tryn," he added, a glimmer of hope cutting through the darkness.

"There are friends of your father's in the city, Princess. Once we arrive, I will reach out to them," Belfor interjected, his voice steady and reassuring.

"Okay, but we need to act quickly. Father will be back soon, and Eron and Sharl will fill him with lies," Charlotte agreed, her tone laced with urgency.

"The king is returning!?" Belfor exclaimed, the surprise evident in his voice.

"Lead the way, Henry," she continued, her voice tinged with sadness as she dismissed Belfor's question, her mind already consumed with the impending challenges ahead.

Henry began to gently shake the rusty iron bars blocking the opening to the sewers until he found one that began to move slightly. With careful precision, he gripped the bar and slid it up until the bottom was free. Pivoting the bar towards him, he applied steady pressure, gradually loosening it from its concrete footing.

As he looked out over the water, Henry watched as the sun timidly peeked at the horizon, casting a faint glow over the sky. A thick, gloomy fog enveloped the port, its tendrils weaving around the ships like ghostly veils.

Sliding through the gap, Henry emerged underneath the docks. The air was thick with the scent of brine and decay, and the sound of lapping waves echoed in the dimness. He beckoned the others to follow as he observed the narrow space between the concrete pipe and a small wooden dock to his right. With a fluid motion, he leaped through the air to the dock, landing with practiced grace on both feet.

The princess mimicked Henry's movements and jumped, her elegant demeanour momentarily disrupted as her footing faltered upon landing. Henry instinctively reached out to steady her, his touch offering reassurance.

"I've had too many wines for this," Belfor remarked with a nervous chuckle as he leaped through the air, landing with a heavy thud and tumbling into a clumsy roll across the damp, waterlogged wood. The last boy followed suit, his movements swift and agile, offering Belfor a hand up with a grin that betrayed his amusement at the spectacle.

"Just there, Princess," Henry said, his finger pointing towards a looming silhouette, a large wooden ship tethered to the dock, its crow's nest the only visible feature against the dense fog.

"Here," he continued, his hand disappearing into a crevice in the stone wall of the dock. With a deft movement, he retrieved two large, deep brown cloaks, their fabric heavy with the musk of sea salt and dirt.

"Put these on, just in case the fog clears," he advised, passing the cloaks to Belfor and Charlotte.

Charlotte and Belfor cloaked themselves, pulling the hoods low to obscure their faces, blending into the shadows as they followed Henry towards the ship.

Henry signalled with a sharp whistle, piercing through the thick mist. From its depths emerged a figure. A weathered sailor stepped into view, his features etched with years of seafaring and smoke enveloping his head as it rose from the wooden pipe in his mouth.

"Quickly," Henry urged, his arm sweeping towards the gangway leading to the ship.

"Thank you, Henry," Charlotte acknowledged, pausing to offer her gratitude.

"There will be time later for that. You must leave now," Henry insisted, a smile playing at the corners of his mouth as he watched them ascend the gangplank with hurried steps.

"Inside, Princess," the sailor grunted, his voice roughened by the salty sea air as he removed the pipe from his mouth.

Charlotte nodded and disappeared into the ship's cabin, the wooden planks creaking beneath her feet as she vanished from sight. Outside, the chaos of the dock intensified, the thud of ropes being hauled, voices shouting commands, and the distant clang of metal against wood signalling the urgency of their departure.

Suddenly, Charlotte felt a jolt reverberate through the ship as it began to move, stirring her from her thoughts. She peeked her head outside the cabin to witness Henry and his friend standing solemnly on the dock, watching as the vessel set sail.

As the ship drifted further away, Charlotte's heart quickened, and a sinking feeling gripped her chest. Her gaze fixed on a large group of men gathering at the edge of the dock. Powerless to intervene, she watched in horror as the men descended upon Henry and his friend.

Two guards charged towards the boys, wrestling them to the wooden structure before binding them in iron shackles. Charlotte gasped, her hand flying to her mouth as she witnessed the scene unfold.

"What is it?" Belfor asked, noticing Charlotte's expression of concern.

"They have Henry!" she exclaimed, her voice trembling with fear.

Belfor peered past Charlotte, his eyes narrowing as he took in the chaos unfolding on the dock. "He's a smart lad, I'm sure he will figure a way out," he reassured her, though his own worry was evident.

Charlotte's thoughts were shattered by the shrill caw of a bird, drawing her gaze skyward. A black raven circled ominously above the ship, its presence sending a glimmer of happiness into her mind as it descended lower and lower.

"Malk," Charlotte murmured under her breath, her voice barely audible over the noise of the ship.

"Huh?" Belfor turned to her, his brow furrowed in confusion.

But Charlotte was only focused on the bird as it swooped down towards her, its talons clutching a rolled parchment. With a swift movement, the bird released its cargo, sending it sailing towards Charlotte, who instinctively reached out and caught it.

"What's that?" Belfor inquired, his curiosity piqued as he watched Charlotte holding the parchment, her hands trembling with anticipation.

Ignoring Belfor's question, Charlotte's heart raced, as she hurried to the corner of the cabin. With trembling fingers, she untied the blue ribbon. As she unfolded the parchment, her eyes widened, oblivious to the fact that the wax seal had already been broken. In her haste, she was consumed by the urgency of the moment, her focus solely on the words written before her.

Charlotte's breath caught as she read the words on the parchment, her heart fluttering with a mix of relief and hope. The familiar handwriting brought comfort as she absorbed each line:

"My dearest C,
I am safe, I pray the same for you.
I have it and I'm on my way to an old friend to decode it.
We will be traveling to your home to resupply at some point,
I long to feel your embrace.
Forever yours

A wave of emotions washed over Charlotte as she read the message, her heart pounding with a mixture of relief and apprehension. He's coming to Serpentia, Charlotte thought, a look of horror crossing her face as she considered the danger her beloved might face.

"What is going on?" Belfor asked, still seeking answers amidst the chaos.

"Just a friend, soon to be in trouble," Charlotte replied, her voice strained with worry. With trembling hands, she dropped to the ground of the cabin, her back sliding down the wooden wall as she sank, the letter tightly gripped in her hands.

"I must reply," she declared, unrolling the note on the floor, her mind racing with the words she had to choose carefully to convey her own safety and urgency.

"A quill!" Charlotte demanded towards Belfor, clicking her fingers together in urgency.

"I don't just carry around a quill," Belfor responded, casting a puzzled look at Charlotte's insistence.

"Well, find one!" Charlotte commanded, her eyes welling up with tears and bloodshot with worry.

Belfor scrambled around the cabin, rummaging through cupboards and drawers until he finally discovered an ink pot and quill nestled in the drawer of an old desk.

"Here, Princess," Belfor said, relief evident in his voice as he handed the items over to her, his own concern mirrored in his expression.

Charlotte quickly scribbled a response on the back of the parchment, her hand trembling. With swift motions, she rolled it up and tied the ribbon back around to secure it.

Hurrying to the cabin door, Charlotte spotted the bird still circling above. With an outstretched arm, she shook the letter towards the bird, which instinctively began a dive toward her.

Tossing the letter into the air, Charlotte watched as the bird swooped past, clasping it in its claws before letting out a loud caw and disappearing into the horizon, swallowed by the rising sun.

"Oo rum," Charlotte heard from beside her, as Belfor continued to explore the ship's nooks and crannies.

"There's no glasses, but care to join me?" Belfor offered, gesturing toward a bottle he had found.

Turning to him, Charlotte shot a questioning look, her mind still racing with thoughts of the message sent.

The pair sat down against the wall of the cabin on some rolled-up hessian sacks Belfor had acquired from under the old desk, finding solace in each other's company amidst the uncertainty of their situation.

"I don't know what you and Gwen had planned, but I'm assuming it isn't this?" Belfor ventured, breaking the silence that hung heavy in the air.

"No, it is not. If only she were here," Charlotte responded wistfully, taking a swig from the old, dusty bottle before handing it back to Belfor.

"It will be alright. Tryn is a nice city," Belfor reassured her, his tone hopeful amidst the uncertainty.

Shaking thoughts of Gwen from her mind, Charlotte extended her hand to hint for Belfor to pass the bottle back. With a smile, he complied, placing the bottle into her hand and watching as she gulped it back with determination.

"Ease up, Princess. I like rum also," Belfor chuckled, his laughter filling the cabin with a sense of camaraderie.

The pair settled back against the wall, swapping old stories of the king and the city, their laughter mingling with the gentle rocking of the ship. However, their conversation was soon interrupted by the unexpected arrival of the captain.

"I see you found my stash," the captain said with a hearty chuckle, his weathered face illuminated by the warm glow of his pipe as he took in a big puff before exhaling a cloud of smoke that swirled in the air.

"We are close to Tryn; the wind favoured us," he announced, his voice carrying a reassuring tone amidst the gentle creaking of the ship. "You are safe to leave the cabin now; no one is out here except for us."

Charlotte and Belfor exchanged nods of acknowledgment, a sense of relief washing over them. With cautious steps, they rose from their seats, the anticipation of stepping out onto the deck palpable in the air.

"Sorry about the rum," Charlotte apologized, her voice carrying a hint of regret.

"Don't be. Plenty of rum stored away," the captain responded with a wide grin, his eyes twinkling with amusement as he gestured towards a hidden cache of bottles gleaming in the dim light.

"You didn't say you had more!?" Belfor exclaimed with a mixture of surprise and excitement as he approached the captain, his steps eager while he watched Charlotte exit the cabin.

"You didn't ask," the captain replied with a hearty laugh, the sound mingling with the rhythmic sounds of the waves as he followed the two companions out onto the deck.

A rush of sea breeze filled Charlotte's lungs as she inhaled deeply, the salty air filling her chest. The symphony of water crashing against the sides of the ship reverberated through the air, punctuated by the rhythmic flapping of the large white fabric sails as they caught the wind.

Walking to the side of the ship, Charlotte leaned over the railing, her eyes tracing the swirling patterns of the water below. The foam-capped waves rushed past, their frothy crests tinged with white as the ship sliced through the cerulean expanse.

Her gaze drifted to the horizon, where the vastness of the ocean met the endless sky in an unbroken line of blue.

"I hate the sea," Belfor's voice broke the serene moment, his discontent evident.

"It's beautiful, Belfor," Charlotte countered softly, her eyes still fixed on the horizon as she walked toward the front of the ship.

"There's nothing out here," Belfor persisted.

"Exactly," Charlotte replied with a knowing smile, her appreciation for the solitude of the open sea clear in her eyes.

Turning toward the captain, she asked, "Which way is Tryn?"

The captain gestured toward a shadowy outline on the distant horizon. "See that shadow, way off in the distance in front of us? That marks the shipping trench. We hit that, then go south."

Charlotte squinted her eyes, trying to discern the elusive mark on the horizon. "Won't be much longer, Your Highness," the captain reassured her.

"Call me Charlotte," she corrected him with a warm smile.

As the ship sailed onward, the trench marker gradually emerged into view, a grandiose monument carved from white marble, depicting a towering figure clad in ornate armour and wielding a spear with regal grace.

"King Rindell," Belfor remarked with reverence, admiring the intricate craftsmanship of the statue as the vessel sailed closer.

"He's a good friend of your father's, Princess," Belfor added, his voice carrying a note of respect amidst the awe-inspiring sight, while the ship executed a sharp turn to follow the dredged pathway.

"Still, I wouldn't reveal yourselves just yet. Who knows how far the prince has spread his lies," the captain interjected, his words a sobering reminder of the precariousness of their situation.

The sails crackled with renewed vigour as they caught the wind, propelling the ship swiftly down the shipping lane. Ahead, large sandstone blocks were piled together, forming a formidable barrier that guided the vessel towards a walled inlet leading into the dock.

"Back into the cabin, please," the captain instructed the pair, their agreement swift as they hastened to seek refuge once more within the confines of the cabin.

Within the cabin, the air was alive with a symphony of sounds. Creaking and cracking of the wooden ship, the calls of sailors as they manned the ropes, and the rhythmic thud of the vessel being guided towards the wooden docks.

Skilled sailors moved with precision and expertise, each attending to their tasks with practiced efficiency. They deftly tied off the ship to the dock and brought it to a gentle rest before sliding out the gangway with practiced ease.

"The coast is clear. This is Arthur; he will guide you," the captain announced, introducing a young, scruffy sailor who stood ready to assist.

"Thank you, Captain," the princess acknowledged, pulling up her hood to conceal her delicate features once more.

"Anytime, Charlotte," the captain responded with a warm smile, his eyes reflecting a sense of understanding and solidarity.

"This way," Arthur guided the pair, leading them briskly down the gangway and onto the bustling dock below.

Workers scurried about, their movements purposeful as they loaded and unloaded wares and produce from the ships moored at the dock. Fishermen lined the edges of the wooden jetty, each one engrossed in conversation as they cast their lines into the shimmering waters.

"Through here," Arthur continued, steering them through the throngs of people and down an alleyway that opened into a bustling bazaar.

The air was thick with the aroma of spices and the clamour of vendors hawking their goods, their voices blending into a cacophony of sound as they navigated past carts laden with colourful fruits and fragrant herbs, all set against the backdrop of white marble blocks that lined the city streets.

"The trade here is unlike any other city," Arthur remarked. "Just in there," he pointed to a small stone building nestled amidst the bustling marketplace.

Intricately patterned rugs hung from the balcony above their heads as they entered through the weathered wooden door, the dim interior offering a stark contrast to the vibrant chaos outside.

As they stepped inside, they were greeted by an older woman dressed in a flowing tan gown, a pale purple scarf wrapped elegantly around her hair, her warm smile welcoming them into the sanctuary of the humble establishment.

"Downstairs," the lady beckoned, gesturing towards the stairwell leading into the basement, her voice gentle yet commanding as she stood at the top of the steps.

"Pleased to meet you finally, Princess. I'm a friend of Gwen's." she said softly, her words carrying a weight of sympathy as she led the trio down the stairs into the dimly lit basement.

As they descended, Belfor's thoughts wandered, pondering the depth of the underground chambers they traversed, passing multiple closed doors lining a long corridor.

The lady paused, her hand reaching out to pull back a large tapestry hanging on the wall at the end of the corridor, revealing an entrance to another room hidden behind.

"Through here," she invited, her gaze steady as she watched them climb into the opening and through the open door before following them through, the heavy tapestry falling back into place behind her, shrouding the entrance once more in secrecy.

Charlotte's eyes widened in astonishment as she stepped out onto the ledge overlooking the expansive room below. People bustled about, engaged in various tasks and conversations, their movements purposeful yet filled with an undercurrent of urgency. Weapons and provisions lined the walls, their presence a stark reminder of the gravity of their situation, while makeshift tents dotted the outskirts of the room, their structures symbolizing the resilience and adaptability of those who had sought refuge there.

A hush descended upon the room as Charlotte's figure emerged into view, her presence commanding attention as all eyes turned to her with a mixture of anticipation and reverence. In that moment, amidst the quietude, the weight of responsibility settled upon her shoulders, and she realized the significance of her role in this clandestine sanctuary.

"What is this?" Charlotte's voice trembled with shock and confusion as she turned to the lady who had led them here, her expression mirroring her bewilderment.

"We are here for you, Princess. Eron's rule over Serpentia has affected us all," the lady explained solemnly, her gaze steady as she met Charlotte's incredulous eyes.

"For me?" Charlotte's voice was barely above a whisper as she turned to face the assembled crowd below, their expectant gazes fixed upon her with unwavering determination.

"Welcome to the rebellion, My Lady,"

18

Sweat beads glistened on Leyla's brow as she twisted and turned in her sleeping bag, her face contorted with a mixture of fear and concern. Abruptly, she jolted awake with a gasp, sitting upright and panting heavily.

"You okay?" Theo's voice drifted from the other side of the tent.

"I'm fine, just a bad dream," Leyla responded, wiping the droplets of sweat from her eyes.

"Care to talk about it?" Theo's inquiry hung in the air.

"Just past stuff," Leyla replied, her voice trailing off.

"Well, I won't press, but I'm here," Theo reassured her.

Leyla fell silent, lost in her thoughts. After a moment, she began to speak, her voice tinged with emotion.

"When I first arrived in Serpentia, I was quite young, and it wasn't under my own will," Leyla started, drawing Theo's full attention as he turned in his sleeping bag to face her.

"I came in on a slave ship and was sold at the market to a very wealthy noble. Life was okay at first, just house chores and tending to the family. But then..." Her voice faltered, tears welling up in her eyes as she struggled to continue.

"When I was sixteen, I managed to catch the eye of my possessor, Winston," she finally confessed, her voice trembling with emotion as she rubbed her eyes.

"You don't have to, Leyla," Theo interjected softly.

"It's okay, you should know," she insisted, her voice wavering with vulnerability.

"Each night, he used to come into our chambers, wildly drunk, and choose one of us to please him. He wasn't a gentle man," Leyla continued, her fingers absentmindedly tracing the deep scars on her upper arms as she lost herself in the memories.

"Anyway," she pressed on, "one night, me and the other slaves had enough and came up with a plan to escape."

"It went horribly wrong. The others managed to escape, but Winston caught me and dragged me into the cellar of their large estate."

"For three months, I was kept down there, chained to a stone pillar in the darkness. I can still smell the dank mold," she said, her words catching in her throat as she recalled the harrowing experience. A tear fell down her cheek, unnoticed until Theo spoke up.

"Leyla, if it's too much, it's okay," he offered gently.

"No, it's okay. You're the only person I have ever told," she replied, her voice trembling with emotion.

"It was his nightly routine to come down to the cellar. But I waited. As he came close, I pounced and managed to wrap my chain around his pudgy neck, squeezing it tight until I felt all movement disappear. I laid there in relief for God knows how long," she continued, her words weighted with her past trauma.

"I grabbed the key from his lifeless body and freed myself. I was spotted by the house servant running from the cellar, who alerted the nearby guards. I managed to make it to the tree line and vanish."

"Since then, I have been living off the land and thieving what I could from the city, until I met you. And here we are," she finished with a brave smile.

"Well, as long as you are with me, I will let nothing like that happen to you," Theo reassured her.

"I will let nothing like that happen again, but thanks for the offer," Leyla responded, her tone determined. "Enough of that, now let's go see these adventurers," she added, eager to move past the painful memories and focus on the present.

Emerging from their sleeping bags, Leyla and Theo meticulously packed up their belongings. They deftly bundled their possessions into neat parcels before strapping and stuffing them into their packs, the morning sun projecting shadows through the cracks in the tent's canvas.

"Uhh, can we get some breakfast first?" Leyla's stomach grumbled audibly, betraying her hunger.

Theo chuckled softly. "Feeling a bit under the weather, are we?"

Leyla gave Theo a playful yet weary look as they made their way toward the a large rectangular tent. The tantalizing aroma of freshly cooked food wafted out from the opening, enveloping them in its delicious scent.

Stepping inside, they found themselves amidst a bustling scene. Malkhia, Horethian, and Atlas sat at a long wooden table, surrounded by villagers. The table itself was a feast for the eyes, laden with an array of dishes—from steaming plates of eggs and sausages to succulent chunks of pork. The villagers chattered animatedly, their laughter mingling with the sounds of sizzling food and clinking utensils.

"Over here!" Atlas called out, her voice cutting through the hubbub. She waved to Theo and Leyla, beckoning them to join the gathering.

"Look at all this food!" Theo exclaimed, his eyes widening in amazement at the bounty spread out before them.

"Apparently it's normal," Atlas said with a nonchalant shrug, her gaze already fixed on a mouth-watering chicken leg. She sank her teeth into it with relish, the savoury juices dribbling down her chin.

"Dig in," Theo invited, his eyes twinkling with amusement as he watched Leyla's plate already piled high with the greasiest delights from the table.

Leyla, mouth already full, managed a muffled, "Did I need to wait?" as she eagerly devoured a piece of fried egg.

Turning his attention to Atlas, Theo asked, "Where are we off to then?" as he began to load his own plate with an assortment of dishes.

"Malk said we needed to see an old friend, then head off to Serpentia for supplies," Atlas responded matter-of-factly between bites.

At the mention of Serpentia, Theo's gaze shifted to Leyla, a silent reassurance conveyed through the gentle squeeze of his hand on her leg and a warm smile that met her worried gaze.

Once they had all polished off their meals, the group gathered outside the tent, ready to embark on their next adventure. The desert sun cast long shadows across the sandy ground as the companions stood together, the air tinged with anticipation.

"I'm Malkhia, nice to meet you. Atlas and Horethian tell me you're good people," Malkhia said, extending a hand in greeting to Theo and Leyla.

"I'm Theo, and this is Leyla," Theo replied with a warm smile, returning the handshake.

"Welcome," Malkhia said, his eyes scanning each member of the group with a keen gaze.

"So, just a ways outside the desert is an old, burned ruin. We need to see someone who lives nearby, then we can head into the city to restock," Malkhia continued, his tone steady and focused. The group nodded in agreement, understanding the task at hand.

"The elder has been kind enough to give us some horses. I didn't expect two more, so we'll have to pair up," Malkhia said, glancing around at the group.

The companions set about preparing the horses. Weapons and supplies were secured to the saddles, the horses shifting restlessly in anticipation of the journey ahead.

Horethian clambered up onto the horse, its sturdy frame shifting slightly under his weight as he settled into the saddle. The horse responded with a loud bray, its breath warm against the desert air.

"Shh," Horethian soothed, his hand gently stroking the mane of the horse as he calmed its nerves. With practiced ease, he offered a hand down to Atlas, who grasped it firmly. In one swift motion, Horethian effortlessly lifted her into the air and lowered her down onto the saddle in front of him.

"Can this horse take both of us?" Atlas asked, adjusting her position to find a comfortable seat.

"Of course it can," Horethian replied with a hint of uncertainty, his eyes briefly flickering with doubt.

Theo extended a hand to Leyla, assisting her as she climbed into the saddle before kneeling down before Jolly.

"All right, boy, it's only for a short while," Theo said as he produced a small purple bottle from his pack and opened the cork stopper, releasing a large cloud of smoke that engulfed Jolly.

Theo let out an audible sigh as he leaned over to pick up the small dog statuette on the ground before placing it into his pack.

"What about your boat?" Leyla asked, curiosity colouring her voice as she looked to Theo.

"Eh, Ramsay has it. I can call him if we need it," he replied as he climbed onto the horse, positioning himself behind Leyla.

The group headed out of the village entrance and into the desert, following Malkhia's lead. The morning sun slowly rose, its warmth beginning to permeate the air around them.

❖ ❖ ❖ ❖

"**S**ylvaris! They're leaving," Durnek called out from the rocky outcrop where they had been camped.

"Sekt, go with Durnek and follow them. Nymira and I will head to the city to prepare for their arrival," Sylvaris instructed, rolling up his bedding before giving Durnek a stern look. "And Durnek, just follow. I trust you can manage that."

Sekt nodded in acknowledgment, slinging his pack over his shoulder.

"Sure, just follow. Got it," Durnek replied in a mocking tone.

The pair set off, with Sekt leading as he tracked the trail left by the horses.

"Trea Ango Mov," Nymira chanted, opening a glowing portal before the remaining two stepped through, the portal vanishing as they entered.

"Always doing the grunt work," Durnek grumbled to Sekt. "I should have become a blacksmith like my brother. I'd be sitting all pretty with a king and not in this hot, miserable place chasing horses on foot," he continued, trudging through the soft sand in an attempt to keep up with Sekt.

"Also, why send the two with the smallest legs? Surely, they would have caught up quicker," he muttered.

Sekt brought a finger up to his mouth and hushed Durnek.

“Great conversationalist,” Durnek replied with a sarcastic tone.

Malkhia guided his steed forward, the ruins looming closer on the horizon. "Almost there," he called out, the anticipation evident in his voice as the group followed suit, slowing their horses to match his pace.

"About time. Don't know how much longer this horse can take our weight," Horethian grumbled, adjusting himself in the saddle.

"You're taking up all the room. I can't feel my arse," Atlas complained, shifting uncomfortably and trying to nudge Horethian aside.

"It's actually not that bad," Leyla remarked, finding a comfortable spot leaning against Theo's chest.

"I thought you said he wasn't your boyfriend. You're looking mighty comfortable," Horethian teased with a chuckle, his eyes twinkling mischievously.

Leyla's cheeks flushed with embarrassment as she realized her body's position and quickly sat up, but Theo's smile remained warm and reassuring as he looked at her.

"Oh, leave them alone," Atlas chided Horethian, rolling her eyes.

Horethian quickly waved off the tension. "What? I didn't mean anything by it," he clarified, hoping to ease any discomfort as they rode toward the ruins.

At the edge of the burned village, Malkhia paused, his hand absently rubbing the back of his shoulder and up his neck. "You alright, Malk?" Atlas inquired with genuine concern as the others caught up to him.

"Yeah, just slept funny," Malkhia assured, his hand dropping back down to the reins as he noticed Atlas's worried expression. "Nothing to worry about," he added, offering her a reassuring smile.

"Just through here, there should be a stream that runs off into the forest," Malkhia pointed to the centre of the village. "Down that stream will be the man we need to see about this map," he explained, gently nudging his horse forward.

"Map?" Leyla's curiosity piqued, her tone carrying a hint of intrigue.

"We found a map in the Dungeon of Echoes; some people are after it. About all I know," Horethian explained with a casual shrug, his tone carrying a hint of nonchalance.

Theo's interest was piqued. "A map in the Dungeon of Echoes?" he asked, his brows furrowing slightly with curiosity. The mention of the Dungeon of Echoes triggered a memory in his mind, conjuring images of whispered legends.

"Yeah, why, you know it?" Atlas responded, her expression now reflecting a mix of intrigue and curiosity, her eyes scanning the faces of the group for any hints of recognition.

"I've heard tales of a map to some lost world in that dungeon. I just thought they were tales," Theo admitted, a note of scepticism in his voice, though there was a flicker of excitement in his eyes.

"Forgotten Lands," Malkhia corrected Theo with a knowing smile, his gaze distant as if he was recalling memories from long ago.

"Ha, next you're going to tell me Amethystite is real," Theo chuckled, his scepticism still evident as he brushed off the notion of mythical treasures.

"Believe what you want, my friend. We'll see if it's real soon enough," Malkhia replied, his smile unwavering as he looked back at the group, his eyes glinting with determination.

As they traversed the ruins of the village, Malkhia brought his horse to a sudden stop outside a large sandstone villa in ruins. His hand instinctively began to rub his neck again, and he drifted into his thoughts, the weight of past memories pressing down on him like heavy chains.

"Your neck that bad?" Horethian rode past Malkhia, breaking him out of his reverie, his concern evident in his voice.

Malkhia didn't respond immediately, lost in the flood of past memories. Suddenly, he snapped back to reality, turning his horse to rejoin the others.

"What happened here?" Leyla's voice cut through the solemn atmosphere as she surveyed the devastation, her eyes drawn to the charred remnants of what was once a sturdy barn.

"These remains look to have burned quickly. No normal fire would have done that," Atlas observed, her sharp eyes scanning another ruined house nearby, her expression grim with understanding.

"A daemon did this," Malkhia stated as he rode up beside Atlas and Horethian, his gaze lingering on the desolate landscape.

"No one's seen a daemon for centuries," Theo interjected, his disbelief evident in his voice.

"This one was summoned," Malkhia replied, a tinge of regret colouring his tone as he recalled past events.

"How do you know so much about this place?" Atlas queried, her eyes narrowing as she regarded Malkhia with suspicion.

"I do my research," he responded, a flicker of mischief dancing in his eyes as he offered her a smile that didn't quite reach his eyes.

"There's the river," Leyla pointed out, breaking the tension as she gestured toward the flowing water at the edge of the village.

"You guys wait at the water. He's not partial to visitors," Malkhia instructed, his gaze lingering on the forest ahead as he prepared to ride off.

"Will he be alright?" Leyla's concern was evident as she took Theo's hand, preparing to dismount and join him by the river.

"He can handle himself," Horethian reassured her, his gaze fixed on Atlas as she dismounted, her hands rubbing furiously against her behind in an attempt to alleviate the discomfort from the long ride.

ekt stopped at the edge of a large pile of rubble, his finger pointing to distant shadowy shapes on the horizon.

"A ruin?" Durnek questioned, squinting to make out the details.

Sekt nodded, still pointing towards the ruins of a village.

"This is Arndell, isn't it? Why would they be going there? Nothing has lived there for years," Durnek mused, puzzled by their destination.

Sekt offered only a shrug in response as they continued their approach.

As they drew closer, the charred remains of the once-bustling farming village came into view. Large sandstone blocks, melted at the top, lay strewn about among the old wooden beams and dilapidated farming carts.

Sekt began pointing to the river against the forest backdrop.

"Follow the river?" Durnek asked, receiving a small nod from the gnome.

"But it's getting darker. Why not head into the village and find some shelter?" Durnek suggested, his concern evident.

Sekt pointed to the river once more, insisting.

"Fine," Durnek conceded, deferring to the gnome's expertise.

They made their way to the left of the village, arriving at the quick-flowing river. The trees loomed overhead, their branches casting long shadows as the sun began its descent, painting the sky with fiery hues of red and yellow.

Sekt stopped once more as he pointed to a small, fallen-down house on the outskirts of the town. Its walls were weathered by time and neglect.

Durnek nodded in agreement, the weight of his pack causing the wooden floorboards to creak beneath his heavy footsteps. With a grunt, he dropped his pack onto the dusty ground, sending a cloud of particles into the air.

Sekt pressed a finger to his lips, the urgency in his gesture evident as he motioned for silence, the faint sounds of movement echoing from outside.

❖ ❖ ❖ ❖

alkhia's horse snorted softly, its hooves splashing through the cool waters of the river as he approached the small, weather-beaten cabin.

"It's been a while, old friend," Malkhia murmured to himself, a faint sense of nostalgia tugging at his heartstrings as he guided his horse towards the cabin.

As they crossed the river, the water rose around them, caressing the horse's underbelly. With measured steps, they reached the opposite bank, the damp earth squelching beneath their feet.

"Cre Igni," Malkhia intoned softly, a subtle shimmer enveloping him as he invoked his magical abilities. The world around him seemed to shift and brighten, allowing him to discern the details of his surroundings even in the dim light of dusk.

But before he could proceed further, a sudden incantation echoed behind him, sending shockwaves rippling through the ground. Malkhia's senses tingled with danger as he realized he was ensnared in a paralysing spell, his body frozen in place along with his horse.

19

"My Liege," the guard began, his voice reverent as he knelt before the prince, head bowed in deference. "The Princess and Belfor have escaped."

The prince's reaction was immediate, his anger flaring as he rose from his throne, towering over the room in his fury. "Escaped!" he bellowed, his voice echoing off the ornate walls.

"Yes, my Prince," the guard confirmed, "They were followed into the cellar and made their escape through the sewers. However, we were able to apprehend two young boys who aided them."

"Bring them to me!" the prince commanded, his eyes blazing with rage as he settled back onto his throne, the air heavy with tension.

Henry and his companion were escorted into the throne room, their hands and feet bound in heavy iron chains that clanged ominously with every step. They shuffled forward, flanked by guards brandishing spears.

Upon reaching the foot of the throne, the guards forced the boys to their knees, their faces grim beneath the weight of their predicament.

"Do you know her?" the prince demanded, his voice cutting through the air like a whip as he rolled a severed head across the floor. The gruesome sight left a trail of blood as it rolled, coming to a stop before Henry, its lifeless gaze fixed upon him.

Henry's jaw clenched as he took in the sight of Gwen's severed head, her expression of terror frozen in eternal torment. Despite the tumult of emotions swirling within him, he remained silent under the prince's scrutiny.

"Do you, boy!" the prince thundered, his fury palpable as he rose from his seat once more, his regal facade crumbling in his wrath.

Henry met the prince's gaze, his own features marred by bruises and blood. With a defiant gesture, he spat a ball of bloodied saliva toward the prince.

The prince's eyes narrowed with contempt as the spittle landed on his polished boots, his anger simmering beneath the surface. He strode purposefully toward Henry. "I just cleaned these," he snapped, his hand raised high before delivering a stinging blow to the already battered cheek of the young captive.

Pain lanced through Henry's face, but he gritted his teeth against the torment, refusing to show weakness before his oppressor.

"Take them away," the prince commanded with a dismissive wave of his hand, his ire momentarily sated as he returned to his throne.

The guards seized Henry and his companion, hoisting them to their feet and prodding them forward with the sharp points of their spears. With heads bowed and spirits battered, they trudged toward the exit, leaving behind the oppressive atmosphere of the throne room.

"They will never talk, my lord," Sharl asserted, stepping forward from the shadows to stand beside the prince.

"We will see, and if not, we haven't had a good hanging in a while," the prince responded with a smile, beckoning a servant over with a large flagon of wine.

"We have news from our unsavoury friends as well," Sharl continued.

"They found them!?" the prince interjected, his anticipation evident as he shifted in his chair and snatched the flagon from the servant to fill his cup.

"They have, and they are tracking them until they know they have the map," Sharl confirmed.

"Ah, good. I knew I could trust you. If it weren't for your knowledge of this treason, I would be in Gwen's position," the prince remarked, taking a large mouthful of wine.

"About that, shall I sort the disposal out?" Sharl inquired.

The prince brought his hand to his chin, contemplating his next move before taking another sip of wine.

"No, place it at the bridge. Let it be a warning to the city," the prince decreed.

"Very well, is that all?" Sharl asked.

"For now," the prince replied.

With a bow, Sharl moved toward the severed head, deftly seizing a handful of hair to carry it out of the throne room before disappearing from sight.

"Come here," the prince beckoned to the servant once more, his voice carrying a sinister edge that sent a chill down her spine.

The young woman hesitantly walked towards the prince, her steps cautious as his intense gaze locked onto her. The flickering torchlight cast eerie shadows across the grand throne room, amplifying the tension in the air. "Yes, my prince?" she asked, her voice barely above a whisper, her heart pounding with trepidation.

"We never got to have our rendezvous," the prince said with a dastardly smile, his eyes gleaming with anticipation as he gestured for her to approach.

"Apologies, my prince," the woman said, her head hanging low with deference, her fingers fidgeting nervously at her sides.

"Come closer," he commanded, his voice low, a predatory glint in his eye.

As she got within arm's reach, the prince extended his hand, gripping her forearm with a firmness that bordered on possessive. With a swift motion, he pulled her onto his lap, the ornate throne groaning under their combined weight. The young woman let out a small shriek as she landed in his embrace, her body tensing with apprehension.

The prince held her tightly, his touch sending a shiver down her spine as his fingers trailed up her thighs, lifting her long dress with deliberate slowness. The room seemed to close in around her, the oppressive atmosphere suffocating her senses.

"I still plan to scrutinize every inch of you," he said with a wicked smile, his voice dripping with menace, his gaze raking over her form with hungry intent.

She fought the urge to resist him, knowing the dire consequences if she did. With a sense of resignation, she shut her eyes tightly as she felt his hand move from her thigh up to her face; his fingers brushed over a small tattoo down her cheek before stopping at her jaw. He forced her head back, her pulse racing with fear and revulsion.

"Open your eyes and look at your prince," he commanded, his grip tightening on her chin. She felt her neck throb from the forcefulness of his movements, a shiver running down her spine.

Reluctantly, she obeyed, cracking open her eyes to find the prince's face mere inches from hers. The scent of stale wine filled her nostrils, making her struggle to maintain her gaze under his intense scrutiny. His eyes bored into hers, dark and penetrating.

"My Prince!" a voice echoed from the entrance to the throne room, interrupting the tense moment. The sudden call startled the prince, and his hand released its grip on the woman's jaw. She exhaled softly, relieved to be free from his grasp.

"Pardon the interruption, but we have news of the king. His party is just over one moon away," the guard announced as he approached the throne, dropping to one knee in deference.

The prince's demeanour shifted abruptly as he sat up straighter on his throne, his grip on the woman's arm tightening momentarily before he threw her off his lap.

"Are you certain?" the prince demanded, his voice laced with tension.

"Yes, my lord," the guard confirmed, his expression serious.

"Damn it," the prince cursed under his breath. "Leave," he commanded, dismissing the guard with a wave of his hand.

Turning his attention back to the woman, he added with a sinister grin, "Oh, and you, we'll finish this later."

As the guard exited the room, the prince muttered to himself, "Just over a moon away. This puts a dampener on things," before refilling his cup with wine.

Commander Sharl strode across the stone bridge, his heavy boots echoing against the ancient stone pillars lining the way. He approached the entrance, fixing his steely gaze on the guards stationed there, their expressions tense under his scrutiny.

"Where are the boys?" he demanded, his voice cutting through the quiet of the castle courtyard.

"They were taken to the cells," one of the guards responded, but Sharl barely acknowledged the answer, his mind already racing ahead to his next task.

He continued his determined march through the labyrinthine corridors of the castle. The stone walls seemed to close in around him as he navigated the dimly lit passages, his hand resting on the pommel of his sword. He headed towards a small tower nestled at the rear of the fortress, its weathered stones bearing the weight of centuries of history.

With each step, the sound of his boots reverberated through the narrow stairwell, accompanied by the occasional clink of his armour. The climb felt endless, the winding staircase seemingly leading him ever upward into the heart of the tower. Finally, he reached two large wooden doors at the top, their surfaces weathered and worn from years of use.

With a grunt, Sharl pushed one of the doors open, revealing a small walkway bathed in the soft glow of torchlight. The air was heavy with the musty scent of stone and iron, and the faint sound of dripping water echoed off the walls. Flanking the walkway were cages, their rusted metal bars a stark reminder of the tower's grim purpose.

Sharl's sharp eyes swept the room, his gaze settling on the figure curled up in one of the cells. He watched intently, observing the slight rise and fall of the boy's chest against the dim light filtering through the narrow window. Satisfied that the boy was alive, he turned his attention to the other cell.

In the dim light, Henry sat on a wooden chair, his face streaked with blood from a recent beating. Despite the pain etched across his features, he busied himself with cleaning the wounds on his face, using a damp undershirt and a bowl of water.

"Henry, is it?" Sharl's voice cut through the stillness, drawing the boy's attention. Henry met Sharl's gaze with a mixture of defiance and resignation, his eyes reflecting the weariness of someone far beyond his years. He nodded silently in response before returning to his task, his hands trembling as he continued to clean his face.

Sharl watched as Henry shifted in his chair to a defiant stance with a mix of frustration and admiration. "You know this will all be over if you just tell us where they went," he pressed, attempting to break through the boy's resolve.

"You're going to kill us anyway," Henry retorted, his voice tinged with bitterness as he set the bowl of bloody water down, the pinkish liquid spilling onto the cold stone floor.

"It will be quicker if you talk," Sharl insisted, his tone edged with impatience.

But Henry remained resolute, rising and walking toward the bars to confront the commander face to face. "I have time," he declared, his defiance unwavering.

Sharl's gaze shifted to Henry's friend lying in the adjacent cell, the boy's breaths shallow and laboured. "Your friend doesn't have much," he warned, hoping to leverage Henry's concern.

"He knew the risks," Henry replied, attempting to mask his worry with bravado.

"You're not bad with a blade. Why don't you come work for me?" Sharl proposed, his tone softer now, almost pleading.

Henry laughed incredulously. "Ha! And bow down to that entitled frail twat?" he scoffed.

Sharl's patience began to wear thin at Henry's insolence. "You know I should kill you right now for talking like that," he threatened, his hand instinctively reaching for his sword hilt.

"Ehh, do it then. Now, later, it doesn't matter," Henry retorted dismissively as he took a seat.

"Very well then, have it your way, boy," Sharl conceded, turning toward the door.

As Sharl neared the door, Henry's words hung in the air like a grim prophecy. "This is bigger than me or him," Henry called out defiantly, his voice echoing in the confines of the tower. Sharl pivoted on one foot to shoot Henry a glare, a silent acknowledgment of the

weight of his statement, before he exited. The heavy
wooden door slammed shut behind him, sealing Henry
and his friend once more within their cold, stone
confines.

20

"Home, sweet home," Sylvaris sighed as he stepped out of the portal, with Nymira close behind. He crossed the room to a large, two-seater bench nestled against the back wall. Books lay scattered across the floor and piled haphazardly around the room. Above the chair, a large tapestry hung askew, adding to the room's disarray. With a heavy thud, Sylvaris lowered himself onto the bench, stretching out his legs and settling in.

"You really need to clean up these books," he remarked to Nymira, who responded with a mocking gesture.

"Yeah, yeah," she retorted, her tone dripping with sarcasm.

"What's next?" she inquired, taking a seat in a smaller chair beside him and grabbing a book from the top of a pile, dust clouding into the air as she blew it off.

"We wait," Sylvaris replied, leaning further back into the chair and closing his eyes.

"We're always waiting. I'm going to the tavern," Nymira announced, rising to her feet and placing the book back down.

"Don't do anything I wouldn't do," Sylvaris said with a smile as he watched Nymira exit the house.

The bustling street teemed with villagers going about their daily routines as Nymira navigated through the throng. The city air, heavy with the mingling scents of sweat, cooking, and refuse, assaulted her senses like a blunt force. She pulled her cloak tighter around herself, covering her mouth and nose to shield against the noxious odours.

"I forgot how bad this place smells," she muttered to herself, her voice muffled by the fabric of her cloak.

Pushing through the crowd, she finally arrived at her destination: a large stone building with a weathered wooden sign depicting a fierce, snarling dragon swinging lazily in the breeze.

"Nymira, the usual?" called out the bartender as she stepped inside the tavern.

Nymira nodded in response, taking a seat at a small table near the window. The bartender hurried over, placing a glass on the table and filling it with a clear liquid.

"Leave the bottle," she requested as the bartender moved to leave.

He complied, setting the bottle down with a thud. "Tough day then?" he asked, his voice tinged with concern.

"Mmm," Nymira replied noncommittally, tossing back the contents of the glass in a single swift motion.

"I'll leave you be," the bartender said, sensing her desire for solitude, before turning to attend to other patrons.

"Before you go, any news on the princess?" Nymira inquired, her voice cutting through the din of the tavern, drawing the bartender's attention.

The man paused, wiping a frothy mug with a rag, before turning to face her. "What news isn't there these days," he sighed, weariness etched into the lines of his face.

"Just a summary," she insisted, leaning forward slightly, her eyes intent on his.

"Well, after Gwen, the princess, and Belfor fled the city, they caught the poor dock boys who helped them," he recounted, his voice tinged with sympathy for the unfortunate youths.

"Any idea where they went?" Nymira probed further, her curiosity evident.

"Rumour is Tryn, but who knows," he responded with a nonchalant shrug, already turning away to attend to other patrons clamouring for his attention.

Nymira nodded pensively, absorbing the information as she swirled the liquid in her glass, lost in thought. With a swift, practiced motion, she knocked back the shot, feeling the fiery liquid trail a path of warmth down her throat, and refilled her glass.

"Nymira, fancy seeing you back in town," a deep voice interrupted her solitary reverie, pulling her attention away from the swirling depths of her thoughts.

She raised an eyebrow as a large man adorned in fur armour settled into the seat across from her, his presence casting a shadow over the table. "Can I help you, Talon?" she asked, the edges of her tone tinged with a hint of scepticism.

"I figured you would be after the princess with the sizable increase to the bounty," Talon remarked casually, his eyes glinting with curiosity.

"Increase?" Nymira's interest was piqued, and she leaned forward, the wood of the table cool against her palms.

"Aye, they raised it to 30,000 gold pieces," Talon revealed, punctuating his words with a gulp of ale.

"Why aren't you after it?" she probed, her gaze narrowing slightly as she studied him.

"Haven't been able to track her yet. Rumour is Tryn, but I'm not too welcome there at the moment," Talon explained, his tone tinged with a hint of frustration.

"Trouble with the Rindell's again?" Nymira smirked behind her glass, a knowing glint in her eye.

"You could say that" Talon responded with a chuckle, his demeanour relaxed despite the underlying tension.

"As much as I love your company, I must be off," Nymira announced, rising gracefully from her seat and downing the remainder of her drink in a single swallow.

She tossed ten gold pieces onto the table with a deliberate clatter. "Here's for the bottle," she declared to the bartender, her voice ringing out clear and commanding over the din of the tavern.

"Be careful out there, Nymira. Wouldn't want that pretty face scarred up," Talon remarked with a smirk as he, too, rose from his seat.

Nymira disregarded Talon's comment and strode back out into the bustling street, navigating her way through the crowd of villagers before retracing her steps to the house.

"Sylvaris," she called out as she burst through the door, her voice echoing through the cluttered room.

The abrupt entrance startled Sylvaris from his slumber, his eyes snapping open as he stared wide-eyed at his sister, who stood in the doorway.

"They increased the princess's bounty to 30k," Nymira blurted out, her words punctuating the air as she hurriedly gathered her belongings, stuffing potions and scrolls into her pack with practiced efficiency.

Sylvaris reclined in his seat, his demeanour calm despite the news. "What about it?" he inquired, his tone betraying a hint of curiosity.

"I'm going to Tryn to see what I can find out," Nymira declared, her voice resolute as she finished packing her essentials.

"You really can't sit still, can you?" Sylvaris remarked, his eyes closing once more as if he was already drifting back into sleep.

"Val Agi Mov," Nymira chanted, her form vanishing into thin air, leaving behind nothing but a small cloud of dust where she once stood in the room.

❖ ❖ ❖ ❖

The bustling marketplace enveloped Nymira as she materialized in its corner, surrounded by a kaleidoscope of sights and sounds. Stalls adorned with colourful banners lined the cobbled streets, each vendor vying for the attention of passers-by with their array of goods. The air was alive with the chatter of merchants hawking their wares, the clinking of coins exchanging hands, and the tantalizing aroma of freshly baked bread and pastries that wafted through the bustling throng.

"Ah, much better," Nymira murmured, drawing in a deep breath to savour the sweet fragrance that filled her lungs, mingling with the myriad scents of spices, flowers, and exotic fruits that permeated the air.

"Val Cre Ren," she softly chanted, invoking a spell, her form shimmering momentarily before seamlessly morphing into that of a petite human woman. Her long blonde hair cascaded in gentle waves over her shoulders, clad in a flowing green dress hugging her frame that billowed around her feet with each graceful step.

"This will do," she mused to herself, her gaze sweeping over the bustling marketplace as she navigated her way through the crowd. The sunlight filtered through the colourful canopies overhead, casting dappled patterns of light and shadow on the cobblestones below.

Nymira spotted two men stationed outside a building on the fringe of the market. "Hmm, rather equipped for townsfolk," she mused to herself, studying the armour of the two men and noting the weapons hanging from their belts. Her gaze shifted to the surrounding buildings, where she spotted two more men dressed similarly, positioned on opposing rooftops overlooking the marketplace.

"The princess must be here," she mumbled to herself, her suspicions growing.

She continued to watch the house as another man in the same attire stepped out of the door. The two guards gave him a nod as he walked off into the crowd. Nymira quickly began to follow the man as he weaved his way through the marketplace before disappearing from sight.

Her eyes darted back and forth amidst the labyrinth of stalls and vendors until she spied the man entering a large sandstone building nestled at the far corner of the marketplace. Its wooden sign, weathered by time and adorned with faded images of two ale jugs clinking together, swayed gently in the breeze.

Making her way through the throng of townsfolk, Nymira stopped at the building, her eyes raising to the hanging sign, watching as it creaked with each small swing. "This must be the tavern. Changed a bit since I was last here," she remarked with a hint of nostalgia as she spotted a notice board hung on the side of the building.

Wanted posters overlapped along the top, filling almost every inch of the board, while the bottom layer was a mix of monster bounties and help-needed advertisements. Her eyes caught an intriguing flyer, and her hand shot up to rip it from the wall, bringing it closer for inspection.

"Help Wanted. The Brass Griffon is looking for workers. Lodgings and food provided as payment. Enquire within," she read aloud, considering her options.

"This could work," she said to herself, a plan forming in her mind as she pushed open the tavern door, the warm glow of the interior spilling out onto the bustling street.

As she entered, the patrons' eyes turned toward her, their gazes lingering in appreciation of her beauty. The interior of the tavern was bathed in a soft, amber light, the air thick with the scent of ale and the sound of merry laughter. She offered a small smile in return, her presence commanding the attention of all who beheld her.

She made her way to the bar, where the barman shot her a sidelong look. "What can I do for ya?" he said, allowing an unsettling smile to cross his face.

"I'm here about the job."

21

The townsfolk greeted Charlotte with fervent praise as she made her way through the bustling crowd of the rebellion, their voices blending into a chorus of support beneath the underground's shadowed archways.

"Thank you," Charlotte gracefully acknowledged a small girl with a nod, her eyes reflecting genuine gratitude as the child curtsied in reverence to the princess, welcoming her.

"What is all this?" Charlotte inquired, turning to the elderly lady who stood amidst the throng.

"This is the rebellion, the people's army," the elderly woman replied, her voice steady with conviction.

"And you're their leader?" Charlotte's curiosity persisted, her gaze searching for clarity amidst the fervour of the gathered assembly.

"We have no singular leader, Princess. We stand as a united front. We have come together to combat the tyranny your brother is imposing upon us. Should he seize control of Serpentia, the rest of the realm will inevitably fall under his oppressive rule," the woman explained, her words resonating with both urgency and determination.

"I don't even know where to begin," Charlotte confessed, feeling overwhelmed by the enormity of the task before her.

"Begin by resting, Your Highness. Much has transpired, and I'm certain both you and your friend are weary," the lady gently advised, taking a step forward and gesturing for Charlotte to follow her lead.

"Speaking of my friend, have you seen where Belfor went?" Charlotte inquired as she followed the lady through the crowd of rebels.

"He's over by the mead barrels," Arthur chimed in, approaching the princess.

"Of course," she responded with a sigh, her mind still swirling with the weight of their situation. She followed the woman through a doorway, concealed behind a heavy curtain.

"It's nothing royal, but it's comfortable and warm," the woman remarked, gesturing toward a simple straw bed tucked into the corner of the makeshift bedroom.

"It's perfect, thank you..." Charlotte paused, realizing the woman hadn't introduced herself.

"Oh, how rude of me. I am Hilda," the woman interjected with a warm smile.

"Pleased to meet you, Hilda, and thank you for the hospitality," Charlotte replied graciously, sinking onto the straw bed with a sense of relief.

"I will leave you to it," Hilda said kindly as she disappeared through the curtain, leaving Charlotte to her thoughts.

Charlotte rested her head on the soft, straw-stuffed pillow, her mind racing with uncertainty. "What am I going to do?" she wondered silently as exhaustion washed over her, pulling her into a deep and dreamless sleep.

"**M**ore wine!" Belfor's voice rang out with laughter, his goblet swaying precariously as he leaned back in his chair.

"There isn't any left," Arthur responded with a sigh, turning the tap on the wine barrel, hoping for a miracle that never came.

Belfor raised a hand to his chin, contemplating, then gulped down the last remaining drops of wine from his cup. "Surely there's a tavern nearby," he declared, a mischievous glint in his eye.

"You can't be seen," Arthur reminded him, his tone tinged with caution as he set his empty goblet down on the worn wooden table.

"They don't know who I am," Belfor insisted with a cavalier shrug.

"Lead the way, Arthur. We'll be fine," he urged, gesturing for his friend to guide the way out of the underground tunnels.

"Fine, but cover up at least," Arthur relented, watching as Belfor pulled the hood of his cloak over his head, obscuring his features.

"Is this good?" Belfor mumbled through the cloth, adjusting the neck to conceal his mouth and nose.

"It'll have to do," Arthur conceded, resigned to their impromptu excursion.

The pair navigated the labyrinthine tunnels, emerging into the bustling marketplace, where the aroma of sizzling meats and spices filled the air.

"It's just over there," Arthur pointed, indicating a weathered sign swinging in the breeze, depicting two clinking ale jugs.

Making their way through the throng of townsfolk, they finally reached the tavern's wooden doors. But before they could step inside, a drunken man stumbled over, his grip firm on Arthur's shoulders.

"Arthur! Fancy meeting you here," he slurred, a lopsided grin spreading across his face.

"Sir! I wasn't aware you were here," Arthur replied, his voice strained with deference as he attempted to raise his hand in a salute, only to have it forcibly pushed back down by the man's grip on his wrist.

"No need for formalities," the man grunted dismissively, pushing the doors open and staggering away toward a table littered with empty glasses.

"Who was that?" Belfor inquired, adjusting the scarf over his face to ease his breathing.

"I'll tell you later when it's safer," Arthur replied cryptically, brushing off Belfor's curiosity as he followed the man inside and made his way toward the bar.

Belfor's attention was quickly drawn to a young woman standing at the bar, engaged in animated conversation with the barman. Her long, flowing blonde hair cascaded down the curve of her petite frame, which was encased in a tight green dress, accentuating her delicate features.

"Go around the back and speak to the other barmaids, they'll sort ya," the barman gruffly instructed the woman, dismissing her with a wave of his hand before turning his attention to Arthur.

"Two pints," Arthur ordered, placing two gleaming gold coins onto the worn wooden bar. The barman nodded, grabbing a jug and expertly filling it from the tap before slamming the two brimming jugs down in front of Arthur.

"Anything else?" the barman inquired, wiping his hands on a stained rag.

Arthur shook his head in response as he lifted one of the jugs to his lips, taking a long, satisfying sip of the ale.

"Here," Arthur offered, turning to Belfor and breaking his friend's gaze from the departing woman as he placed the full cup into his hand.

"I like the view here," Belfor remarked with a grin, taking a sip of the ale.

"We can't stay long," Arthur reminded him, following Belfor's lead as he made his way to an empty table by the window.

"Did you see her, Arthur?" Belfor slurred, waving his cup in the air and accidentally spilling its contents onto the already damp wooden table.

"She's out of your league," Arthur teased, taking a sip of his own drink and chuckling at his friend's antics.

"Pfft, no one is out of my league," Belfor retorted, straightening his tunic with false confidence.

"So, who was that man that made you stand so stiffly?" Belfor queried; his words slightly slurred as he swayed in his seat.

"He's one of the four captains of the rebellion," Arthur explained, his gaze fixed on the drunk captain from across the room. "It's unusual for them to be out in public like this."

As the conversation shifted, a dainty voice interrupted their discussion. "Freshen your jugs?" the young woman asked, appearing at their table with a shy smile.

"I won't say no," Belfor replied with a wink, his charm overshadowed by the alcohol's influence.

The young woman smiled shyly as she placed two filled jugs on the table, her hand extended, awaiting payment.

"Keep the change," Belfor insisted, placing three gold pieces into her palm.

"How kind of you, sir," the young woman murmured, offering a curtsey before turning away.

"Not so fast, young lady. I need more time to admire your beauty. I'm Belfor, and it's an honour to be in your presence," Belfor declared with a wobbly bow, attempting flattery in his inebriated state.

Arthur attempted to quieten Belfor's exuberance, but to no avail.

"I'm Maryanne, pleased to meet you," the young woman replied politely, though a hint of amusement danced in her eyes.

"What a moron, introducing himself while in hiding," Nymira thought to herself as she watched Belfor stumble through the bow.

"I must get back to work, but I could come see you after?" Maryanne offered with a polite smile, attempting to extricate herself from the situation.

"Maybe another time," Arthur interjected hastily, trying to prevent Belfor from making any more mistakes.

"Now, now, Arthur, no need to be jealous," Belfor retorted with a smirk, oblivious to the tension mounting around him.

"We are staying just over…" Belfor began to say before Arthur's fist connected with the side of his jaw, sending him tumbling to the floor in a daze.

"What are you doing, boy!" Belfor shouted, rubbing his throbbing jaw as he glared up at Arthur from the ground.

"What's the commotion?" the bartender inquired, striding over to the table with concern etched on his face.

"Just a jealous little boy," Belfor muttered, scrambling to his feet and brushing off his pants with a scowl.

Before Belfor could retaliate, Arthur launched another punch, only to have his arm seized from behind by the strong grip of the rebellion captain.

"That'll do, Arthur," the captain interjected firmly, pulling Arthur away from the brewing altercation.

"You, upstairs!" the bartender commanded, gesturing to Nymira. "And both of you, out!" he added, pointing towards the door with no patience for further disturbances.

"Fine! Until next time, Maryanne," Belfor declared with a theatrical bow, offering a playful wink as he was ushered toward the exit by the bartender's firm hand.

Nymira hurried to the staircase, making her way upstairs to a small room with a balcony overlooking the bustling marketplace.

From the balcony, Nymira observed with a mixture of curiosity and amusement as the men were shoved unceremoniously onto the street, struggling to maintain their balance in the aftermath of the tavern turmoil.

"What is going on?" the captain demanded, his voice gruff as he barged through the tavern door, his eyes narrowed with suspicion.

"He was about to tell that barmaid where we are," Arthur explained tersely, shooting Belfor an accusatory glare.

"You just wanted Maryanne for yourself," Belfor retorted, his expression stern as he locked eyes with Arthur.

"My god, you are simple," Arthur muttered in frustration, shaking his head in disbelief.

"Enough, you two. We are not to make another scene. Go back and sleep it off. Hopefully, no damage control is needed, but I'll make sure," the captain intervened, his tone authoritative as he turned from the men to head back inside the bar.

"Let's go, you've already said too much," Arthur urged, leading the way into the now-quiet marketplace, the glow of the setting sun casting a warm, golden hue over the scene.

"Damage control? He just wants to drink more," Belfor grumbled under his breath as he begrudgingly followed Arthur's lead.

"What a beautiful sunset," Belfor remarked, joining Arthur's side and gazing wistfully at the painted sky.

As the men walked across the market and disappeared into an old sandstone house adorned with intricate woven rugs, Nymira watched from a distance, her thoughts swirling with intrigue.

"What fools," she thought to herself, the door to the room creaking open as she shifted her gaze from the spectacle unfolding below to the door.

Nymira listened to the bartender's furious tirade, his words dripping with anger as he accused her of stirring up trouble among the patrons. With a dismissive wave of her hand, she approached him, her expression cool and determined.

"I don't have time for this," she declared, her voice cutting through the tense atmosphere like a blade.

"Trea Fir," she chanted softly, her eyes glowing with a fierce intensity as she summoned a ball of fire that erupted from her outstretched hand, engulfing the bartender in flames.

The room was filled with the agonized screams of the bartender as the fire consumed him, the sound echoing off the walls before abruptly falling silent as his charred body collapsed to the floor with a heavy thud.

A bright reddish hue filled the room, casting eerie shadows against the charred floorboards and the pile of ash that remained in the wake of the inferno.

"He would have had it coming," Nymira remarked coldly, stepping onto the remains of the bartender as she made her way out into the hallway of the upper floor.

"Now I need a way into that building," she thought to herself, her mind already racing with plans as she descended the stairs and stepped out into the bustling street, leaving the chaos of the tavern behind her.

22

The young boy jolted awake, shooting upright in the small bed. His eyes darted around the modest wooden shack as he rubbed the sleep from the corners of his eyes.

"Where am I?" he asked himself, his vision beginning to clear. A sharp pain shot through his body as his hand instinctively reached for the back of his neck, feeling the soft cloth draped over it. He winced as his fingers brushed against the tender skin beneath the bandage.

Suddenly, the door burst open. "Ahh, you're awake," a deep, groaning voice announced from a shadowed figure standing in the doorway.

The young boy rubbed his eyes again, straining to see through the dim light cast by the flickering candles scattered around the room. An older man, dressed in long, flowing brown robes covered in dark green vines and wearing a pointed hat, entered the room. He set his bag and hat on the cluttered round wooden table at the centre.

"Didn't know if you would," the man said, peering towards the boy before turning his back and heading towards a bench piled high with old dishes. The young boy noticed the man walked with a slight limp, leaning heavily on a long, gnarled wooden staff entangled in vines and topped with a large round gem.

"Hungry, I presume," the man said, grabbing a plate from the top of the pile and dusting it off before placing *it on the table. "Cre Hea Vlas," he chanted, and a small puff of smoke rose from the plate, revealing a large bushel of bright red apples.*

"It's not a normal breakfast choice, but that spell is quite random," the man said, picking up an apple and brushing it against his long, ragged brown robes before taking a bite. "Still, quite tasty. Come now, boy, don't be scared," he continued, watching as the young boy cautiously clambered out of bed.

"Who are you? Where am I?" the boy asked timidly as he walked over to the older man.

"Hmm, memory loss," the man murmured, turning to a small workbench cluttered with vials of different coloured liquids, scrolls, and books strewn across the top. He began to sift through the piles of books, muttering to himself. "Aha!" he exclaimed, blowing the dust off the cover of a book and flicking through the pages.

"You didn't answer me," the boy said, biting into one of the apples. A surprised look crossed his face as the burst of flavour lit up his mouth.

The old man continued to mumble to himself before turning to the boy. "You have what we call Mana sickness. It's been many years since I've seen it; surprised I forgot the symptoms," he said.

"Mana sickness?" the boy questioned, a puzzled expression crossing his face as he took another bite of the apple.

"When you deplete your body's mana pool, you start to get some nasty side effects. Consider yourself lucky it's only memory loss," the man explained, putting the book back down on the bench and walking towards the boy. He pulled out a chair and lowered himself onto it.

"I don't really like apples," the man said, chanting another spell. The apples disappeared in a cloud of smoke. "Cre Hea Vlas," he chanted again, and this time a pile of cooked bacon and eggs appeared on the plate.

"Ahh, that's better," the man said, dusting another plate off before loading it up with food.

The boy followed the man's lead and took a seat at the table before eagerly devouring his food.

"You are hungry," the man chuckled, watching the boy shove piled forkfuls of food into his mouth.

"That was good," the boy said, leaning back into the chair and admiring the empty plate in front of him. "So, where am I?" he asked, looking at the old man.

"Not far from your old home," the man replied, laying his utensils down neatly on the plate.

"Where is my home?" the boy asked, trying to remember.

"You will see soon enough. Now, what is your name?" the man inquired.

"I don't remember," the young boy replied.

*"Hmm, do you remember how you came to be here?"
the man continued.*

*"Not really. I remember screaming and fire," the boy
said.*

*"Interesting," the man muttered, running his long,
slender fingers through his flowing grey beard,
brushing over the sprouts of small plants sticking
through.*

*"I don't remember much, actually. Is this permanent?"
the boy asked, his face filling with a mixture of panic
and anxiousness.*

"It may or may not be," the man replied.

*"Do you ever give straight answers?" the boy asked, a
hint of anger creeping into his voice.*

*"Now, now, young one. Don't be too hasty," the man
admonished, rising to his feet and giving the boy a stern
look. The boy slinked back into his chair as the look
penetrated deep into him.*

*"You have much to learn," the man said, grabbing his
hat and bag before heading toward the door. "Come
now," he said, beckoning to the boy while pushing the
door open with his staff.*

*The boy clambered to his feet, watching the old man
walk out the door. He quickly moved around the table
and rushed to join him outside. He raised his forearm
over his eyes as the sunlight blinded him, shining
through the surrounding trees and illuminating the area
around him.*

A serene river flowed steadily in front of the shack, its clear waters shimmering under the sun's rays. The gentle current carried leaves and twigs downstream, creating a soothing, babbling sound. The riverbanks were lined with lush greenery, ferns, and wildflowers in shades of blue and yellow, adding bursts of colour to the scene. The air was fresh, filled with the scent of pine and damp earth.

A stone pathway, worn smooth by time and weather, led from the door down the side of the river. It wound gracefully through the dense forest, where ancient trees stood tall with their canopies forming a protective arch overhead. Sunlight filtered through the leaves, casting dappled shadows on the ground. The path continued until it reached a clearing where the forest began to thin out, revealing glimpses of distant hills.

The man busily dug through his bag, mumbling to himself. "I knew I had a spare one here," he said, finally stopping and producing a large book bound in deep red leather with a golden pentagram embroidered on the cover.

"Here," he said, tossing the book to the boy. The boy caught it and quickly began to turn the pages.

"Initiate, Adept. This book just has titles in it," the boy said, shooting the old man a puzzled look.

"Well, you need to fill it," the man said, turning away and beginning to walk down the stone path. "Here, use this for a start," he added, throwing a scroll over his shoulder toward the boy.

The boy ran to catch the scroll, his hands fumbling through the air but failing; the scroll bounced off the wet stone pathway. He quickly picked it up and untied one of the blue ribbons holding it closed.

"I've seen this before somewhere," the boy said as he read the words.

"I don't doubt it, after you stole my chest and all," the man replied, not bothering to look back at the boy. "Just touch it to the book."

The boy held the unravelled scroll up to the book. Suddenly, a bright light shone, and the scroll began to combust. Shocked, the boy dropped the book to the ground.

"Don't treat your spell book that way," the man admonished, turning to pick up the book and handing it back to the boy.

The boy opened the book to see the word "Heal" imprinted under the Initiate title. "What does this mean?" he asked.

"Your first spell," the man replied. "Now come on, much to do," he continued, walking briskly down the path.

The man stopped by the stream where it bent around. The other bank of the river stretched out into a large clearing. Smoke billowed from what appeared to be the charred remains of a farming village.

"What is this place?" the boy asked as he joined the old man.

"Curious," the man said, looking down at the boy.

"What is? You're crazy," the boy said.

"Ha, indeed, some would say I'm mad," the man responded, handing the boy another scroll and a small pouch before beginning to chant. "Brez Mov Rai," he chanted as his feet began to rise inches from the ground.

The man took a step and began to walk across the river, floating just above the waterline. "Come now," he said, looking back at the boy as he stepped onto the opposite riverbank.

Holding the thin parchment up to the sun, the young boy noticed the incantation the man had said inscribed on it. He pressed it to his book, and it combusted. Keeping a tight grip on the book this time, the boy quickly turned the page to see the word "Levitate" now appearing below "Heal" under the Initiate tier.

"What's in the pouch?" the boy asked. "Reagents. They're used for spell casting. Now hurry up," the man replied.

"Brez Mov Rai," the boy chanted. Suddenly, his feet lifted off the ground, and he flailed his arms to keep his balance.

"Very good, you may be of use after all," the older man said from the other side of the river.

With slow, deliberate steps, the boy walked towards the man, watching as the water flowed quickly beneath his feet, splashes bouncing up and covering his worn leather shoes in droplets of water. The gentle current below created a mesmerizing dance of light and shadow, adding to the surreal experience of walking on water.

He jumped the last step, landing firmly on the ground next to the man.

"Impressive," the man acknowledged, giving a nod of approval. "Now, let's see what else you can do. We have much to accomplish and little time to waste."

As they reached the opposite bank, the boy could see more clearly the extent of the devastation. The once-thriving village was now reduced to ruins, blackened timbers and smouldering ashes painting a grim picture.

"Now, that spell only lasts a short period and consumes your mana as you use it," the man said before turning away and walking towards the ruins.

"What happened here?" the boy asked, walking beside the man and scanning his eyes over the smoking timber beams and fire-scarred sandstone blocks.

"A daemon," the man replied. "When a creature is summoned that is above the power of the mage, it turns wild and uncontrollable."

"A summoned daemon? Who would summon one of those?" the boy asked, a look of confusion crossing his face.

"Hmm," the man said, looking down at the boy. "Worse than I thought," he added as he looked back up at the ruins.

"I've had enough of the riddles, old man. Just tell me already!" the boy spat angrily.

"I will, when the time is right. Gather what you can and meet me back at the hut," the man said as he walked off, leaving the boy behind in the ruined village.

"Do this, do that. Seems familiar," the boy muttered, rummaging through one of the burnt-out houses and collecting food and items untouched by the flames.

As he turned to leave, he noticed a large beam across the floor of a small room. Red embers still alighted along its length as smoke rose into the air. Beneath it, he spotted the large body of a man trapped.

Suddenly, his mind raced with flashbacks of memories. Images flashed before his eyes of the fire raging through the village and the falling debris.

"I did this," he said, falling to his knees and clutching his head in pain. He felt the fingers of a large hand dig into his ankle as a hand gripped his leg.

Terror filled him as he realized the body beneath the beam was not lifeless. The man's eyes flickered open, filled with pain and desperation. "Boy," he rasped, his voice barely audible over the crackling embers.

The boy's heart pounded in his chest. He scrambled to lift the beam, but it was too heavy. "I... I can't do it alone, father," he cried out, tears welling up in his eyes. He felt the weight of guilt and responsibility pressing down on him as heavily as the beam itself.

Summoning his courage, he remembered the spell the old man had taught him. "Cre Hea," he whispered, placing his hands on the injured man's chest. A cloud of smoke emanated from his palms. The man's breathing remained laboured, his life slipping away.

"Malkhia..." the man murmured, his grip on the boy's leg loosening. "I forgi..."

The boy's eyes widened in horror as he realized the man was beyond saving. "No, please," he begged, but the man's eyes glazed over, his body going limp.

A cold shiver ran down the boy's spine as he looked at the lifeless figure before him. He felt slender fingers press into his collarbone as a hand clasped his shoulder.

"Come now, Malkhia," the man's voice sounded from behind him.

❖ ❖ ❖ ❖

alkhia's eyes shot open as he saw an old man holding his shoulder, attempting to wake him up. His instinct kicked in, and he threw a fist towards the man.

"Ahh, too slow," the man chuckled, stepping to the side to avoid the punch.

"What, where am I?" Malkhia said as he sat up quickly, his heart pounding.

"I've heard that before," the man chuckled once more, taking a seat at the small table in the centre of the room.

"Eldric?" Malkhia asked, rubbing his temple to ease the headache.

"The one and only. What brings you back here, young one?" Eldric said, taking a drink from a small cup.

"I was looking for your help. You didn't need to paralyse me and knock me out," Malkhia said, swinging his legs off the bed.

"Had to be sure you weren't followed, which you were," Eldric replied.

"Followed? They would just be my party, no threat from them," Malkhia said, trying to understand the situation.

"Aye, the four are no threat. But the other two. Must be after the item you possess," Eldric said, his tone serious.

"Other two?!" Malkhia asked, his voice tinged with urgency and shock.

"A gnome and a dwarf. I could smell them from a mile away. You've grown weak, Malkhia," Eldric said, rising to his feet, his weight heavily resting on an old, gnarled wooden staff.

"I need to get back to them!" Malkhia said, panic rising. He ran towards the door, pushing it with enough force to almost break it off the brass hinges. Bursting outside, he was greeted by the dense forest, the distant sounds of a struggle echoing through the trees.

23

A loud whoosh reverberated through the cavern as the enormous, glistening battle axe sliced through the air. Eric's sinewy fingers tightened around the supple leather handle, his weathered face breaking into a wide grin that peeked through the thick tangle of his beard.

"Seems you're rather pleased there, Eric," the king remarked with a playful glint in his eye.

"The finest work of my craft," Eric replied, his voice tinged with pride as he swung the axe high, the weighty head thudding against his shoulder.

"Sir, the carts are nearly filled," a guard interjected, standing stiffly at attention and saluting the pair.

"So soon? Impressive work," the king acknowledged with a nod, dismissing the guard with a wave.

"Shall we press on or retreat?" the king inquired, turning to Eric for counsel.

"The carts won't squeeze through that passage, my lord," Eric pointed out.

"Ah, a valid observation. Backwards it is," the king conceded, deftly slinging his pack onto his back.

The company swiftly dismantled their camp, the dimly lit mine amplifying the sounds of creaks and groans as the men strained against the weight of carts laden with freshly mined Amethystite ore. Water sloshed around their boots with each step, the cavern floor dotted with shallow puddles reflecting the flickering torchlight.

"I wonder how Serpentia is managing in my absence," the king pondered aloud, walking alongside Eric beside one of the laden carts.

"I'm certain all is well; Belfor is there to assist your son, and you know Charlotte and Gwen are more than capable," Eric reassured him, casting a glance up at the king.

"You're likely right. But that boy... not cut out for leadership, yet he's my only heir. Why must children be so perplexing?" the king chuckled softly, shaking his head.

"Nevertheless, I'd say this venture has been a success. Would you not agree, Eric?" the king asked, scanning the surroundings.

"Eric?" the king called out suddenly, realizing Eric had vanished from sight.

"Men! Halt!" The king's command echoed through the cavern, bringing the party to an abrupt standstill. Ore clattered against the sides of the carts, causing several men to stagger forward from the force.

A piercing yell reverberated through the dimly lit tunnels, drawing everyone's attention towards its source.

"Quickly, men!" the king shouted, throwing his pack to the ground and unsheathing his exquisitely crafted longsword. With urgency driving their steps, the king and a group of men sprinted towards the fading cries, the sound leading them to a crossroads within the mine.

"This way!" the king directed sharply, veering left at the intersection.

"Eric!" The king's voice rang out, punctuated by laboured breaths and the heavy thud of his steel boots against the stone floor.

Rounding the corner, the king's gaze fell upon Eric, ensnared by thick, purple thorny vines, being dragged by a large shadowy figure. A guard swiftly followed the king, his bow drawn and an arrow nocked, taking aim at the creature.

The arrow struck true but rebounded harmlessly off the creature's hide, leaving it unscathed.

"Leave me!" Eric's voice rang out as he watched the king charge toward the beast. With a swift motion, the creature turned, its massive arm swinging towards the king and knocking him sideways into the cavern wall.

From the creature's other arm, thick, purple vines shot out towards the king, wrapping tightly around the lower half of his abdomen. The coils squeezed fiercely, pressing the air from the king's lungs.

Footfalls echoed as the remaining guards rushed into the fray. A volley of arrows rained down on the beast, eliciting a deep, guttural growl that reverberated off the cavern walls. The sound was so intense that loose stones rattled and fell, forcing the guards to drop their weapons and cover their ears to shield themselves from the powerful soundwaves.

The vibrations from the guards' assault caused the vines entwined around Eric's legs to loosen, allowing him to shuffle free from the creature's grip. With swift determination, he slung his axe over his shoulder and swung it with all his might down onto the creature's arm.

A resounding crunch filled the chamber as the axe cleanly sliced through the limb. Purple blood oozed from the wound, staining the floor as the creature let out an even louder roar of pain, retracting its injured appendage back into itself.

The deafening roar echoed in Eric's ears, causing a warm liquid to trickle from them. He glanced over at the king, seeing him teetering on the edge of consciousness, his strength waning.

Eric sprinted towards the king, his axe raised high. With a swift, powerful swing, he brought the axe down on the vines ensnaring the king. The sharp blade severed the thick, purple tendrils, causing them to slacken, and the king gasped for air, relief washing over his face.

Meanwhile, the creature recoiled against the cavern wall, emitting a piercing shriek. Eric pivoted towards it, determination etched on his face. He charged forward, axe held aloft, and leaped into the air. With a primal yell, he drove the axe deep into the creature's shoulder.

Locked in a fierce gaze with the creature, Eric felt the weight of its deep purple eyes staring into his soul. The creature's gaping maw snapped towards him, trying to dislodge the axe. Eric's grip began to falter under the creature's relentless assault, and he fell to the ground, stumbling back, watching as the beast dropped heavily to its knees with a resounding thud.

Seizing the moment, Eric lunged at the beast once more. He planted his foot on its knee, using it as leverage to launch himself high into the air. With a swift, fluid motion, he grasped the axe handle and wrenched it free. Momentum carried him in a full circle, and with a mighty swing, he brought the axe down upon the creature's bulky neck.

In a single, clean stroke, the axe severed the head from the body. Eric landed on his feet, chest heaving with exertion, as he watched the creature's head roll across the cave floor. The body slumped limply to the ground with a heavy thud, purple ichor flowing freely from the gaping wound and pooling on the rocky ground.

"King!" Eric called out, rushing towards the king, who was slumped against the cavern wall, his breath laboured and his body weakened.

Eric slid to his knees beside the king, placing a steadying hand on the king's chest and tilting his head up to meet his gaze. The king coughed violently, a spray of blood bursting from his lips and splattering the ground between them.

"Think I'll have a rest now," the king murmured with a weary smile, his voice a mere whisper against the backdrop of the cavern's eerie silence.

"You'll be okay, we can get you out of here," Eric insisted, his voice trembling with urgency. "Quickly, empty a wagon and bring it here!" he barked, turning his head towards the guards.

"There's no need, Eric," the king replied, his tone softening with a touch of finality. "This is it, old friend. It's been good." He struggled to draw breath, each word laborious, punctuated by painful coughs that sprayed blood across his lips and chin.

Eric glanced down at his blood-stained hands; fingers slick with crimson from the deep gashes in the king's abdomen caused by the thorns of the vines.

"You found it, though. I'm glad," the king continued, his eyes shimmering with a mix of pride and sorrow as he coughed again, blood pooling at the corners of his mouth despite Eric's efforts to staunch it.

"Just hold on," Eric said, his voice breaking as he gently shook the king, trying to keep him awake. The king's head began to droop, his eyes losing their light.

"Look after Charlotte," the king said, his voice barely a whisper, as he locked eyes with Eric. A faint smile touched his lips before his body went limp, the last breath escaping his lungs, leaving his eyes staring vacantly into the abyss.

24

Sekt signalled Durnek with a quick, precise hand motion as they manoeuvred along the jagged remains of a ruined building. The cold stone pressed against their backs as they edged closer to the unsuspecting party, their footsteps muffled by the debris underfoot. The air was thick with tension as they navigated through the eerie silence of the shattered structures.

"Are we killing them? Sylvaris said to follow only," Durnek asked in a hushed tone, barely audible amidst the quiet rustling of leaves, flowing river, and distant forest sounds.

Sekt shook his head decisively, his expression serious, and brought a finger to his lips to silence Durnek. From his pack, he retrieved a pair of bolas crafted meticulously from sturdy vines and smooth, rounded rocks.

"Ahh, worth more alive," Durnek said, spotting Sekt holding the weapon.

Sekt stepped into the open and began to swing one bola overhead, building momentum before releasing it with practiced precision. The weapon sailed through the air, finding its mark with a sharp snap as it ensnared the torso of a large, bald man, immobilizing his arms against his waist.

Swift as a shadow, Sekt swiftly launched the second bola. This one found the legs of a small, blonde elven woman, causing her to stumble and collapse with a startled gasp.

Meanwhile, Durnek surged forward, his warhammer spinning like a deadly dance of steel and fury. The handle connected with one of the party members, a resounding thud echoing through the ruins as the blow struck the man's temple, rendering him unconscious instantly.

Unfazed, Sekt calmly aimed his crossbow. With a quiet hiss, a small, blue-tipped arrow shot forth and struck a slender, black-haired woman in the arm. She crumpled to the ground, her body going slack as she succumbed to the tranquilizing poison.

"I'll kill you all!" the large man roared in defiance, his struggles against the entangling vines of the bola growing more desperate by the moment.

"Ha! Good luck with that," Durnek retorted with a grim chuckle, delivering a swift, decisive blow to the man's head with the handle of his warhammer. The man slumped unconscious.

With a grunt of effort, Durnek heaved the unconscious woman onto his broad shoulders and sprinted towards Sekt, who was already darting away into the dense foliage of the surrounding forest.

"You won't get far!" a female voice shouted after them, the urgency in her tone echoing through the ruins.

"Should have killed them," Durnek muttered breathlessly as he caught up with Sekt, their pace relentless as they plunged deeper into the dense undergrowth.

"How do we get away, anyway?" Durnek asked between laboured breaths, his voice tinged with urgency and determination as they navigated the winding paths through the ancient woods.

Sekt reached into a small pouch at his side and withdrew a scroll tied with a vibrant red ribbon, handing it swiftly to Durnek.

"Ah, Nymira gave you a portal scroll. Lucky," Durnek exclaimed with relief, his grip tightening on the scroll as they pressed onward, the pursuit echoing faintly in the distance behind them.

The pair came to an abrupt halt behind the trunks of a cluster of towering trees, their breaths laboured from the frantic sprint through the dense forest. Durnek gently lowered the unconscious woman to the forest floor, his hands trembling with urgency as he unfurled the scroll.

"Tree Angle Movie," Durnek chanted, his voice echoing faintly through the quiet woods. Nothing happened.

Sekt furrowed his brow, giving Durnek a puzzled look, and tapped the words on the scroll with a sharp, curved finger. "Alright, alright, I'm no good at magic, or reading," Durnek muttered in frustration, clearing his throat before trying again.

"Trea Ango Mov," he intoned once more. This time, a bolt of shimmering blue light shot down from the scroll, striking the ground before them. The air around the impact point began to swirl and shimmer, gradually coalescing into a shimmering portal.

With a swift, practiced motion, Durnek turned to scoop up the unconscious woman into his arms. As he did, an arrow whizzed past his head, embedding itself deeply into the trunk of a nearby tree. Without hesitation, Durnek hefted the woman onto his shoulders and dashed towards the portal, Sekt close on his heels.

The swirling energies of the portal crackled and hummed as they approached, its threshold pulsating with arcane energy. With a final burst of speed, Durnek and Sekt leaped through the portal just as it began to shrink and vanish behind them, leaving the forest eerily silent once more.

Malkhia leapt onto his horse and urged it into a gallop, racing back through the dense forest towards the river and away from the secluded hut. The rhythmic pounding of hooves echoed against the trees, mingling with the distant sounds of struggle and hurried footfalls.

As Malkhia drew closer to where he had left his companions, the forest suddenly fell silent. Without hesitation, he spurred his horse forward, leaping into the swift-flowing river. The horse fought against the current, its powerful legs churning water as it clambered onto the opposite bank.

Reaching the spot where he had last seen his friends, Malkhia's heart sank. Horethian lay bound and unconscious, his head bearing large, bloody contusions from a blunt object. A few feet away, Theo lay in a similar state, unmoving.

Quickly dismounting, Malkhia rushed over to them, his mind racing with questions. "What the hell happened here?" he muttered to himself, scanning the area for any signs of their assailants.

"Malk! They took Leyla!" a voice called out from the edge of the forest.

Malkhia's head snapped up at the sound of Atlas's voice. He rose to his feet, concern etched on his face as she approached, panting heavily from her run.

"What happened, Atlas?" Malkhia demanded, his voice tense with worry and urgency.

"A gnome and a dwarf ambushed us," Atlas gasped between panting breaths. "They tranquilized Leyla with something and fled into the forest. I almost got one, but they escaped through a portal."

Malkhia's brow furrowed deeply with concern as he knelt beside Horethian, the urgency in Atlas's words sinking in. Placing his palm gently on Horethian's forehead, he began to chant a quick healing spell, his voice a steady murmur against the tense silence of the forest. Horethian's eyes snapped open with a jolt, and Atlas swiftly cut away the bindings with her dagger, her eyes darting around nervously as she watched him rub his head in confusion.

"What the hell was that?" Horethian muttered, his voice groggy as he scanned their surroundings, trying to piece together what had happened.

"We were ambushed," Atlas explained, her tone edged with frustration and worry as she stood up, her eyes never leaving the forest's edge where the ambushers had vanished. She watched intently as Malkhia repeated the healing process with Theo, his palm glowing softly with healing energy.

"Leyla!" Theo's voice rang out, full of panic and concern as he shot upright, his eyes wide with fear and confusion.

"They took her," Atlas confirmed with a heavy sigh, her shoulders slumping slightly with the weight of their predicament.

"Where?! We need to get her back! I promised to protect her," Theo exclaimed, springing to his feet. He grabbed his bag, slinging it onto his back with a determined expression.

"Mercenaries," a gruff voice called out from a distance. The group turned to see an old man approaching, leaning heavily on a gnarled vine-covered staff. His weathered face was partially obscured by a long, unkempt beard dotted with plant leaves, and his eyes glinted with a mix of wisdom and mischief. "No doubt after the map you have," he continued as he joined the group, his presence commanding attention.

Atlas instinctively drew an arrow and notched it, her bowstring taut as she aimed at the approaching figure. Her eyes narrowed with suspicion. Malkhia's hand came down gently on her bow, pushing it toward the ground.

"This is Eldric, who we came to see to decode the map," Malkhia explained, his voice calm but firm.

"Eldric the Mad?!" Atlas echoed in shock, her gaze darting between Malkhia and the old man, her grip on the bow loosening but her stance still wary.

"Haven't heard that name in a while," Eldric said with a chuckle, his voice gravelly but warm. He leaned more heavily on his staff, the wood creaking under his weight.

"How do you know so much, old man?" Atlas asked sceptically, sliding the arrow back into her quiver but keeping a cautious eye on Eldric.

Malkhia nodded in agreement. "Yes, how do you?"

Eldric chuckled softly, his eyes twinkling with ancient wisdom. "Ah, you forget so much, young Malkhia. Knowledge is power," he replied cryptically, his voice carrying a hint of mystery.

He lowered himself onto a flat pile of sandstone, settling in with the ease of someone accustomed to the ways of the wild. "They will be heading to Serpentia with your friend. The prince hired them quite some time ago to find you," Eldric continued, his gaze distant as if peering through time itself.

Eldric tossed Malkhia a small pouch, the weight of it familiar in his hand. "This will top up your reagents. I sense you're low. Also, I cannot help with decoding this map, but I have a contact in Helge who can help. Seek out Ruela; she will be able to assist you," Eldric explained with a knowing look, his voice carrying the weight of his years.

"Thank you," Malkhia replied gratefully, his gaze dropping to the pouch of reagents in his hand, his thoughts already turning to their next steps.

"Be careful, Malkhia, that is no ordinary map. This will be the last we meet, young one. I'm not long for this world," Eldric grunted as he rose to his feet, leaning heavily on his staff for support.

"I hope you find your friend and what you're looking for with that map of yours," he continued, his eyes distant as if pondering times long past.

"Thank you again, Eldric, for everything," Malkhia said sincerely, his voice filled with respect and gratitude.

Eldric waved Malkhia's thanks away with a dismissive gesture and began to shuffle back down the riverbank toward his humble hut, disappearing into the dense forest beyond.

"How do you know him?" Atlas asked, her expression a mix of curiosity and puzzlement as she turned to Malkhia.

"He took me in when I was just a boy," Malkhia answered quietly, his eyes following Eldric's fading figure into the shadows of the forest. "But there's no time for stories now. We need to get Leyla back," he said firmly, his voice resolute as he flipped open his rune book.

"Gather your belongings quickly. We're heading to Serpentia," Malkhia commanded, his tone leaving no room for debate as he began to chant the intricate portal spell, the runes glowing softly under his touch.

25

The prince let out a heavy sigh as he sank into the plush armchair by the grand window of his chamber. His fingers drummed impatiently on the armrest before he snapped his gaze toward the servant lingering in the doorway.

"Bring me that wench from the throne room!" he barked, his voice laced with irritation.

The servant stiffened. "At once, Sire," he replied, bowing before turning swiftly on his heels.

"And more wine!" the prince added, shaking the nearly empty flagon, watching the last dregs swirl at the bottom.

"Of course, Your Grace," the servant acknowledged before disappearing down the hall.

With another weary sigh, the prince poured the remaining liquid into his goblet and took a slow sip, his gaze drifting toward the sprawling city beyond his window. The flickering torches and moonlight cast long shadows over the grey cobblestone buildings stretching into the distance. A smirk curled on his lips.

"My city," he murmured, savouring the thought. "All mine."

A deep voice cut through his reverie.

"My Grace."

The prince turned slightly, recognizing the speaker. "Ah, Sharl. What news do you bring?"

"The boy still refuses to talk," Sharl reported, his tone edged with certainty. "Unfortunately, I believe he is on the verge of mentally breaking."

"Push him harder," the prince ordered, raising his goblet to his lips. "We need to know where my sister fled and what plans they have."

"As you wish," Sharl responded, his face betraying no emotion.

He stepped aside as another servant entered, clutching a fresh bottle of wine in one hand and dragging a woman behind him with the other. She was striking, bronzed skin, long waves of dark hair cascading over her shoulders, and deep, defiant eyes that flickered with anger.

The servant set the bottle down beside the prince, then shoved the woman forward before dropping to one knee in a respectful bow. Without another word, he retreated, leaving the chamber.

The prince leaned forward slightly, his tongue running over his lips as his gaze roamed over the woman's form.

"Get the information, Sharl," he said, not taking his eyes off her. "Leave me."

With a silent nod, Sharl turned and exited, the heavy wooden door closing behind him with a resonant thud.

"You have been evading me, yes?" the prince said, his voice cutting through the silence like a blade.

"Of course not, my prince," the woman replied, though hesitation wove through her words. Her hands fidgeted in front of her, eyes cast downward, avoiding his piercing gaze.

The prince rose from his chair with slow, deliberate movements. In a flash, he seized her wrist and yanked her forward, forcing her onto the bed. She gasped, her back pressing into the silk sheets as he loomed over her.

"No evading this time," he murmured, placing a knee on either side of her before leaning down, his weight pinning her in place.

His fingers moved to his belt, unfastening the buckle, and sliding it free. The leather hissed as it left the loops, a slow, deliberate sound. His other hand reached for the fabric of her blouse, gripping it firmly at the collar. His fingers curled around the fabric, holding it taut as he studied her expression, his smirk deepening at the fear flickering in her eyes.

"My prince!" a voice bellowed suddenly, the heavy wooden door flying open with a crash.

The prince's head snapped up, his expression darkening.

"For heaven's sake, what now?" he barked, irritation seething in his tone.

The man in the doorway kept his gaze fixed on the ground, his posture tense. "Apologies, my lord.

Mercenaries have arrived. They claim to have a captive of importance."

The prince exhaled sharply; his patience worn thin. He cast one final, lingering glance at the woman beneath him before rolling off the bed, sliding his belt back through its loops with slow, practiced movements.

"Show them to the throne room," he ordered, fastening the buckle with an audible snap.

Then, turning back to the woman, his lips curled into a smirk.

"We will continue later."

He straightened, adjusting his clothes with a haughty air before stepping away from the bed. As he approached the door, he glanced over his shoulder, his gaze cold and unbothered.

With a final, dismissive flick of his fingers, he turned the handle and stepped out, the heavy door slamming shut behind him. The sound echoed in the empty room, leaving the woman alone in the dim, oppressive silence.

❖ ❖ ❖ ❖

A tall elven warrior strode down the red-carpeted throne room, his movements fluid and measured. One hand rested lightly on the hilt of his katana, fingers idly brushing the leather grip. Behind him, a small gnome and a stocky, bearded dwarf followed closely, leading a captive woman by a short rope. A rough hessian sack concealed her head, her posture tense beneath her bindings.

Sharl, standing at the base of the throne, watched their approach with mild amusement.

"Sylvaris," he greeted with a nod. "A pleasure, as always."

Sylvaris halted at the foot of the dais, dipping his head in acknowledgment.

"The prince will be with us shortly," Sharl added.

As if on cue, the prince stepped through the grand archway, his sharp gaze sweeping over the assembled mercenaries before settling on Sharl. He moved leisurely toward his throne, his expression one of intrigue and expectation.

"Good news, I hope," he mused, lowering himself onto the cushioned seat.

"My prince," Sylvaris said, bowing deeply. "I am Sylvaris, and I believe we have something of interest to you."

"Out with it, then," the prince snapped, impatience flickering in his eyes.

"Of course, my lord," Sylvaris replied smoothly, straightening. "We located the adventurers. They have the map you seek, but it is encrypted. We were unable to steal it, but we did manage to capture one of their own."

He gestured toward the dwarf, who promptly passed him the rope. With a swift, practiced motion, Sylvaris yanked the captive forward, forcing her onto her knees before the throne. He reached down and tore the sack from her head.

The woman gasped, her eyes darting around the room, her breath hitching as she took in her surroundings. Panic flickered in her gaze.

The prince leaned forward, resting his elbows on his knees as he studied her.

"And who might you be?" he asked, his voice smooth but laced with amusement.

She lifted her chin, her expression hardening. "Piss off."

A chuckle rumbled from the prince's throat. "Feisty one, I see."

His smirk widened as he reclined lazily into his throne.

"Take her with the others. See what you can extract from her," he ordered, waving a dismissive hand.

Two guards stepped forward, grabbing the rope from Sylvaris's grasp before dragging the woman toward the corridor. She struggled briefly, but they held firm, hauling her out of the throne room.

The prince exhaled, his fingers tapping idly against the armrest. "I must have that map. Retrieve it!"

"As you wish, my lord," Sylvaris said, bowing once more.

The prince shifted his gaze to Sharl. "See that they are paid, at least in part, for their troubles."

Sharl smirked. "Of course, my prince."

The prince settled back into the throne, a satisfied gleam in his eyes.

Leyla crashed onto the cold stone floor of the hallway, twisting against the rough rope cinched tightly around her torso. She fought against the guard's grip, pressing her arms hard against her body to resist his pull.

"I don't have time for this," the guard muttered, tightening his hold and dragging her across the floor.

"Let me go!" she cried, her legs kicking wildly as her feet scrambled for purchase, trying to slow him down.

"It's easier if you come willingly," the guard grunted, barely glancing at her struggles as he hauled her forward.

With a huff of frustration, he turned to his companion. "Sort her out. I can't drag her the whole way."

The other guard nodded, stepping forward without hesitation. He gripped his halberd, raising it high before slamming the blunt end against the side of her head.

A sharp burst of pain exploded through Leyla's skull. She barely registered the warm trickle of blood before her vision blurred the world around her, spinning as everything faded into darkness.

A loud clang jolted her awake. The unmistakable sound of a heavy steel door slamming shut echoed through the damp space. Her breath came in shallow gasps as she blinked groggily, the pounding in her head making it hard to think.

Her hands, now free of their bindings, pressed against the slick, wet stone floor. Slowly, she lifted herself upright, her muscles aching from the rough treatment.

As her vision adjusted, she took in the iron bars surrounding her.

Her pulse quickened as she shuffled back against the wall, pressing into the cold stone for stability. Two other cells came into view, just beyond hers. Swallowing hard, she called out.

"Where am I?"

A voice, young but sharp with defiance, answered from the shadows.

"I will tell you nothing!"

Leyla's head snapped toward the voice, her eyes scanning the dimly lit cell. In the corner, a malnourished young boy sat curled up, his tattered clothing clinging to his frail frame. Dried blood crusted his skin, his hollow eyes filled with defiance.

"Who are you?" she asked, her voice cautious.

"I will tell you nothing!" the boy shouted again; his tone sharp with mistrust.

Leyla exhaled, deciding not to press him further. Instead, she shifted her gaze across the room, her eyes adjusting to the darkness. Another cell sat just beyond the boy's, its occupant deathly still.

She squinted, trying to make out the shape. Another small boy, motionless on the floor. Then, without warning, the stench hit her. A wave of rot filled her nostrils, making her recoil, her head snapping back as her hands shot up to pinch her nose.

Her stomach twisted. "How long has this one been here?" she murmured.

Turning back to the living boy, still huddled in the corner, his silence felt heavier than before.

"Please hurry, Theo," she sobbed to herself, her voice barely above a whisper as she buried her face in her hands.

Before she could dwell on her thoughts and past trauma, the heavy creak of a door swinging open made her lift her head.

A tall man strode into the chamber, his polished armour gleaming even in the dim light. His hand rested idly on the pommel of his sword, his movements slow and deliberate as he took in the scene before him.

"Awake and settling in, I see," he said, his voice carrying the confidence of someone in complete control.

His gaze flickered toward the boy in the corner. "Are you being a good roommate, boy?"

"Nothing!" the boy spat back.

The man chuckled. "As usual. Apologies for the company. He's not much for conversation."

Leyla scoffed, glaring up at him. "You could do something about the smell in here."

The man's amused expression didn't waver. Instead, his eyes drifted lazily to the corpse in the nearby cell.

"We could," he said, tilting his head slightly. "Or we could not."

His gaze snapped back to her, his smile fading. "Now, tell me your name."

Leyla straightened, meeting his eyes with a smirk. "I will tell you nothing."

The man let out a soft laugh, shaking his head. "You two will get on well, I see."

Without another word, he turned to the guards standing by the door.

"Dispose of the corpse," he ordered, gesturing toward the rotting body. "We have enough rats in this castle as it is."

Then, without sparing her another glance, he strode out of the room, the door slamming shut behind him.

26

Eric's boots thudded against the wet cave floor, each step sending droplets of water splashing against the rough stone walls. The air was thick with dampness, carrying the scent of salt and earth. His head hung low, his thoughts as heavy as the lifeless body beside him, wrapped tightly in a large white sheet, a king reduced to a fragile burden.

"Not long now, sir," one of the guardsmen called back, his voice echoing in the cavern's depths.

Eric barely heard him. His gaze lingered on the shrouded form.

"I told you to leave me, you fool," Eric muttered, but his words carried no real anger, only exhaustion.

The cave mouth yawned open ahead, spilling harsh, blinding sunlight into the gloom. The group squinted as they stepped out onto the beach, where the world was loud and restless. Waves crashed violently against jagged black rocks, spraying mist into the salty air. In the distance, gulls cawed overhead, circling the anchored ship that waited like a silent sentinel in the bay.

On the shore, men worked swiftly, pushing ore-laden carts across the damp sand toward the waiting rowboats.

"Load the boats. We set off before nightfall," Eric commanded. His voice was firm, cutting through the crashing surf, and the men obeyed without hesitation.

Crates of ore were heaved into the small wooden boats, the wood groaning under the weight. One by one, the vessels shoved off, their oars slicing cleanly through the waves as they made for the large ship. High above, the crow's nest swayed atop the towering mast, bobbing with the ocean's restless rhythm.

A deep, resonant horn bellowed from the ship's hull. A low, mournful sound that rippled across the water, announcing the return of its crew. Thick rope ladders unravelled down the side, slapping into the churning sea.

"That's all the ore, sir," one of the men reported.

"Very good. Now help me with the king."

With care, they lifted the king's body and carried him to the last remaining rowboat. Eric stepped aboard last, the wooden planks creaking beneath his weight.

As they reached the ship, rough hands pulled them up one by one. A sailor grasped Eric's forearm, steadying him as he climbed over the railing. "Sir, what happened?" the man asked, eyes darting to the sheeted corpse.

"Elemental," Eric said flatly, brushing past him without another word.

He barely heard the murmurs of the crew as he strode across the deck. There was no time for grief, nor for questions that led nowhere. "Raise the anchor and lower the sails. We head home."

The ship stirred to life. At the bow, two men turned the massive wooden wheel, the thick chain groaning as it hoisted the steel anchor from the depths. Around them, the crew worked in practiced unison, loosening ropes, tightening knots, unfurling sails.

With a final tug, the last binding was loosed, and the dark red sails billowed open. The fabric snapped taut, swallowing the wind and transforming the ship from a stagnant relic into a force of motion.

The crew's rhythmic chant filled the deck, their voices rising with purpose. Each man knew his task, his duty etched into calloused hands and sun-worn skin.

As the ship surged forward, the coastline shrank behind them. A ghost of frantic moments past. Before them, the sea stretched vast and untamed, a realm of peril and promise. The prow sliced through the whitecaps, sending a fine mist spraying over the deck, a baptism of salt for the journey ahead.

Inside the captain's quarters, Eric stood alone, his back to the door, his shoulders heavy with unspoken burdens. Through the small window, he watched the ocean churn beneath the setting sun, the waves shifting endlessly, as merciless as fate itself.

 ❖ ❖ ❖ ❖

Charlotte's eyes fluttered open, adjusting to the dim glow filtering through the makeshift curtain that separated her small room from the bustling resistance hideout. The muffled sounds of conversation and clattering dishes filled the air beyond the heavy fabric.

She sat up, swinging her legs over the edge of the bed, rubbing the sleep from her eyes before stretching her arms overhead, stifling a yawn.

"I haven't slept that well in a while," she murmured to herself.

Pushing herself to her feet, she walked towards the curtain, gripping its edge and pulling it aside just enough to peek out. The underground refuge was alive with movement. Townsfolk hurrying about their tasks, voices overlapping in steady chatter.

"Ahh, you're awake," Hilda's voice came from the side. Charlotte turned just in time to see the woman approach; arms crossed but with a welcoming expression.

"We weren't sure when you'd wake up."

Charlotte stepped out and let the curtain fall back into place, offering a sheepish smile. "I'm sorry, I must have been exhausted."

Hilda waved a hand dismissively. "No apologies, Princess. It's perfectly fine."

She gestured toward the main area. "Come, let's get some food in you. Then, I have someone for you to meet."

Charlotte followed as Hilda led her to an empty table near the edge of the room. Before she could sit, a young boy rushed over, balancing two plates piled with bacon, eggs, and bread. He set them down carefully, then turned to Charlotte and dropped into a quick bow.

Charlotte's lips curled into a smile. "Thank you."

The boy hesitated for a moment, eyes wide with curiosity, before darting back into the crowd. He didn't go far, though—lingering just enough to sneak another glance.

Hilda let out an exaggerated sigh and swatted at the growing crowd of onlookers. "Back to work! Stop your gawking."

With reluctant grumbles, the gathered townsfolk scattered, returning to their tasks.

Hilda sat down with a shake of her head. "The nerve," she muttered before nodding toward Charlotte's plate. "Eat up. I imagine it's been days since you've had a proper meal."

Charlotte didn't need to be told twice. She picked up a piece of bacon, watching the way the light glistened off its crisp surface before slicing off a small bite and placing it in her mouth.

Hilda chuckled. "No need for formality, we're humble people here." She bit into a stale bread roll, unconcerned by its toughness.

Charlotte hesitated for only a moment before nodding. Abandoning her measured bites, she began eating with more enthusiasm, cutting into her eggs and stuffing forkful after forkful into her mouth.

Hilda grinned, watching with amusement. "Ha! There you go."

"We need to head into the city. There's a man we must speak with; he'll help us plan our next move against the prince," Hilda said, tearing off another chunk of her bread roll.

"Next move?" Charlotte asked, pausing between mouthfuls.

"Yes. We can't let him get away with this. Now finish up, we have a lot to do." Hilda brushed the crumbs from her pink-and-white blouse.

Charlotte hurriedly finished her meal, letting out a loud belch before slapping a hand over her mouth. "Sorry," she muttered with a sheepish laugh.

Hilda chuckled. "Like I said before, Princess, no apologies needed."

She reached for a large brown piece of fabric and handed it to Charlotte. "Put this on. We must be cautious—you're still wanted, and we don't know how far the news has spread."

With that, Hilda led her through the winding tunnels of the underground camp and out into the bustling city streets.

Perched atop a rooftop beyond a small wall, Nymira narrowed her eyes as she spotted movement below.

"Ahh… Who might you be?" she murmured, watching the two women slip into the crowd, a wicked grin curling her lips.

She rose to her feet in one fluid motion and leapt over the edge of the wall. Her black cape billowed as she descended, landing soundlessly on the cobblestone street.

"Quickly," Hilda urged, gripping Charlotte's hand and pulling her closer.

"Where are we going?" Charlotte asked, breathless.

"No time for questions. It's just around the corner."

They darted through the marbled alleyways, weaving through the labyrinthine streets.

"In here!" Hilda beckoned toward a large red door with a small X carved into the wood.

They slipped inside, slamming the door shut with a heavy thud.

From the shadows of the alley, Nymira tilted her head. "Interesting," she mused, stepping toward the door.

She reached out, only to recoil as a pulse of magic flared from the wood, forcing her to withdraw her hand. A slow, knowing smile curled her lips.

"Very interesting."

Inside, Charlotte and Hilda hurried through the dusty, neglected house. Furniture lay scattered, covered in cobwebs from years of abandonment.

"Your friend lives here?" Charlotte asked, wrinkling her nose.

"Sometimes. He moves around a lot," Hilda answered, leading her up a narrow wooden stairway. The faded carpet runner bore the imprint of heavy use, a thick layer of dust dulling its once-rich colours.

As they reached the top, a voice rang out from behind a small, closed door.

"Enter."

Hilda grasped the handle and pushed the door open, the hinges groaning in protest.

A man clad in long purple robes turned to them, an old leather-bound book in hand. "You're getting sloppy in your old age, Hilda. You were followed."

Hilda stiffened. "Followed?"

The man smirked, flipping through the pages of his book. "It's fine. An elven woman—strong, but she can't enter."

He stopped on a page, muttered a few words, "Ahh, here—Trea Ango Mov," and with a flash of blue light, a portal swirled into existence on the floor.

The air crackled as the portal solidified.

"Quickly, before she figures out how to break the ward." He stepped through without hesitation.

Charlotte hesitated, but Hilda grabbed her wrist, yanking her forward.

"No time to be afraid. Move!"

They vanished into the swirling energy, the portal collapsing behind them just as the door exploded inward. Splinters of wood scattered across the room as Nymira stepped inside.

Her gaze fell to the scorched floorboards, still sizzling with residual energy.

"Hmm… portal."

A smirk played at her lips as she knelt, running a hand over the lingering warmth.

"Very interesting indeed."

Nymira rose to her feet, dusting off her cloak. "Well, no use waiting around," she muttered to herself before slipping out of the abandoned house and making her way back toward the city centre.

The streets were alive with movement, merchants hawking their wares, beggars lingering in alleyways, and armoured patrols weaving through the crowd. Nymira navigated the throng with ease, eventually arriving at the entrance of the building Charlotte and Hilda had emerged from earlier.

Glancing around at the rooftops, she noticed the absence of the overwatching guards.

She traced a gloved hand over the rough wooden door. "Must be something worth finding here."

Murmuring an incantation under her breath, she pressed her palm against the wood. A sharp click echoed as the lock yielded to her magic. With a smirk, she pushed the door open and stepped inside.

Her keen gaze swept over the dust-laden floorboards. Faint footprints trailed toward a staircase leading downward. Nymira's smirk deepened.

"Amateurs."

Descending the steps, she let the shadows wrap around her before uttering, "Cre Igni." A surge of magic sharpened her vision, casting the dim basement into stark clarity as if it were daylight.

The footprints continued, guiding her down a narrow hallway lined with crumbling stone walls. At the far end, a massive tapestry hung against the wall, its fabric stirring from an unseen draft.

Nymira approached, fingertips brushing the embroidered surface. "Hmm… what do we have here?"

With deliberate slowness, she peeled back the heavy cloth, revealing a hidden wooden door, left slightly ajar. She leaned forward, peering through the small gap.

Beyond, a vast chamber sprawled before her. An underground hideout teeming with movement. Townsfolk bustled about, shifting crates of supplies, stacking weapons, and exchanging hurried whispers. Oblivious to the predator watching from the shadows.

A wicked grin curled at Nymira's lips. "Found you."

27

Eldric pushed open the door to his ramshackle hut, its rusted hinges groaning in protest. The flickering glow of firelight spilled from within, casting long shadows over the warped wooden planks of the threshold. He stepped inside, the worn floor creaking beneath his weight, and leaned his gnarled staff against the wall beside the entrance. With a quiet click, he shut the door behind him, sealing out the frosty night winds that howled through the tangled trees beyond.

A rancid odour hung thick in the air, a sickly blend of decomposing flesh, bitter oils, and melted wax. The mingling scents clung to the damp walls, sinking into the very bones of the hut.

"I was wondering when you'd come," Eldric muttered, his voice carrying a note of weary amusement as he turned to face the intruder.

A figure sat at the small, uneven table near the hearth, draped in heavy robes as black as a starless night. Shadows pooled within his hood, swallowing his face entirely. His presence seemed to drink in the warmth of the fire, the very air around him laced with a chilling stillness.

"Mind if I join you?" Eldric asked, making his way toward the table.

"By all means," the figure rasped, his voice like charred parchment scraping against stone.

Eldric lowered himself onto the chair, its aged wood creaking beneath him. He leaned back, easing the weight from his aching legs, and folded his arms. "You won't get the map."

The figure remained motionless. "We will."

"Did you decipher it?" The stranger leaned forward slightly. The dim candlelight wavered, struggling against the encroaching darkness within his hood. For the briefest moment, the glow threatened to reveal his features, before a single frozen breath from the figure snuffed it out entirely. The room was left in the ember-glow of the dying fire, the hut suddenly feeling much smaller.

Eldric smirked and tapped the side of his nose twice, his pale eyes glinting with mischief.

"Do it or leave," he said, settling deeper into his chair as if daring the figure to make his move.

"Very well."

The figure raised a hand and snapped his fingers. A spark of reddish light bloomed at his fingertips, pulsing like molten ember before it streaked across the room. It struck Eldric in the chest, and in an instant, his body crumbled into dust. His ragged robes collapsed, settling lifelessly over the chair, and spilling onto the wooden floor.

The figure exhaled slowly, standing. "Old fool."

As he turned toward the door, his gaze lingered on the staff leaning against the wall. A relic of old wood and engraved runes, its aura hummed faintly in the dim light. Without hesitation, he reached for it, curling his gloved fingers around its worn grip.

The moment his hand met the staff, a faint pulse of energy surged through it, like the last heartbeat of something ancient.

The figure hesitated for only a breath, then wrenched open the door and stepped into the frigid night, vanishing into the darkness. Behind him, the silence swallowed the hut, leaving only the lingering scent of death and the soft, dying crackle of the fire.

❖ ❖ ❖ ❖

The city was deathly quiet beneath the pale glow of the moon, its light filtering through the towering trees that loomed over the streets. Shadows stretched across the grey cobblestone, shifting with the breeze. In a secluded alleyway, nestled between the roots of ancient stone walls, a blue light flickered to life, growing brighter until it spilled over the alley like liquid flame.

"We must get her!" Theo burst through the shimmering gateway; his urgency barely contained. The rest of the group followed close behind, their forms briefly silhouetted in the fading glow.

"We will, Theo," Malkhia said firmly, stepping to his side. He placed a steadying hand on the younger man's shoulder. "But we need to scout the castle first, rushing in blind will only get us caught."

"There's no time for that! We need to go now!" Theo's voice wavered between desperation and frustration.

"If you charge in without a plan, you'll end up in a cell right next to her," Horethian muttered, adjusting his pack with a grunt.

Malkhia exhaled slowly, eyes scanning their surroundings before nodding toward a small stone building at the end of the alley. A weathered wooden sign hung above its door, swaying gently in the night breeze. The image of a bubbling cauldron was painted onto its surface.

"We can rest here for the night," Malkhia said. "Regroup, plan our next move."

Theo clenched his jaw but finally gave a short nod. He followed as the group stepped inside.

The warm glow of candlelight greeted them, held aloft by an aging man whose lined face flickered with recognition.

"Malkhia," the man said with a knowing smile. "To what do I owe the pleasure at this hour?"

"Good to see you again, Adrian." Malkhia's expression softened. "We just need a place to stay for the night."

"Of course. Your room is as you left it." Adrian turned toward a door at the back of the room. "I was just heading to bed myself. Take care, Malkhia."

With that, he disappeared into the shadows, leaving the group to their own devices.

Malkhia led them to a small chamber on the second floor. With a snap of his fingers, the dormant candles sputtered to life, their golden glow revealing a room coated in layers of dust. Old, timeworn furniture sat undisturbed, and in the corner sat a rickety table, cluttered with potion bottles, faded scrolls, and brittle books.

"It's not much," Malkhia admitted, setting his staff and bag atop the table. "But it's safe."

A loud growl interrupted the moment. Horethian clutched his stomach.

"Time for food yet?" he asked, casting a hopeful glance at the others.

"We don't have time for this!" Theo snapped.

Atlas stepped forward, placing a calming hand on his chest. "It's okay, Theo. We'll get her back."

His breath hitched, and she noticed the unshed tears pooling in the corners of his eyes.

Malkhia raised a hand, murmuring an incantation under his breath. "Cre Hea Vlas."

Thick smoke curled from the centre of the room, swirling like a living thing before dissipating to reveal a modest pile of fresh fruit and roasted meat. Horethian wasted no time, dropping to the floor and grabbing a large leg bone, gnawing at it loudly while the others sat around the feast.

Atlas wiped a clear patch onto the dusty floor, drawing rough lines with her finger.

"Alright," she said, looking up at them. "Here's the plan."

❖ ❖ ❖ ❖

"**G**et up!" A rough voice barked, followed by a freezing rush of water crashing over Leyla's face. She gasped, jolting awake, her body stiff from the cold, unforgiving stone beneath her.

She wiped the droplets from her face, blinking away the grogginess. "What do you want?" she muttered, her voice hoarse.

"Commander wants to speak with you," the guard grumbled, fumbling with a heavy ring of keys. The iron lock clanked, and the cell door creaked open.

Before Leyla could react, the guard seized her by the arm and yanked her into the dimly lit corridor.

"Tell them nothing!" A boy's voice rang out from a nearby cell.

The guard scoffed and shot a glare toward the bars. "Oh, shut up." With a firm tug, he dragged Leyla forward, her feet stumbling over the uneven stone as they left the cells.

Outside the cell door, the guard turned and stopped before a thick wooden door, its brass handle worn from years of use. "In here," he said, twisting the handle and shoving Leyla inside. The scent of damp stone and mildew mixed with blood filled her lungs.

The door slammed shut behind her, and a cold presence filled the room.

"Sit down." The voice dripped with quiet menace.

Leyla hesitated, scanning her surroundings. The chamber was bare, save for a single wooden chair in the centre. Beside it, a small table sat draped in cloth. The fabric sagged over odd, jagged shapes beneath.

She swallowed hard and sat.

Before she could react, Sharl strode forward, pulling a length of rope from his belt. His grip was firm as he bound her wrists together, tightening the knot until the coarse fibres bit into her skin.

"Henry spent a long time in this room," Sharl mused, stepping back. "I suggest you cooperate… or end up like him."

With a flourish, he ripped the sheet from the table.

A collection of rusted tools glinted in the candlelight—blades, pincers, hooks dulled with age but stained with use.

Leyla's stomach twisted. "I don't know what you want." Her voice wavered despite her effort to stay composed.

Sharl tilted his head, feigning disappointment. "You know exactly what we want."

He reached down, picking up a pair of corroded forging tongs, opening and closing them with a harsh clack.

"The map?" Leyla breathed, her throat dry.

Sharl's lips curled into a slow, cruel smile. "That didn't take long."

He set the tongs down and turned to face her fully. "Have you decoded it?"

Leyla flinched as he unsheathed a dagger from his belt. The steel gleamed for just a moment before he pressed the tip against her cheek.

"I don't know what you mean," she pleaded, twisting her face away.

Sharl's grip clamped down on her chin, holding her still. "Wrong answer."

Pain seared through her skin as he dragged the blade downward, carving a shallow line from her cheek to her chin. Warm blood trickled down her neck, soaking into her tattered clothes.

"Is it decoded?!" Sharl growled, moving the blade to her throat.

Leyla clenched her teeth, her breath sharp. "We went to decode it before I was taken. I don't know what happened after."

Sharl released her, bringing the dagger to his lips. He ran his tongue over the edge, tasting her blood. "Hmm. I believe that."

Sliding the weapon back into its sheath, he smirked. "I suppose I'll be meeting your friends soon. No doubt they'll come for you."

Leyla's glare hardened. "They'll kill you."

Sharl let out a low, amused laugh. With a swift motion, he struck her across the face with the back of his hand.

Pain exploded through her skull as she reeled, her vision blurring.

"They can try."

28

The prince entered his chambers with a wicked grin, his sharp eyes locking onto the woman standing at the foot of his grand wooden bed. She was small, elegantly tanned and petite, her hands clasped tightly to her chest as if she could shrink into herself.

"You've escaped me three times now," he mused, amusement lacing his voice as he unfastened the heavy cape draped over his shoulders. It slid to the floor with a muffled thud.

He took his time undoing the buttons of his silk shirt, his fingers slow and deliberate. "Wine?" he offered, gesturing toward the polished table by the window, where a collection of glass bottles sat, deep red glistening in the candlelight.

The woman shook her head, eyes downcast.

"More for me," the prince muttered, tossing his shirt atop the cape before pouring himself a generous goblet. The dark liquid swirled as he lifted it to his lips, savouring the taste.

"Make yourself comfortable. It will be a long night," he said, his voice thick with cruel intent.

The woman hesitated before sitting on the edge of the bed, her posture stiff, her gaze never lifting from the stone floor.

The prince smirked, stepping closer. "How long have you been in Serpentia?" His tone was light, almost casual, as if this were any other evening conversation.

"Not long, Your Grace," she answered softly.

"No family?"

She shook her head.

His fingers trailed along the rim of his goblet as he studied her. "How did you wind up here?"

The pause before she answered was almost imperceptible. "I was taken as a child by the slavers from my home village," she said carefully.

"Ah, that's right—the desert village." The prince nodded, recalling the details of her capture as if discussing a piece of livestock.

He turned his back to her, refilling his goblet. "You sure you don't want some? The best wine in all of Serpentia."

Again, she shook her head.

A smirk curled at his lips. He set his drink aside, unbuckling his belt with slow, methodical movements before pushing his trousers to the ground.

"You have too many clothes on," he murmured, his voice dark with anticipation.

Then, sharper.

"Off. Now."

He stepped toward her, his shadow looming over her as the candlelight flickered.

And that was when she moved.

Her hands, which had been trembling against her chest, sprang forward. A flash of silver hidden beneath the folds of her sleeve, gleamed in the dim light.

The prince barely had time to react before she drove the thin dagger upward, aiming for his throat.

His instincts saved him. He jerked back, the blade missing its mark, slicing deep across his collarbone instead.

For the first time that night, the wicked grin vanished from his face.

She lunged again.

The prince sidestepped the blade with practiced ease, his smirk twisting into a snarl. Before the woman could strike again, he brought his fist down hard against the back of her head.

She stumbled, a sharp gasp escaping her lips as she crashed onto the cold stone floor.

"Trying to kill the prince?" he spat, shaking the sting from his knuckles.

The woman rolled swiftly, putting distance between them as she rose to her feet. Her breath came in ragged gasps, her fingers tightening around the dagger's hilt.

"You don't deserve life," she hissed, her voice trembling with fury.

Then, without hesitation, she turned and bolted toward the door.

"Guards!" the prince roared, his voice echoing through the chamber as he clutched his bleeding shoulder.

The woman's bare feet pounded against the stone floors as she burst into the dimly lit corridor, her pulse hammering against her ribs. The hallway stretched before her, flickering sconces casting jagged shadows against the towering stone walls.

"Yes, my lord!" a hurried voice called from the far end of the corridor. Heavy boots clattered against the ground, the sharp clank of metal armour growing closer.

"I've been attacked, you fool!" the prince snapped, his voice seething with rage. He glanced down at his shoulder, where blood seeped between his fingers. "Capture her immediately!"

The guard hesitated only a moment before nodding. "Of course, my lord!" He turned sharply, his polished breastplate catching the firelight, then sprinted down the hallway after the fleeing woman.

Her chest grew tighter as she fled from the growing voices of guards on her tail, their shouts echoing like a relentless drumbeat against the towering stone walls. She wove through the labyrinthine hallways of the castle, her breath ragged, heart hammering like a war drum.

The flickering torchlight barely illuminated her path, casting shifting shadows that played tricks on her eyes. She could hear the heavy clang of armoured boots closing in behind her, their rhythm growing faster.

She turned a corner sharply, nearly slipping on the polished marble floor, and pressed forward, forcing her aching legs to move. The castle was vast, but every corridor felt like a dead end, every doorway a trap. She had studied the layout in secret, but now amid the chaos, it blurred in her mind.

The sound of pursuit grew louder.

Her lungs burned. Her muscles screamed.

She had to escape. She had to find a way out before they caught her, before she was dragged back to the monster she had failed to kill.

❖ ❖ ❖ ❖

The moat water splashed against the jagged stone walls of the castle. The faint smell of wet earth and damp moss hung in the air as Theo grunted, his foot slipping on the slick surface of the stone. His heart pounded as his grip wavered, sending small stones cascading into the dark waters below.

"I'm coming, Leyla," he muttered, bracing himself against the wall and finding a firmer foothold. The ancient stone of the castle seemed to stretch on forever.

With one last heave, he pulled himself over the top of the wall, scanning the castle grounds below. The wind howled faintly through the battlements, carrying the scent of the surrounding pine forests. He crouched low, taking a deep breath. The stone tower in the distance caught his eye. A small, crumbling spire at the rear of the castle grounds.

"That must be it," he whispered to himself, narrowing his eyes. The castle was a sprawling fortress, its walls tall and unyielding. In the distance, the sounds of clangs and shouts echoed from the inner courtyard. He moved stealthily along the outer walkway, his leather boots barely making a sound on the weathered stones beneath his feet.

The castle was alive with activity. The sharp clink of armour echoed down the hallways, carried by the wind. He paused, his body pressing into the shadowed corner of an archway as the glow from a distant torch revealed a lone guard entering a small, square outpost.

Theo's fingers slid into his bag, his heart racing. He pulled out a small wooden figurine. With a steady hand, he tossed it behind the guard. As the figurine hit the floor, purple smoke billowed from it, filling the air with an eerie haze. Moments later, the snake took form. A massive, writhing serpent, its scales shimmering like amethyst. The snake wrapped itself around the guard's legs, constricting quickly and silently. The guard's muffled scream was cut off as the serpent coiled tighter, tightening around his neck with deadly precision.

Theo stepped back, a satisfied smile crossing his face. He held out a small bottle; the purple smoke swirled as the snake disappeared into it, leaving only the figurine behind.

"Good job," Theo whispered, slipping the figure back into his pack. With one last glance at the shadowed courtyard, he moved forward toward the tower, his mind focused on Leyla.

The castle felt like a labyrinth, its winding stone halls and passages designed to confuse any intruder. The air was thick with the smell of burning torches.

A faint noise startled Theo, clanging metal echoed through the halls as a tattered woman darted past one of the tower windows. Guards shouted, but the woman was already gone, lost in the maze of the castle's winding passageways.

"What's going on there?" Theo wondered aloud, but he didn't waste time considering it. The mission hadn't changed. He had to reach Leyla before they moved her, or worse. He continued along the tower's outer edge, his pulse quickening with each step.

He reached the door to the tower, his hand cold as he turned the handle. The old iron door creaked open, and Theo slipped inside, blending into the shadows. The stone walls seemed to close in around him as he made his way silently through the dark corridors.

As he neared the tower's staircase leading to the upper levels, the heavy stomp of boots echoed from above, followed by the sound of voices.

"The prince was attacked, find the woman!" a booming voice rang out.

"Yes, commander."

Theo froze. The castle's thick stone walls muffled the voices, but the urgency was clear.

He waited, his back pressed against the cold stone wall as the guards rushed past, their armoured footsteps fading into the distance. His heart raced, but he didn't waste time. He emerged from the shadows and continued up the winding staircase, the smell of damp wood mingling with the stale air of the tower.

At the top of the stairs, he stopped before two heavy wooden doors. He could hear the soft, broken sobs coming from inside. His heart twisted in his chest. He pushed the door open slowly, just enough to peek inside.

Leyla was bound to a chair in the centre of the room, blood staining her clothes. The dim light from a single torch flickered off the stone walls, casting eerie shadows across the floor. The room reeked of decay, of old stone and blood.

"Leyla!" Theo called out, rushing toward her.

Her tear-filled eyes met his, a flicker of recognition passing through her pained expression. "Theo… is it really you?" Her voice was hoarse, barely more than a whisper.

Theo's hand trembled as he cut the ropes around her wrists. "It's me," he whispered, his voice thick with emotion. He gently cupped her bruised cheek, his thumb brushing over the long cut along her skin. The sight of her injuries made his heart ache.

"What have they done to you?" he asked, his voice breaking as he helped her to her feet.

Leyla winced, the pain evident in her eyes, but she stood on shaky legs, trying to hold herself upright. "They… they know about the map. The prince… he was going to kill me…"

Theo clenched his jaw, fighting the rage building inside him. "It's okay," he reassured her, wrapping an arm around her to support her weight. "I got you."

"Where are the others?" she asked, her voice barely a whisper as she leaned against him.

"Shh," Theo whispered, glancing nervously toward the door. "We don't have much time. We need to get out of here."

29

"Sir! Something ahead!" a voice rang out over the crash of the waves.

Eric steadied himself as the ship's bow lifted from the rolling surf before crashing down with a spray of saltwater. He raised his looking glass, adjusting the focus until the blurred outline sharpened into something unmistakable—a towering marble statue rising from the ocean, half-shrouded in mist.

"Tryn," he muttered, lowering the glass and tucking it away.

"Full speed ahead!" Eric called, his voice cutting through the howling wind.

The crew leaped into action, hauling ropes and tightening sails. The ship's wooden hull groaned in protest as the wind filled the rigging, propelling them forward with renewed speed.

"Fly the Serpentia colours," he ordered. A crewman nodded and rushed to raise the deep green flag bearing the emblem of a coiled serpent. It flapped violently in the salty breeze, marking their allegiance as they surged forward.

Then, a cry rang out from the crow's nest.

"Land!"

A rare smile crossed Eric's face as the outline of the port came into view—a sprawling harbor with tall wooden piers stretching into the water like skeletal fingers. Stone walls loomed beyond, encircling the city that nestled against a backdrop of towering cliffs.

"Bring her in steady," he instructed, expertly manoeuvring the ship through the bay. The scent of brine and fish thickened in the air as they closed in on the docks.

"Release the anchor!"

Two men turned the wooden wheel, and the massive steel anchor plunged into the depths, sending up a spray of water as it struck the seabed. The ship rocked slightly before settling.

"Lower the boats," Eric called out to the crew as rowboats began their descent into the rippling water below.

The crew clambered aboard the rowboats and set out in unison towards the dock.

A group of finely dressed men approached; their robes embroidered with sigils of office. Eric adjusted his coat before stepping out of the boat, his boots hitting the weathered wood of the dock with purpose.

"Warmest welcomes," one of the men said, offering a short bow.

"Thank you. I must see the king at once," Eric replied, wasting no time on pleasantries.

The official's expression tightened. "Apologies, but His Majesty is away on political matters."

Eric's jaw clenched. "When will he return?"

"It is not known, sir." The man's voice was calm, but there was an edge of finality to it. "You are welcome to visit the castle once you've finished your business in town. We will provide boarding should you require it."

With a nod, the official turned and strode away, his entourage close behind.

Eric exhaled sharply. "Men, you have free reign until we set sail in two days. We leave with or without you."

A chorus of "Yes, sir!" echoed from the crew.

Eric rolled his shoulders. "I need a drink," he muttered under his breath before heading down the dock.

The port was alive with the bustle of commerce. Workers lugged crates of fresh fish and exotic goods, merchants shouted over one another, and the air was thick with the scent of spices, salt, and burning oil lamps. The cobblestone alley leading to the market was a whirlwind of colours—bright silks, copper trinkets, and hanging lanterns swayed in the ocean breeze.

Eric wound his way through the market until he spotted a wooden sign swinging gently above a tavern door. Painted upon it were two jugs of ale clinking together.

"This will do," he murmured, pushing open the heavy doors.

Inside, the tavern was dimly lit, the air thick with the scent of ale and roasting meat. Laughter and the occasional clash of tankards filled the room.

Eric strode to the bar, where a burly man was polishing a glass with a rag tucked into the waistband of his trousers.

"Your largest jug," Eric said, slapping a few gold coins onto the counter.

"Coming right up." The bartender pulled the tap, filling the jug until foam spilled over the brim.

"Busy night?" Eric asked as the man slid the ale across the bar.

"Can't say, sir, only recently took ownership," the bartender replied.

Eric nodded absently, taking a deep swig before turning to scan the room. His eyes landed on a man at the far end—a loud drunkard sloshing ale onto the floor as he gestured wildly.

"Belfor?"

The man turned, blinking through the haze of alcohol. Then his face split into a wide grin.

"Eric!" Belfor roared, throwing his arms around him, drenching Eric in ale.

Eric sighed. "What are you doing here? You're supposed to be with the prince."

Belfor's expression darkened, his drunken sway momentarily stilling. "Don't even mention that tyrant. He's taken over, Eric… and it's not pleasant."

"Oh, I must take you to Charlotte," Belfor slurred, a man beside him smacking his arm. "You can't mention her, you fool."

Belfor scoffed, swaying slightly. "Oh hush, Arthur. No one's listening." He took another swig, missing his mouth and spilling ale down his shirt.

Eric stepped closer. "Take me there now and spare no detail."

Belfor hesitated, then nodded, his drunken haze momentarily lifting.

"Follow me," he slurred, wiping his mouth. "You're not gonna believe this."

❖ ❖ ❖ ❖

Charlotte stumbled forward as Hilda's firm grip dragged her through the swirling portal. Moonlight shimmered on the gentle waves that lapped at the shore, the rhythmic sound of water meeting sand filling the quiet night. She looked around, disoriented.

They now stood on a small, deserted island—a perfect circle of white sand surrounding a patch of lush, emerald grass. A lone palm tree swayed in the warm ocean breeze, its silhouette stark against the starlit sky.

Leaning against the tree, a man exhaled a thick plume of smoke, the glowing embers of his ornately carved wooden pipe flickering in the dark.

"Welcome, Princess," he said, straightening as he turned to face them.

Charlotte tensed. "Who are you?" she asked, suspicion lacing her voice as she and Hilda stepped closer.

"Just a humble traveller," the man said with a warm smile. "One who shares your goals." He took another slow pull from his pipe, the scent of spiced tobacco curling in the air.

Then his eyes sharpened. "Have you heard from Malkhia?"

Charlotte froze, her heart hammering at the name. She quickly schooled her expression. "Malkhia?" she echoed, feigning ignorance.

The man chuckled knowingly. "Aye, don't be shy. He was a student of a dear friend. Unfortunately, I sense he is no longer with us."

Charlotte's breath caught in her throat. "What do you mean?"

The man tapped his pipe against the tree, letting the ashes fall onto the grass. "Fret not, Malkhia is still among the living and he carries something of great importance, an artifact tied to the fate of this land. I believe I can aid him—by aiding you."

Charlotte hesitated before admitting, "I haven't heard from him in some time." A flicker of worry passed over her face.

"He is well-trained," the man reassured her. "But time is not on our side. You must return to Serpentia and claim the throne."

Charlotte recoiled. "Return?" she snapped. "My brother will kill me."

The man nodded solemnly. "He will try, yes. But for the good of the people, you must face him."

Charlotte clenched her fists. The idea of walking willingly back into the viper's nest sent a chill through her.

"We will regroup in Tryn," the man continued. "Your pursuer has found the rebellion's hideout, I believe."

Hilda's head snapped toward him. "Who has found it?" she demanded, urgency dripping from her voice.

The man flipped through the worn pages of an old leather-bound book, ignoring her question. "There's no time for that," he muttered before waving his hand. A swirling blue portal materialized before them, its light casting eerie shadows across the sand.

"Quickly," he said, stepping through.

Hilda and Charlotte exchanged glances before following.

The world around them shifted, and in an instant, they were inside Hilda's modest chamber, the air thick with candle smoke and parchment. The portal closed behind them with a quiet shimmer as the man waved his hand.

"Hilda! Thank the gods you're back," a young man called as he rushed toward them. His face was flushed with urgency. "There's someone here to see Charlotte."

Charlotte's brow furrowed. "Someone for me?"

"Yes, my lady. He gave no name, but he's short, stocky, and has a long beard."

Hilda's eyes narrowed. "Fetch him."

The boy disappeared and returned moments later with a stout, battle-worn dwarf striding beside him. Behind them, Belfor followed closely, his usually jovial face tense.

Charlotte gasped. "Eric!"

She rushed forward, throwing her arms around him.

"Aye, my princess," Eric said softly, returning the embrace. "But I bear terrible news."

Charlotte pulled back; her breath caught in her throat.

Eric's expression darkened. "Your father… we were attacked while gathering the ore. He fell in battle."

Charlotte staggered, her hands flying to her mouth.

"Father is dead?" she whispered, her voice barely audible.

Eric lowered his head. "Aye. We must return to Serpentia."

Charlotte wiped at the tears brimming in her eyes. "But my brother…"

"I know," Eric said. "Belfor filled me in. We need to stop him."

"I don't know if I can," Charlotte admitted, her voice unsteady.

"I'll fight with you," Eric vowed.

"And I," Belfor declared, stepping beside Eric, his hand clenched over his heart.

"You have the people behind you, Charlotte," Hilda said gently.

The man from the island exhaled, stepping forward. "Hilda, gather the townsfolk. Charlotte must address them."

"Me?" Charlotte looked up, startled.

"Who else?" he said with a smile. "They believe in you. Now show them why."

Charlotte swallowed hard, nodding as she wiped her eyes. Hilda squeezed her shoulder reassuringly before slipping out of the room. Moments later, the sounds of murmuring voices filled the air as the rebels gathered in the open courtyard below.

The man led Charlotte and Eric up a narrow wooden staircase to a raised walkway overlooking the assembled townsfolk. The sea of faces looked up at them, expectant, hopeful, uncertain.

Charlotte's throat felt tight. "My people…" she began, barely above a whisper.

The crowd remained restless, their voices still carrying conversations.

Eric placed a hand on her shoulder, giving her an encouraging nod.

Charlotte took a deep breath and straightened.

"My people!" she called, raising her hands. This time, the murmurs ceased as all eyes turned toward her.

She swallowed her fear.

"Thank you all for standing by me," she began. "When I fled my home, I never imagined I would find others who shared my struggle. But I know now that I am not alone—just as you are not alone."

She paused, scanning their faces.

"The prince has gone too far. He has taken our homes, our families, our freedom. And if we do not stop him now, he will take even more."

A ripple of agreement spread through the crowd.

"I am scared, just as you are," she admitted. "But fear is not a reason to run—it is a reason to fight."

Her voice grew stronger.

"We cannot live in hiding forever! We cannot let fear rule our lives!" She stepped forward. "Stand with me! Fight with me! We must reclaim our home—we must end his reign of terror!"

A moment of silence hung in the air.

Then, a voice rang out—one man raising his fist in the air. "For the princess!"

Another joined.

Then another.

Soon, the entire crowd erupted into a rallying cry, fists raised, voices echoing through the night.

Charlotte's chest tightened with emotion as she looked out at them. These people were ready.

This was no longer just a rebellion.

This was a war.

30

tlas groaned as she was jolted awake by Horethian's loud, rumbling snores. Rubbing the sleep from her eyes, she glanced around the dimly lit camp, her gaze sweeping over the resting figures. But when her eyes landed on an empty bedroll, her breath caught in her throat.

Theo was gone.

She bolted upright.

Heart pounding, she crawled hurriedly toward the vacant space, her fingers brushing the fabric of his abandoned bedroll. Her stomach twisted as she noticed his belongings were missing as well.

Without hesitation, she spun around and scrambled over to Malkhia, shaking him by the shoulders.

"Malk! Malk! Wake up!"

Malkhia groaned, swatting at her hands. "What is it, Atlas?" he muttered groggily, rubbing his eyes.

"Theo's gone."

That snapped him awake. His eyes flew open, sharp and alert.

"I knew he'd do something reckless," Malkhia muttered, already rising to his feet.

"Horethian, wake up," Atlas hissed, shoving at the large man's broad shoulder.

Horethian grunted and rolled over. "Five more minutes..." he grumbled.

Atlas scowled and delivered a swift kick to his ribs.

"Ow! What was that for?" he groaned, clutching his side as he sat up.

"Theo's gone. He left to save Leyla," she said, urgency in her voice.

"By himself?" Horethian asked, his drowsiness evaporating.

"Yes, it appeared that way," Malkhia confirmed, slinging his pack over his shoulder. "We need to move—now."

Atlas grabbed her bow and quiver, slinging them over her back, while Horethian lumbered to his feet, reaching for his sword.

The three of them hurried out of the small house and into the silent city streets. The darkness pressed around them, the only sound their soft footsteps against the cobblestone. When they reached the castle's main entrance, Horethian suddenly stopped.

"What's that?" he asked, pointing toward a dark shape impaled on a spear near the gate.

Malkhia's expression hardened. "Gwen."

Atlas frowned. "Who?"

"No one," Malkhia muttered, shaking his head as if to push away the thought. "We can't go in through here. If we do, half the army will be on us before we even step inside." He turned away. "I know another way."

Atlas shot him a suspicious look. "Do I even want to know how you know this?"

Malkhia ignored her, leading them along the castle's outer wall. The stone loomed high above them, shadowed by the night. Eventually, they reached a dense patch of trees and shrubs tangled around the base of the wall.

Malkhia pushed aside a low-hanging branch, revealing a narrow hole in the stone. "Through here. It leads to a small garden inside the castle."

Horethian crossed his arms, eyeing the hole with clear scepticism. "Is there another way? I'm not a dwarf."

Malkhia smirked. "No, there isn't."

Horethian exhaled heavily. "Of course not."

"You're too big to fit anyway," Malkhia added. "Stay here and guard the entrance. We won't be long."

Horethian scoffed. "Stay here and guard," he mimicked under his breath, kicking at the dirt. "Fine. But if you take too long, I'm finding another way in."

Malkhia nodded before slipping through the hole. Atlas followed, casting one last glance at Horethian before vanishing into the darkness beyond.

Once inside, Malkhia crouched low, his voice a whisper. "This way."

Atlas nodded, gripping her bow tightly as she moved to follow.

Moving swiftly but silently, Malkhia and Atlas crept along the garden's edge, keeping close to the castle wall. The neatly trimmed hedges and low-hanging fruit trees cast long shadows under the moonlight, offering them cover. A wooden door loomed ahead; its surface was worn smooth by years of use.

Malkhia pressed a palm against the wood, whispering a chant under his breath. A faint shimmer pulsed from his fingertips, followed by the soft click of the lock disengaging.

He eased the door open just enough to peer inside before shutting it again.

"There are two guards," he murmured, turning to Atlas. "One left, one right."

Atlas was already kneeling, an arrow nocked, her sharp gaze meeting his. "I'll take the left."

Malkhia nodded, gripping the door handle. With a slow breath, he muttered another incantation. A small white bolt of light crackled to life in his palm before streaking toward the rightmost guard.

At the same instant, Atlas loosed her arrow. It cut through the air, striking the left guard cleanly in the neck. He barely had time to gasp before slumping against the wall.

"Quickly," Malkhia urged, pushing the door open fully and stepping over the still-smoking corpse of the guard he had struck.

Atlas followed, her steps light and measured.

Malkhia suddenly raised a hand, signalling her to stop. "Footsteps," he whispered.

They pressed against the stone wall, staying out of sight as flickering torchlight cast shifting shadows along the hallway.

A young woman burst into the room ahead of them, her breath ragged, eyes wide with panic. She glanced wildly around before bolting straight toward them.

Malkhia reacted instantly. He caught her by the arm, pulling her into him before clamping a firm but gentle hand over her mouth.

"Shh," he whispered in her ear. "We are not your enemy."

The woman trembled in his grasp but slowly nodded.

Suddenly, the sound of clanking armour echoed down the corridor. Two guards rushed into the room she had just fled, swords drawn, torches in hand.

"She must've gone down here," one of them barked, pointing toward a walkway leading to the castle's centre. Without hesitation, they took off into the darkness.

Malkhia waited, listening intently as their footsteps faded.

Only then did he release the woman. "You're safe," he murmured.

"We need to get out of here," the woman gasped, tears streaming down her face. Her hands trembled as they clenched a small silver dagger.

"We will," Malkhia assured her. "But first, we need to find our friend."

"Do you know where the prison cells are?" Atlas asked.

The woman nodded and pointed toward a dimly lit corridor leading deeper into the castle. "They're close. A small tower at the end of the castle grounds."

"Can you lead us there?" Malkhia pressed.

Another hesitant nod, and she moved in behind them, letting Malkhia take the lead.

They hurried down the winding stone corridor, their footsteps muffled by the thick layer of dust. But then—

A sharp, piercing clang shattered the silence. The castle bell.

The alarm had been raised.

"Well, so much for subtlety," Malkhia muttered. "Move!"

They broke into a sprint.

"Here!" the woman panted, tapping Malkhia on the shoulder and pointing to a sturdy wooden door.

Malkhia pushed it open, revealing a narrow spiral staircase winding up into darkness.

"The cells are at the top," the woman whispered.

Without hesitation, they climbed. The scent of damp stone and rusted iron thickened the air as they neared the top landing. Two doors loomed ahead.

Malkhia reached for one—

It exploded open.

A blur of motion, then a heavy impact.

Theo barrelled into him, knocking Malkhia off his feet. They tumbled backward, nearly rolling down the stairs.

Theo, pinning Malkhia beneath him, had a dagger pressed inches from his throat. His eyes, wild and desperate, squinted in the dim light.

"Malk?" he asked, his breath ragged.

"Who else?" Malkhia grunted, shoving him off.

Theo staggered back; dagger still gripped tight.

"Why in the hells are you here?" he demanded, whirling toward Atlas and the others.

"To help, you idiot," Atlas snapped. "Leyla is one of us now. Just like you." She turned to Leyla with a reassuring smile.

Malkhia's gaze flicked to the woman beside Theo. Blood, dried and crusted, traced lines down her bruised face.

"Are you okay?" he asked, brushing dust from his hat before placing it back upon his head.

Leyla nodded, leaning against Theo for support. "I am now."

"You found your friend," the mysterious woman cut in, stepping forward. "We need to leave."

But Leyla's eyes locked onto her. A flicker of recognition.

"...Aria?" Leyla whispered, as if unsure her eyes weren't playing tricks.

The woman stiffened. Her gaze narrowed.

"Leyla?" she echoed, disbelief laced in her voice.

Leyla's eyes darted to the woman's cheek. "I'd recognize that tattoo anywhere. What are you doing here!?"

"Time for reunions later. We need to move," Malkhia said, brushing past Aria and making his way down the stairway.

The group quickly fell in behind him, their urgent whispers and hurried footsteps the only sounds filling the narrow tower.

As they neared the door where the two guards had fallen, Malkhia suddenly raised a hand, halting them in place.

"They've been moved," he murmured, eyes scanning the shifted bodies. A flicker of unease crossed his face. "Careful."

He pressed a hand to the door, gently easing it open. The scent of damp earth and blooming flowers drifted in from the moonlit garden beyond. He peered into the darkness.

"Looks clear," he said, pushing the door fully open and stepping onto the soft grass. The silver moonlight filtering through the trees mingled with the warm glow of the torch-lit pathways.

"Where do you think you're going?"

The deep voice rang out, freezing them in place.

From the shadows, a group of guards strode into the garden, their armour reflecting the flickering firelight. At their centre stood a towering figure clad in thick, polished plate.

A scout rushed up to him. "Commander, the exits are secured."

Malkhia narrowed his eyes. "Sharl, I presume."

The hulking man smirked, unsheathing his sword in a slow, deliberate motion. "You presume correctly."

He rested the flat of the blade against his shoulder, the edge gleaming wickedly. "Now, hand over the map, and you can all walk free. The wench included."

Malkhia's lips curled into a smirk. "Or not."

Before Sharl could react, Malkhia muttered a sharp incantation—

A blazing fireball erupted from his palm, streaking through the air and slamming into the guard beside Sharl. The man's scream split the night as flames engulfed him, his body collapsing into a smouldering heap.

Taking advantage of the chaos, Atlas swiftly notched two arrows and loosed them in quick succession. They found their marks, piercing the throats of two guards drawing their swords. Their bodies crumpled silently.

Theo rummaged through his bag, fingers wrapping around a small, intricately carved lizard figurine. With a flick of his wrist, he tossed it onto the ground.

A purple haze surged outward, tendrils of magic swirling through the air.

Then, with a deep, guttural growl, a massive fiery-red monitor lizard materialized. Its gleaming scales shimmered in the moonlight, and its wide maw dripped with thick, bubbling saliva. Its tongue flicked, tasting the air.

"Move!" Malkhia barked, leading the group behind the hedges toward the hole in the castle wall.

Theo lingered for a moment at the rear, eyes locked on Sharl.

"Kill."

The lizard reared up, its enormous form towering over the guards.

Sharl barely had time to sidestep before one of his men rushed forward, sword raised high—

The blade came down in a sweeping arc.

With a quick flick of its tail, the lizard disarmed the man, the force of the blow denting his breastplate with a sickening crunch. The guard staggered back, clutching his chest before collapsing to the ground. The monitor's jaws snapped open wide, its forked tongue flicking in the air before clamping down over the man's head.

A gruesome crack echoed through the garden. The lifeless, headless body slumped onto the grass.

Sharl lunged toward the hedges while the lizard was preoccupied, but the creature's tail lashed out, blocking his escape.

"Blasted lizard," Sharl growled, bringing his sword down in a powerful arc. The blade sank deep into the thick tail, nearly severing it.

The monitor shrieked in agony, its fiery eyes locking onto him. Its mouth opened wide, saliva pooling between jagged teeth. A stream of sticky ichor shot from its maw, igniting into roaring flames mid-air.

Sharl barely had time to react before the fire struck him across the side of his face. The searing heat tore through his flesh, the scent of burning skin and hair thickening the air. A ragged scream burst from his throat as he staggered back, his hand instinctively flying to his face, fingers pressing against the charred, peeling flesh.

Blinded by pain and rage, he swung wildly. His blade found purchase in the creature's neck, slicing clean through. The monitor's head thudded onto the ground, its lifeless eyes still smouldering. The body twitched once before collapsing, sending up a final gust of heat.

Sharl gasped for breath, his remaining eye burning with fury. His grip tightened around his sword as he turned toward his men.

"Get them!" he bellowed.

The guards scrambled, searching frantically for any sign of the fleeing intruders.

"Good boy," Theo said sadly, looking back toward the castle wall as he helped Leyla to her feet, her arm wrapped around him for support.

"Took your time," Horethian called from the other side of the trees as the group emerged.

"What happened here?" Atlas asked, eyes widening as she spotted Horethian sitting atop what appeared to be six unconscious guards.

"I guarded the hole," he replied with a grin. "Oh, and I got a new shield too, courtesy of our friends." He waved a shiny heater shield in the air, showing it off to the group.

"We need to hurry," Malkhia urged, leading them into the weaving city pathways.

"I'm out of reagents," he panted, his heartbeat pounding in his ears with every step.

"This way," he said, guiding them down a narrow alley. The ringing of the bell gradually faded as they put more distance between themselves and the castle.

They reached the small house where they had camped earlier and burst inside. The man occupying the house stumbled out of his room at the sudden commotion.

"Reagents," Malkhia gasped.

The man nodded, turning toward a small table in the walkway outside his room. He snatched up a small pouch and tossed it through the air. Malkhia caught it effortlessly, stuffing it into his bag before flicking open a leather-bound book.

With a quick chant, a portal materialized in the centre of the room, flooding it with an eerie blue glow.

31

"Uplifting speech," Nymira remarked dryly as she let the heavy tapestry fall back into place behind her. The thick fabric muffled the sounds of the stone corridors beyond. She muttered a spell under her breath, and a faint fizzle of smoke curled around her form before she vanished from sight.

She reappeared in a dimly lit chamber, dust thick in the air and the scent of old parchment clinging to the walls. The room was cluttered with books, some stacked precariously on tables, others abandoned on the floor, their pages curling with age. The single candle on the desk flickered, casting long shadows against the cracked plaster walls.

Sylvaris jolted awake from the worn two-seater bench at the back of the room, blinking blearily at her.

"Oh, it's you," he muttered, rubbing his eyes before slumping back down.

"You could be more welcoming," she quipped, stepping over a pile of discarded books.

"I told you not to be long." He yawned, stretching. "Sekt and Durnek returned with a prisoner."

Nymira's brows lifted. "Where are they now?"

"Dropped her off with the prince. The pair went off to spend their coin." Sylvaris sighed, tossing an arm over his eyes.

"Well, I have some information worth more than whatever reward money they just wasted." She walked to a small wooden chair, its once-rich upholstery now faded and worn. With a flick of her hand, she dusted the seat before lowering herself into it.

That got Sylvaris' attention. He sat up, boots scraping against the uneven floorboards.

"Oh?" he said, his curiosity piqued.

"The princess is in Tryn, rallying a rebellion," Nymira said, resting her elbows on the chair's armrests. "The king is dead. And Durnek's brother is with her."

Sylvaris' smirk vanished, his expression sharpening. The candlelight reflected in his amber eyes as he processed her words.

"That," he murmured, leaning forward, "is worth some coin." A slow smile crept back onto his face. "We'll head to the castle at first light. Good work, sister."

Outside, the city of Serpentia stirred. The grey stone buildings loomed against the misty horizon as the first rays of morning light pierced through the cloud-laden sky. The narrow streets, still slick with the remnants of last night's drizzle, echoed with the distant calls of merchants setting up their stalls. Smoke curled from the chimneys of the lower quarters, where bakers and blacksmiths stoked their fires, bringing warmth to the cold morning air.

Nymira's eyes cracked open, adjusting to the dim light filtering through the warped wooden shutters. The scent of damp stone and stale ale clung to the decrepit house they had claimed as their hideout. With a groan, she pushed herself up from the creaking mattress and stepped out into the main room.

Durnek and Sekt were sprawled in their chairs, their snores loud enough to shake the dust from the rafters. Empty tankards and a half-eaten loaf of bread sat forgotten on the table between them.

She shook her head in mild exasperation just as Sylvaris entered the room, already fully dressed, his expression unreadable.

"Good morning," Sylvaris said, stretching his arms above his head with a lazy yawn.

"Morning," Nymira replied, rubbing the sleep from her eyes.

"Well, let's get to it," Sylvaris said as he strode toward the door.

"What about these two?" Nymira gestured to Sekt and Durnek, still snoring in their chairs, oblivious to the conversation.

"Let them sleep it off. At least this way, they won't know how much we're getting paid," Sylvaris said with a sly grin, pushing the door open. Sunlight poured into the room, forcing him to squint as he stepped onto the bustling street.

The city was fully awake now, alive with the sounds of merchants hawking their wares, blacksmiths hammering steel, and the occasional outburst of laughter from the taverns lining the streets. The scent of fresh bread mixed with the less pleasant stench of unwashed bodies and damp stone.

"Why do we live in this city?" Nymira muttered, sidestepping a group of children chasing a stray dog. "It's crawling with humans." A glint of disdain coloured her voice.

"It's cheap," Sylvaris replied with a shrug. "And no one asks questions."

They reached the narrow bridge leading to the castle, where the atmosphere shifted. The streets grew quieter, the jovial chaos of the marketplace replaced by the imposing silence of the castle guards. The stone walls of the keep loomed ahead, weathered and cold.

"That's a lovely greeting ornament," Nymira remarked, pointing to a decomposing head impaled on a rusted spear at the castle entrance.

"Believe it or not, that was Gwen," Sylvaris said without breaking stride.

Nymira's gaze lingered on the grisly sight for a moment, her lips pressing into a thin line before she followed her brother toward the guards stationed at the entrance.

The two armoured men stiffened as the elves approached, crossing their halberds in an X to bar their path.

"No entrance," one of the guards said in an authoritative tone, his expression unreadable beneath his helmet.

"We must see the prince at once. We bring important information," Sylvaris stated, unfazed.

"No entrance," the guard repeated, his stance unwavering.

"If we don't speak to the prince, we're all as good as dead," Nymira interjected, frustration creeping into her voice.

The guards exchanged uncertain glances, shifting slightly on their feet.

"Get Commander Sharl," Sylvaris pressed. "We're friends."

"Commander Sharl is indisposed at the moment," one of the guards replied stiffly.

Sylvaris frowned, but Nymira was quicker to respond. "Listen, if you don't let us through, this city will be burning in the very near future." Her voice carried a sharp edge, and for the first time, the guards' grip on their weapons faltered.

"Captain!" one of the men called out.

A figure in ornate armour strode toward them, his expression one of mild irritation. "What do you two need now?"

Recognition flickered across his face as his gaze landed on Sylvaris.

"Ah, Sylvaris," the captain said. "The commander is unfit for visitors today."

"We have urgent news for the prince," Sylvaris insisted.

The captain studied them for a moment before letting out a heavy sigh. "Very well. Let them through."

The guards lowered their halberds, visibly relieved as their arms relaxed at their sides.

"This way," the captain said, turning sharply on his heel. He led them through the grand courtyard, past rows of soldiers sharpening blades and stable hands tending to restless horses. The towering castle walls seemed to close in around them as they approached the grand doors of the throne room.

The heavy wooden doors groaned as they swung open, revealing the vast chamber beyond.

The captain halted at the entrance, gesturing for the pair to continue down the long, carpeted floor toward the throne. At its centre sat the prince, his posture tense, his hand pressed against his collarbone as though nursing an unseen wound.

"Your Grace, we bring urgent news," Sylvaris announced as he reached the foot of the throne, kneeling in a bow. Nymira followed suit, her head dipping in practiced formality.

The prince straightened, giving them his full attention, though his fingers remained firmly against his shoulder.

"Are you injured, Your Grace?" Sylvaris asked, noting the wince that flickered across the prince's face.

"It is nothing," the prince replied curtly. "What have you come to report?"

Sylvaris lowered his head slightly. "My condolences, Your Grace, but your father has perished on his expedition."

The chamber seemed to hold its breath. The prince's eyes widened, his entire body going rigid.

"Condolences?" A slow smile spread across his face, his previous discomfort forgotten. "This is wonderful news!"

Sylvaris and Nymira exchanged quick, questioning glances.

"We must begin the coronation immediately," the prince declared, beckoning one of his advisors forward.

"That is not all," Sylvaris interjected.

The prince paused, clearly impatient. "Go on."

"Your sister has been sighted in Tryn. She is rallying a rebellion to contest the throne," Sylvaris continued. "Eric is with her."

The name landed like a hammer.

"Eric!?" The prince's face twisted in anger. "That traitor!" He scoffed. "I'm not concerned about a band of refugees waving pitchforks."

"They are well-informed and well-armed, Your Grace," Nymira warned.

The prince waved a dismissive hand. "Enough. Fetch the Commander—we must begin my coronation," he instructed his advisor. The man gave a sharp nod before striding briskly from the chamber.

"Is that all?" the prince asked, his tone already shifting toward boredom.

"It is," Sylvaris replied, carefully masking his irritation.

"Then be gone." The prince flicked his wrist as though shooing away a nuisance.

Sylvaris, unshaken, lifted his gaze. "A matter of payment, Your Grace."

The prince blinked, then let out a short laugh. "Ah, yes. Mercenaries and their coin." He leaned back in his throne, entirely at ease. "See the captain on your way out."

Sylvaris and Nymira bowed once more before turning toward the exit.

"He's a prick," Nymira muttered under her breath as they walked.

"Shh," Sylvaris warned, his voice low. "You don't want to end up like Gwen."

Before they reached the doors, a figure entered the chamber behind the returning advisor.

His face was barely visible beneath layers of blood-soaked bandages, the fabric clinging to his skin like a macabre mask.

The prince let out a quiet hiss at the sight. "They really did a number on you, didn't they?"

Sharl's good eye flicked to the prince's shoulder. "I could say the same about you."

The prince straightened, his expression hardening. "My father is dead. We need to begin my transition to king."

Sharl gave a curt nod. "Very well. We will begin preparations." With that, he turned sharply and strode from the chamber.

The prince exhaled, his lips curling into a satisfied
smirk. "King," he murmured to himself, savouring the
word. "I like the sound of that."

32

"Princess!"

A voice called out from the bustling crowd, and a man sprinted toward her.

"Yes?" the princess asked, turning her attention away from a wooden crate filled with freshly forged swords.

"We've gathered all the ships we can, but it's still not enough," the man reported, slightly out of breath.

"Leave it with me," Eric said, placing a reassuring hand on the princess's shoulder.

She nodded, then refocused on the man. "Start loading the ships with supplies," she instructed. The man gave a quick nod before hurrying back into the throng of workers and soldiers.

"Tryn should be able to aid us, Princess," Eric said.

"Do you think they will agree?" she asked, folding her arms as she watched the loading efforts continue.

"I don't know," Eric admitted. "With the king away, it's hard to say. We've been allies for some time, but politics shift like the tides."

The princess offered him a small, confident smile. "I have faith in you, Eric."

Eric dipped his head in acknowledgment before turning toward the exit of the hideout.

before turning toward the exit of the hideout.

Stepping out into the city streets, he pushed through the crowd, making his way toward the towering, elegant castle that dominated the skyline. Its white marbled walls gleamed under the sun, framed by lush, bright green trees. Neatly trimmed hedges and carefully arranged flower beds lined the pristine stone walkway leading up to the main gates.

"Much prettier than Serpentia," Eric muttered to himself as he approached the guards stationed at the entrance.

"I need to speak with the king's advisor," he stated firmly.

"Right away, sir! Raise the gates!" one of the guards called out.

Above them, men worked in unison, turning massive iron wheels. The metal gate creaked and groaned as it lifted, disappearing into the stone archway above.

Eric strode forward, following the smooth, polished stone path until he reached the castle's grand entrance. Two towering, ornately crafted doors stood before him, their intricate carvings gleaming in the light.

Pressing firmly against their centre, he felt the weight of them shift. Slowly, the doors swung open, revealing a vast, well-furnished chamber beyond.

In the centre of the room stood a massive wooden table, surrounded by high-backed chairs. Servants bustled around it, carefully arranging cutlery while others dusted and swept the polished stone floor.

"Preparing for something?" Eric asked as he approached one of the advisors.

"Ah, Eric," the man replied, turning away from the woman he had been speaking with. "We don't know when our king will return, so we must always be ready."

He offered Eric a polite smile. "To what do we owe the pleasure?"

"Can we speak in private?" Eric asked.

"Of course. This way."

The advisor led him through an arched doorway into a smaller, more intimate chamber just off the grand dining hall. The scent of aged parchment and polished oak filled the air. A small window let in slivers of morning light, illuminating the neatly arranged documents scattered across a modest wooden desk.

"Drink?" the advisor offered as he gestured to a side table stocked with bottles of deep amber and crimson liquids.

"No, thank you," Eric declined, taking a seat as the advisor settled into the chair opposite him.

"You have been a friend to Tryn for some time now," the man said, leaning back slightly. "We would be glad to help, if we are able."

Eric exhaled, gathering his thoughts. "I don't know how much you've heard, but while the king and I were on our expedition, the prince took control of Serpentia."

"I've heard rumours," the advisor admitted, his expression darkening. "Both about the prince's rule and your expedition."

"Well," Eric continued, "as you may have guessed, power has gone to his head."

The advisor nodded grimly. "We suspected as much. We were waiting for the return of the King and yourself to set things straight."

Eric's jaw tightened. "That's why I'm here. The king has passed."

A silence settled between them. The advisor's expression shifted, his posture stiffening as the weight of the news sank in. "We had not heard. My condolences, Eric."

Eric lowered his gaze briefly. The loss still sat heavy on him.

"This is troubling news indeed," the advisor continued.

"The princess was driven out of the castle and forced to flee," Eric explained. "She's been living among the refugees here in Tryn."

"Ah, Hilda, I presume?" the advisor said, nodding. "A kind woman. She's caused no trouble for us."

"She's building an army," Eric said. "We intend to retake Serpentia."

The advisor sighed, rubbing his chin. "Eric, without King Rindell, I don't have the authority to commit Tryn to war."

"Is there nothing you can spare?" Eric pressed.

The advisor hesitated for a moment, then a small smile touched his lips. "Now that I think of it, I do have some resources at my disposal—some troops, some ships. No Tryn colours to be flown."

"Anything will help, sir," Eric said sincerely.

"When do you need them?"

"As soon as possible."

"We can have them ready to leave by tonight."

Eric exhaled, relief washing over him. "Thank you."

He stood, turning to give the advisor a respectful bow.

"No need for that, Eric," the advisor said with a nod. "You have been a loyal friend to Tryn, and it is an honour to repay that debt—if only we could do more."

Eric turned to leave as the advisor stood.

"Good luck, Eric," the man said.

Eric gave him a firm nod before stepping out of the chamber.

He left the castle grounds, moving quickly through the bustling streets, his mind focused on the task ahead. As he descended the stone staircase leading to the hideout, he spotted the princess speaking with a group of men.

"Princess," he called as he approached. "We've secured the extra ships and some troops."

A relieved smile crossed her face. "That is great news. I had no doubt in you."

She turned to the group. "Will we be ready to depart tonight?"

"The additional ships and men will be prepared," Eric assured her.

"We've almost finished loading the supplies. Shouldn't be much longer," one of the men added.

"Very good," the princess said with a determined nod. "We set sail at sundown."

The rebels worked tirelessly, hauling crates and manoeuvring carts through a series of underground tunnels that led directly to the docks.

"These are old smuggling tunnels," Hilda said as she walked beside the princess, watching the labourers move back and forth.

The princess glanced at her curiously. "Why didn't we come this way when we first arrived?"

"We only recently opened them up," Hilda replied.

"Good timing," the princess remarked with a small smile.

Hilda smirked. "Good timing indeed."

Just then, a worker pushing a cart laden with cannonballs passed by. "This is the last of it, Princess."

"Thank you," she said, offering him an appreciative nod.

They followed him through the tunnels until they reached a heavy iron grate, swung open to reveal the docks beyond.

Charlotte stepped forward, gazing out over the bay where their fleet awaited. The harbor was alive with activity—sailors shouting orders, rebels loading provisions, and rowboats ferrying supplies to the waiting ships. Onlookers lined the docks, murmuring amongst themselves as they observed the flurry of movement.

The princess took a deep breath. Soon, they would reclaim what was rightfully hers.

"No backing down now," a voice said from behind the princess.

Charlotte turned to see Eric approaching, his expression calm yet resolute.

"Are we doing the right thing?" she asked, a note of uncertainty creeping into her voice.

Eric placed a reassuring hand on her shoulder. "If we weren't, would this many people be standing behind you?" He gave her a small, confident smile.

Before she could respond, a man approached. "Everyone's boarding now. I suggest you do the same, Princess."

Charlotte inhaled deeply, steeling herself before nodding. Stepping out into the dimming twilight, she made her way toward the small boats ferrying people to the waiting ships.

"This is it," she murmured to herself as she climbed into the boat alongside Eric and Hilda.

The oars sliced through the water, sending ripples across the bay as they neared the fleet. Charlotte's gaze swept over the ships, their masts swaying gently with the tide. Her father's flagship stood at the centre, its presence both familiar and heavy with meaning.

As they pulled alongside, she reached for the rugged rope ladder hanging over the hull. Gripping the rough rungs, she hoisted herself up, her arms trembling slightly.

Eric reached the deck first, turning back to steady her as she climbed over the railing.

"Ready the sails!" he called to the crew.

Without hesitation, he led Charlotte and Hilda toward the captain's quarters.

The moment she stepped inside, her breath caught.

"Is this him?" Charlotte's voice was barely a whisper as her eyes landed on the shrouded form lying on the bed. The body was wrapped tightly in a white sheet, still and silent.

Eric exhaled heavily. "Aye."

Charlotte's legs gave out beneath her, and she sank to her knees beside the bed. Gently, she placed her head against the covered form.

"I'm sorry, Father," she murmured, her voice breaking as tears welled in her eyes.

Hilda knelt beside her, resting a comforting hand on her back. "It'll be okay," she said softly, rubbing slow, reassuring circles as Charlotte's quiet sobs filled the room.

Eric lingered for a moment before turning away. "I'll be back. We need to ready the ships." He stepped out, closing the door behind him.

Outside, the deck was alive with movement. Sailors rushed to secure the rigging, their calls and commands echoing across the fleet.

"Raise the anchor!" Eric bellowed, gripping the ship's wheel with both hands.

The ship groaned as the heavy chain reeled in, the vessel shifting as it was freed from its mooring. Slowly, Eric turned the wheel, guiding the bow toward the open horizon.

His eyes swept across the fleet behind him, watching as each ship followed in turn, their crimson sails unfurling and blending into the fiery hues of the sunset.

A slow smile spread across his face. "This is it."

33

unlight streamed through the prince's window, striking the gilded edges of the ornate furniture and shimmering against the polished stone floor. Dust motes danced lazily in the air, disturbed only by the soft rustling of silk sheets as the prince shifted in his bed.

"Ughh." He groaned, rolling to the side—and, in doing so, shoved one of the women beside him off the mattress.

She hit the floor with a dull thud, letting out a startled whimper.

The other woman bolted upright, her face pale as she clutched the sheets to her chest.

"Leave me," the prince muttered, rubbing his eyes.

The women scrambled to gather their clothes, slipping into their dresses with practiced haste before fleeing through the chamber doors. The heavy wooden panels slammed shut behind them, leaving the prince alone with the quiet morning.

Blinking against the golden light, he stretched his limbs and smirked to himself.

"Coronation day."

His pulse quickened. It was finally here.

With a surge of excitement, he threw off the covers and stood, his bare feet sinking into the thickly woven rug. Servants had tended to his chambers long before sunrise, laying out fresh garments over a carved wooden chair near the window. The scent of lavender lingered in the air, mixing with the faint traces of wine and perfume from the night before.

He reached for his tunic, sliding one arm through the sleeve—but as he did, pain flared through his shoulder, sharp and hot.

His smirk twisted into a scowl. "That damn woman," he muttered under his breath, rubbing the tender spot.

A voice called from the doorway.

"My lord."

The prince turned. A steward stood at the entrance; his hands clasped neatly before him.

"What?"

"The tailor is waiting."

The prince scoffed. "Let him wait." He sat on the edge of his bed, fastening the intricate golden clasps of his boots. "I'll go when I'm ready."

The steward bowed and departed, leaving the prince to his thoughts.

He rose from his bed, stretching his arms above his head, letting out a loud groan.

Stepping out into the grand corridor, lined with towering stained-glass windows. Between them, emerald green banners hung from the high-vaulted ceiling, each emblazoned with a golden serpent entwined around a sword. The air carried the faint scent of burning incense, mingling with the rich fragrance of polished oak and old stone.

Servants flitted about the halls, dusting the portraits of past rulers, their gazes averted as the prince strode past.

"Morning, ladies," he said with a playful smirk, offering them a lazy wave.

At the corridor's end, he paused before a massive oil painting framed in gold—the likeness of his father, King Aldric, depicted in full regalia, his piercing eyes staring down with a gaze both cold and commanding.

The prince chuckled under his breath. "Your time is done, old man." His eyes flicked to the empty space beside it—soon to bear his own portrait, even grander.

"Morning, your grace."

He turned to find one of his advisors approaching, dressed in deep green robes embroidered with silver.

"Bring me the commander," the prince ordered.

The advisor hesitated. "The commander stepped out, my lord."

The prince's smile vanished. "On my coronation day?" His voice hardened. "He'd better be back in time."

The advisor gave a quick bow. "Apologies, my lord. If you'll follow me, the tailor awaits."

The prince allowed himself to be led through a side hall, past doors of dark mahogany carved with intricate sigils of the royal house. They entered a smaller chamber where a tall, thin man awaited. He wore a well-used leather apron, its front pocket bristling with chalk, pins, and measuring tape. Rolls of rich fabric—velvets, silks, brocades—lined the walls, shimmering beneath the soft glow of candlelight.

"Your grace." The tailor bowed deeply. "If you would stand here, please." He gestured to a mark before a tall mirror framed in gold.

The prince stepped into place, his grin returning as he admired his reflection.

"The usual coronation colours, my lord?" the tailor asked as he began measuring.

"Gold and red."

The tailor paused briefly before nodding. "A break from tradition, I see."

The prince merely smirked.

The tailor worked quickly, his hands deft as he adjusted the prince's posture, taking careful measurements and scribbling notes in a small leather book.

At last, he straightened. "I have all I need. We will begin work immediately."

The prince's smirk faded. "You have four hours."

The tailor stiffened, his fingers tightening around his chalk. "Uhh… as you wish, my lord." His voice held a tremor, but he bowed low, nonetheless.

The prince strutted out of the chamber, his boots clicking against the polished stone floor as he made his way toward the exit of the grand hall.

"Your grace," a voice called from behind.

He exhaled sharply, rolling his eyes as a man hurried toward him.

"What now?" the prince drawled; his tone laced with irritation.

The steward bowed his head respectfully. "The guests have begun to arrive."

The prince frowned. "They're early. Show them to their rooms." He waved a hand dismissively before pausing. "Any news of Sharl?"

The steward shook his head. "None as of yet, my lord."

The prince clicked his tongue in frustration, then turned on his heel, heading toward the courtyard.

Stepping outside, he was met with a striking contrast— luscious green grass spread neatly across the courtyard, bordered by vibrant beds of flowers, carefully trimmed hedges, and fruit-bearing trees. Against the dull grey stone of the towering castle walls, the garden was a rare pocket of life amidst the fortress's cold, imposing architecture.

But near the far wall, a blotch of deep, red-stained grass and singed branches caught his eye. A scarred patch where the earth had yet to recover from some abrupt fire. He lingered for a moment, staring at the scorched ground as his thoughts drifted toward the ceremony mere hours away.

"Where the bloody hell is Sharl?" he muttered, shaking his head before making his way to the castle's front gates.

The guards standing watch straightened as he approached, stepping aside in rigid silence to allow him passage.

The moment he stepped outside, he was hit by a wave of rancid air—thick and putrid, it clawed at his nostrils and sent a sharp sting through his sinuses.

"Dear gods, that's awful," he gagged, raising a sleeve to his nose. His gaze darted across the courtyard until it landed on the culprit. A decomposed head, its flesh rotted to the bone, still impaled on a spear just beyond the gate.

With a disgusted sneer, he gestured to one of the guards. "You there. Get rid of that. Guests are arriving."

The soldier nodded briskly, stepping forward to remove the gruesome display.

The prince let out a dry chuckle, shaking his head as he resumed his stride. "You've let yourself go, Gwen," he murmured to himself, smirking at the memory of the poor soul who once owned that head.

Stepping onto the grand stone bridge leading away from the castle gates, he ran a hand over the intricate carvings lining its pillars—each one depicting the serpentine sigils of his house intertwined with scenes of conquest and war.

"All mine," he whispered, relishing the moment.

"Your grace!" Another voice rang out, hurried footsteps pounding against the stone behind him.

The prince groaned audibly, turning with a glare. "Can't I just have a morning of peace?"

A nervous-looking steward bowed deeply. "Apologies, my lord, but you are needed in the kitchen."

The prince sighed, rubbing his temple before nodding. "Very well."

Without another word, he turned and followed the man back through the courtyard, re-entering the castle and making his way toward the bustling heart of the kitchen.

"Your grace, we need to go over the menu."

The voice belonged to a large man in a grimy apron, his face glistening with sweat from the roaring fires of the castle's kitchens. The air was thick with the scent of roasting meat, fresh bread, and the sharp tang of spilled wine, but beneath it all lurked the ever-present musk of unwashed bodies and old grease.

The prince barely concealed his disgust as he wrinkled his nose. "You dragged me here to go through meals!?"

He spat the words like they were something foul. "Can't you use your head and figure it out?"

Before the cook could sputter out a response, the prince turned on his heel and stormed out, his boots striking against the stone floor with impatient clicks.

"Surrounded by fools," he muttered under his breath, shaking his head.

As he rounded a corner, a young servant emerged from the opposite direction, his arms trembling under the weight of a towering silver tray piled high with breakfast dishes. The moment he spotted the prince, his face drained of colour.

He tried to step aside—too fast...

A split second later, metal clattered, glass shattered, and warm slop splattered across the prince's elegant tunic.

The air in the corridor turned heavy, thick with tension. The nearby servants and guards instinctively stepped back, as if afraid of being caught in the impending storm.

The prince lowered his gaze to the mess. Then to his clothes. Then to the boy.

The young servant was frozen in place, his breath coming in short gasps. His hands trembled as they hovered over the wreckage, uncertain whether he should try to clean it up or simply beg for mercy.

A slow, wicked grimace curled across the prince's lips.

"How dare you."

The servant barely had time to react before the back of the prince's hand struck his cheek with a sharp crack, sending him sprawling into the pile of broken dishes.

Thin rivulets of blood beaded across his palms where they had scraped against shattered glass, but he didn't dare make a sound. His shoulders rose and fell with quick, panicked breaths as he clutched his hands to his chest.

"Stupid, useless little wretch," the prince sneered, looming over him like a wolf over a wounded rabbit. "You can't even carry a tray properly? Tell me, what good are you?"

The boy, eyes wet with unshed tears, dropped his gaze to the floor. "I—I'm sorry, your grace—"

"Sorry?"

The prince crouched down, seizing the boy's chin between his fingers and jerking his face upward, forcing him to meet his gaze.

"Sorry won't clean this mess."

He shoved the servant's face aside and straightened, flexing his fingers as if shaking off the mere thought of touching someone so lowly.

"You'll scrub this floor until it shines, and if I find so much as a speck left, I'll have you executed."

The boy nodded frantically, already reaching for the shards of glass with shaking hands.

Satisfied, the prince turned and strode down the hall without another glance, leaving the servant trembling on the floor, crimson drops of blood mixing with spilled broth and shattered porcelain.

As the prince strode into the grand main hall, his advisor waved him down with an urgent expression. "My prince, your royal robes are ready. We need you dressed, your guests are already taking their seats."

"About time," the prince muttered, though his mind was elsewhere. He leaned in slightly. "Any word on Sharl's whereabouts?"

The advisor shook his head. "Still nothing, my lord."

The prince clenched his jaw. "Damn it, Sharl." He turned on his heel, his boots clicking sharply against the polished marble floor as he stormed down the hallway toward his chambers.

Throwing open the door, his gaze immediately landed on the magnificent robe draped across his bed. The fabric shimmered in the dim candlelight—deep, regal gold, its surface adorned with intricate red embroidery in patterns of coiling snakes and laurel crowns. The sheer wealth stitched into every thread sent a rush of satisfaction through him.

"Not bad." A grin flickered across his face as he stripped off his stained tunic and moved toward the washbasin by the arched window.

The salty breeze from the ocean rolled in, ruffling the sheer curtains. He scooped handfuls of cool water, splashing them over his face and torso, scrubbing away the grime of the morning's irritations. As he reached for a linen towel to dry himself, something out beyond the waves caught his eye.

A cluster of thin, dark poles poked through the misty horizon, barely discernible against the bright midday sky.

Frowning, he squinted, his instincts suddenly on edge.

His breath hitched as he leaned in, trying to get a better view. Ships. And not just any ships, an entire fleet, their silhouettes growing sharper as they sliced through the distant waters.

The prince didn't bother finishing drying himself. He grabbed his trousers and rushed out the door, nearly colliding with a passing servant. Ignoring the startled yelp behind him, he turned sharply and took the nearest spiral staircase two steps at a time, ascending to one of the highest lookout towers.

"Eyeglass," he barked at the guard stationed there.

The poor man fumbled with his belt, nearly dropping the instrument before finally handing it over. The prince snatched it impatiently and raised it to his eye, twisting the brass dials to sharpen the blurred horizon.

The first thing he saw was the flag.

A coiled black serpent, snapping in the wind. His blood ran cold.

His grip tightened around the eyeglass as he swept over the approaching vessels, stopping when he spotted a familiar ship at the fleet's centre.

His breath grew shallow as he adjusted the focus.

Through the dissipating fog, three figures emerged at the bow of the lead ship.

The prince's stomach twisted into knots.

His father's ship, leading a fleet flying the Serpentia banner. And standing at its helm…

His fingers trembled against the brass rim as the figures came into view, sharp and unmistakable.

A woman. Dark curls whipping in the wind. A royal blue cloak trailing over her shoulders.

His breath caught in his throat.

"Charlotte."

His eyes burned with disbelief as he stared at the ship drawing closer. With a violent shout, he slammed the eyeglass against the stone, shattering the lens with a deafening crack.

"How dare she!"

Epilogue

oud footsteps echoed off the cold, damp cavern walls as a towering figure, muscles bulging beneath his dark cloak and polished armour, strode down a narrow, wet stone path. His heavy boots splashed against the puddled ground, each step a dull thud that seemed to resonate through the cavern's depths. At the end of the path, a dark figure perched upon a jagged stone throne, shrouded in shadows.

As the large man reached the foot of the throne, he dropped to one knee, his head bowed in reverence. "My Lord," he rumbled, his voice deep and commanding. "They are yet to decode the map but have managed to escape once more."

The dark figure's voice slithered from the depths of his cloak, raspy and cold. "Stand."

The man rose to his full height, the flickering blue torchlight casting eerie shadows across his broad frame.

"You failed me," the shadowed figure hissed, his fingers snapping with a quick, sharp motion. A red spark danced briefly between his fingertips.

The large man flinched, instinctively raising a hand to his face. His fingers brushed over the still fresh wounds that marred his skin.

"I would give you a reminder if these pesky adventurers hadn't already," the dark figure cackled, his voice dripping with disdain.

The man's jaw clenched, but he said nothing.

"Bring me my map," the dark figure ordered, the finality of his voice sending a cold shiver through the cavern.

"As you wish, my lord," the man replied, bowing low before turning on his heel. His hand rested on the pommel of his sword as he strode off into the darkness, the distant echo of his boots fading behind him.

The group tumbled out of the portal and into the small wooden cabin, where the chill of the deep snow outside crept through the cracked windows. The smell of old pine and dampness filled the air, and the sight of shattered furniture scattered across the floor made the cabin feel abandoned, like a memory frozen in time. A chair lay upturned, one of its legs snapped, and the remnants of a once cosy fire pit lay cold and ashy.

"Where are we?" Theo asked, rising to his feet and helping Leyla up. The snow on their clothes clung to them like a reminder of the harsh cold outside.

"Our old house," Atlas said, a small, bittersweet smile tugging at her lips. "Well, what's left of it," she added, her voice tinged with a mix of nostalgia and sorrow.

"My shield!" Horethian bellowed, dropping his current shield without a second thought. He rushed across the room to an old kite shield leaning against the wall, pulling it into his arms with a triumphant grin, like a lost treasure found. The familiar weight seemed to reassure him.

Atlas shook her head, a soft chuckle escaping her lips as she watched Horethian.

Malkhia stepped away from the group, his eyes scanning the broken remnants of what had once been his home. Books, scrolls, and shattered glass littered the floor, the remnants of his life's work scattered like forgotten fragments of his past. He crouched by his workbench, fingers brushing over the wreckage with a quiet sadness.

"What do we do now?" Leyla asked, her voice laced with uncertainty, her breath visible in the cold air as she looked to Malkhia for guidance.

"First, we rest," Malkhia said, standing up and brushing the dirt from his robes. "They've already checked here. There's a good chance they won't come back."

Horethian let out a frustrated grunt. "Can't we just give them the map?" he asked, the question hanging in the air with more hope than reason.

"You saw how badly they want it," Atlas replied, her gaze hardening. "It's obviously important. If we give it to them, we'll never know what's at stake."

Aria, still unfamiliar with the group, furrowed her brow in confusion. "Who are you people?" she asked, her voice quiet but full of curiosity and concern.

Malkhia sighed, rubbing a hand across his face. "Let's rest first, then we can discuss everything," he said, his tone firm but weary. "We've all been through enough for now."

The group settled into what little peace the battered cabin could offer, each lost in thought, the weight of their journey pressing down like the cold itself. In the silence, only the soft creak of timber and the distant howling wind through the snow broke the stillness. The map, hidden away for now, seemed to pulse with unanswered questions.

Malkhia stood in the open doorway, the warm glow of the hearth at his back. He drew from his pipe and let out a long, curling plume of smoke into the night air. A shiver crept through his bones from the icy air.

The burden of leadership had settled on his shoulders once more. He had made his choice. But he knew it wouldn't be long before the world demanded more from them than they could possibly give.

"Rest," he said quietly to no one and everyone.

Above, clouds swallowed the moonlight. A shape circled in the dark sky—a black bird, wings silent against the wind, a rolled parchment clutched in its claws.

It dipped low, releasing its grasp. The scroll fell without sound, tumbling through the air until it landed at Malkhia's feet in the snow.

He stared down at it.

The smoke from his pipe faded into the cold.

What's Next...

A storm sails toward Serpentia.

Onboard, a princess once cast aside now marches with fire in her heart and an army at her back. Her return is no quiet one—Serpentia will burn before she kneels before her brother. But reclaiming a kingdom is no simple task.

The throne she seeks is steeped in blood, and not all who fight beside her want to see her wear the crown. Some serve loyally. Others wait for the right moment to strike. Will her coup forge a new future—or drown the realm in fire and tyranny?

Elsewhere, the adventurers find a moment's peace. Their wounds are healing, but the map they carry is far from silent. It pulses with ancient whispers, pulling them toward lands long buried and truths best left forgotten.

The Forgotten Lands are stirring. And when they wake, the world may never be the same.

Will the princess take back what was stolen? Will the adventurers survive what waits beyond the map?

The journey continues in the next chapter of *Echoes of Exile*.

About the Author

Blake Noack lives and works in the rugged expanse of remote Western Australia, where the vast landscapes offer the perfect backdrop for building fantasy worlds.

A lifelong gamer and TV addict, Blake's stories are inspired by the characters created and adventures experienced through video games and films.

Echoes of Exile – The Prince's Pursuit began as a tribute to those in-game moments—the epic choices, the near-misses, and the unforgettable party dynamics. Now, it marks the beginning of a larger saga filled with danger, discovery, and magic.

This debut is only the first step in a journey that's far from over.

Have thoughts about the book?

Want to chat, leave a review, or share your Favorite part of the adventure?

Reach out anytime at:

echoesofexile@outlook.com

feedback, fan theories, and friendly banter are all welcome.